G000167826

'I had thought to offer you my sympathy.'

Mr. Wyckham's sardonic tone made Amy blush, and Eleanor leapt to her defence.

'Because you heard us laughing, do you think we mourn our father any the less?'

'It is not for me to judge, ma'am. I understand that ladies can become hysterical when overwrought.'

'I am never hysterical, and nor is my sister. And no, it is not for you to judge. You cannot have known Papa, if you do not know how much he is missed by all, and how especially by us.' To her annoyance she felt the tears rising in her eyes, and lowered her head so that he should not see them.

'Naturally you miss him. And you are about to be turned out of your home, are you not?'

Tears forgotten, Eleanor raised her head furiously.

'How dare you, sir! How dare you imply that we have no other feeling, no other reason for missing him!'

A DISTANT CONNEXION

Petra Nash

MILLS & BOON LIMITED
ETON HOUSE   18-24 PARADISE ROAD
RICHMOND   SURREY   TW9 1SR

All the characters in this book have no existence outside
the imagination of the Author, and have no relation
whatsoever to anyone bearing the same name or names.
They are not even distantly inspired by any individual
known or unknown to the Author, and all the incidents
are pure invention.

All Rights Reserved. The text of this publication or any
part thereof may not be reproduced or transmitted in any
form or by any means, electronic or mechanical,
including photocopying, recording, storage in an
information retrieval system, or otherwise, without the
written permission of the publisher.

This book is sold subject to the condition that it shall not,
by way of trade or otherwise, be lent, resold, hired out or
otherwise circulated without the prior consent of the
publisher in any form of binding or cover other than that
in which it is published and without a similar condition
including this condition being imposed on the subsequent
purchaser.

First published in Great Britain 1989
by Mills & Boon Limited

© Petra Nash 1989

Australian copyright 1989
Philippine copyright 1989
This edition 1989

ISBN 0 263 76514 8

Set in Times Roman 10 on 11½ pt.
04-8908-77669 C

Made and printed in Great Britain

CHAPTER ONE

'IT IS over, then? Oh, poor Nell, how pale you are!' Amy
rose from her seat by the window, laying aside her prayer-
book and the old shawl, which she had huddled round
her shoulders against the draughts that the worn brown
velvet curtains could do little to mitigate, and hurried
forward to her sister. Her movements were graceful, and
her form slender in its gown of unrelieved black. The
uncompromising severity of this garment enhanced,
rather than hid, her fair beauty, and she wore it with an
unconscious elegance that many a society lady might have
envied, thought her sister inconsequentially. Eleanor
knew that her own dress, though identical in every way,
only made her skin look sallow instead of having its usual
creamy glow, while sorrow and tiredness had dulled the
gloss from her brown hair and reddened her hazel eyes.
Amy continued, 'You should have let me come with you.
It is not right that you should have gone alone to poor
Papa's funeral. Are you faint? You are so pale. Come
and sit down.'

Eleanor gave a weary shake of her head.

'You know I never faint—I am far too robust,' she
said with the ghost of a smile. 'It is only the cold—the
wind cuts like a knife today. Let me just sit by the fire
and get warm, and I shall be well enough.' She sank into
the corner of a shabby sofa and held out her hands to
the small fire. 'Would you unbutton my gloves and take
off my bonnet? My hands can hardly feel the strings.'

Amy laid aside the plain black bonnet and pulled off
her sister's gloves, folding them neatly, before taking one

5

of Eleanor's hands in her own and rubbing it. She sat close beside her.

'Your hand is like ice. Oh, Nell, you should have let me come with you.'

'In this weather, and with you hardly well from your last cold? It was bad enough that I was there. A lot of people were shocked to see me, though no one actually said that I should have stayed at home, as most women do. You know as well as I do that Papa would never have permitted it, so careful as he was with you.'

Amy nodded sadly, and reached across for the other hand.

'Indeed, you both take—took—care of me too well. I wish I were stronger, Nell.'

'You are stronger, dearest, much stronger now, if you will only take care of yourself and keep away from colds.'

'I do not want to be a burden on you.'

'Never that, you goose, even if you were a complete invalid, which you are far from being! I know how much you wished to stand at Papa's graveside, but in this bitter weather it would have been most unwise, and how could I bear to lose you, too? You are all the family I have in the world.' In spite of herself her voice shook, and for a few minutes the sisters clung together while Eleanor allowed herself the luxury of shedding some of the tears which she had held so firmly in check all day. Presently she sat up straighter, wiped her eyes, and blew her nose in a determined fashion.

'As for my going alone, the very reverse is true! I should think nearly the whole parish must have been there. Papa would have been so pleased. There were faces there which have not seen the inside of a church for many a long year. That wicked old man Jackson was there, quite clean of soot, though only last year Papa was so angry with him, and threatened him with the magistrate when he tried to bring that poor little boy into the house to sweep chimneys.'

Amy was distracted from her sadness, as Eleanor had hoped she would be. Although the younger by a year, Eleanor had always protected and cared for her sister, who at nineteen was slight and still delicate from a series of childhood illnesses that had several times threatened to carry her off. It was, in fact, mostly due to Eleanor's careful nursing that Amy was still alive, for the Manchester of the mid-1840s was known to be one of the unhealthiest places in the country, even for those of the middle and upper classes who lived there.

'That horrible old man! I don't know how he could!'

'Well, he did. And Mrs Hughes, who was so angry when Papa told her she should buy milk for the children rather than gin for herself, she was there too. She came and spoke to me.'

'Oh, Nell, what did she say?'

'She said he was the best man who ever lived, and that he would be sorely missed. There were tears in her eyes, too.'

'Poor thing, perhaps we have judged her too harshly. Papa always said that it was ignorance, not vice, that kept such people in misery.'

'There were so many there. If only they could have come to church while Papa was alive, how happy he would have been. He wanted so much to help them, and gave so much of himself, yet it wasn't until he was dead that they showed they had noticed. If he could but have known how his death would move them, I believe he would have been happy to die.'

'I am sure he does know it, dearest.' Amy spoke with the simple piety that was her father's legacy. 'As for his being happy to die, I think that if he had not had us to care for, he would have welcomed death any time these last thirteen years.' She looked pensively into the glowing coals at the heart of the fire. She still held one of Eleanor's hands in her own, stroking it almost unconsciously as she spoke. Her face was thoughtful but serene, her body held erect but without strain, relaxation and calm showing in the curve of her neck, the soft droop of her shoulders. 'We were so young when Mama was taken. You were only five, but do you remember how he was before?'

'Oh, yes, so full of jokes and always laughing. I remember he played mad games with us all around the house until we were worn out with excitement, and Mama would say "Gently, Edward, gently," and have us sit quietly with her until we were calm. But he was always cheerful, and still enjoyed our play and fun after Mama died, though he did not join in as he used to.'

'Dear Papa, that cheerfulness was all for our sake. Do you recall how he would not let us wear mourning for Mama? He said it was wrong for children to grow up in a house of sorrow. But I think that when Mama died a part of him died with her, and all he really wanted was to be with her again.'

Eleanor was surprised.

'You are right, Amy, I am sure you are. I had not thought of it in that way, but now that you say it I feel sure that it was so. Poor Papa.'

'I am not clever, like you, Nell, but living quietly as I do I have had more time to notice how people feel, while you were busy helping Papa with his work.'

Eleanor kissed her.

'You have something a great deal better than cleverness, and that is wisdom, and a loving heart. Not that you are not clever, too, and do not let me hear you say otherwise! But now we must use all the wisdom we possess, for we must soon decide where we are to live, and how.'

'Must we? So soon?'

'I am afraid so. Of course, we may stay here for a while, but naturally this house will be needed when a new vicar is appointed to take Papa's place. We cannot call this home for many more weeks, and must be prepared to leave.'

They both looked round the room. Everything in it was old, and some things were downright ugly, yet how many memories were held within those four walls. The Reverend Edward Hunter had had no worldly ambitions: his God had called him to help the poor in this working district of Manchester, and he had never wanted to move to a wealthier or a more comfortable living. There had been times when his family had been close to actual want, but somehow they had always managed, and the room, though shabby, was as homely and cheerful as a slender purse and clever fingers could contrive. The furniture might be simple and plain, judged by the standards of an age that considered ornate opulence and a profusion of decorative objects the height of fashion, but it gleamed with polish. The uncomfortable hardness of the horsehair sofa and chairs was softened and brightened by a profusion of lovingly embroidered cushions, and, even when there was little in the larder, they always contrived to have a few fresh flowers and leaves to brighten and scent the room. Eleanor knew that in the weeks to come all her strength of will and ingenuity were to be stretched to their utmost, but here in this quiet room she seemed to find the strength she needed.

'We must think of something. Dear Papa was never a wealthy man, and his nature was too open and generous for him to have money put by—indeed, were it not for the doctor's kindness we should be hard put to it to pay his bills of the last few weeks, while Papa was so ill. There is our money from Mama's jointure, but that will not bring us more than twenty-five pounds a year, and we cannot live on that alone.'

'Then we must work. My plain sewing is good, and so is my embroidery. Perhaps I could take in needlework?' suggested Amy.

'I fear there are already too many gentlewomen in straitened circumstances trying to live by their needles. We should need to rent a room, and that alone would cost us several shillings a week, apart from the cost of coals and lamp-oil, for we could not sew if the room were cold, and the daylight is short in winter. It is only the middle of October; there are many months of winter ahead of us. No, it will not do. I must try for a post in some well-to-do household. As a housekeeper, perhaps. I am sure I should be a most saving one, for Papa always said I was most economical.'

'In a well-to-do house they might not have a taste for mutton broth, though yours is so good.'

'Then I should have recourse to Mrs Acton's book of receipts, and serve up ten courses with the best of them. I should wear black bombazine, and a great many petticoats, and have a big bunch of keys hanging at my belt. The cook and the butler would be in awe of me, while the housemaids would quake in their shoes when they heard me coming, I should be so severe!'

'How droll you are—as if anyone could quake at you! But I am afraid that even the bombazine and the petticoats could not make you look half old enough to be a housekeeper.'

'Perhaps not. But a governess? Papa taught us so well, and I have always helped him in his factory schools. I have enough Latin to prepare a little boy for school, and if my accomplishments were lacking you could supplement them, for both your needlework and your drawings are very fine. Yes, a schoolroom full of delightful children, what fun we should have!'

'A schoolroom of spoiled, wilful children, as like as not,' corrected Amy with her gentle laugh.

'No, no, it is all planned. Two little girls with golden curls, and two little boys in short coats. And a kind mama who is in want of a companion to help her with her embroidery and to read to her. We should both be needed.'

'But do you think, dearest, that experience in teaching factory children will be enough of a recommendation to this kind mama? I feel sure she would want references.'

Eleanor looked at her sister, who sat wrinkling her brow over these problems, and reflected that the main problem was likely to be neither lack of references nor of years, but Amy's beauty, which the kindest of mistresses might well regard with suspicion. The mourning dress, though unfashionably cut and of cheap fabric, could not hide her graceful figure, nor detract from her fine complexion—indeed, the black which made Eleanor look sallow and pale only served to bring out the delicate whiteness of Amy's skin, and to make the gold of her plainly dressed hair shine all the brighter. Her eyes, along with her lashes were a deep brown, in startling contrast to her otherwise fair colouring, and even after weeping were clear and bright, though Eleanor was ruefully aware that her own were puffy, and her nose red beneath the sprinkling of freckles that so unfashionably marred it.

She was sincerely proud of her sister's beauty and had no regret for her own mid-brown hair and hazel eyes. In most circles she would have passed for a tolerably pretty girl, but beside her sister her looks faded into insignificance, a fact for which she was glad, for, as she had once remarked to her father, 'One beauty in the family is quite enough.' To which Papa had replied that to him both his daughters appeared equally beautiful. This, since he had never been known to deviate from the strictest truthfulness, his daughter could only attribute to the eyes of love. For the rest, Amy was gentle, loving, and totally unfitted to take care of herself, a task which Eleanor was cheerfully prepared to undertake, though she felt less than confident of her ability to succeed.

She thought, not for the first time, that it was a pity that so much beauty and goodness should be hidden away in a working district of Manchester. It was not that she was ambitious for a brilliant match for Amy—no daughter of Papa's would be swayed by considerations of worldly wealth or power—but a man of comfortable fortune, who would love and cherish Amy—how gladly she would entrust her sister to such a one!

'You are so quiet, Nell. Have you thought of a plan?' Her train of thought interrupted, Eleanor shook her head and smiled.

'Not a plan, precisely, just thinking. I do so wish we had a wider acquaintance.'

'Yes, indeed, for then we might get references. But you will manage something, I know. You always do.'

Eleanor laughed.

'Such faith in me! But references were not what was on my mind. When I referred to acquaintances, I should more properly have said gentlemen!'

Amy blushed.

'It seems hardly the time to be thinking of such things, dearest,' she said in gentle reproof.

'It is not, I know, but I must think of it,' retorted Eleanor with decision. 'You cannot deny that matrimony is the only career other than that of governess or paid companion that is open to women of our class. We cannot find work in the mills.'

'No, indeed,' Amy shuddered. 'Though it seems a little indelicate to refer to the Holy Estate as a career. You would surely not wish to enter into a marriage merely as a business proposition?'

'No, though you must be aware that very many do. I feel I am far too dull and practical to feel the kind of romantic attachment that one reads about in novels. I am not the languishing kind! I think I should be very well satisfied if there were respect and liking. Don't look so shocked! Since we do not know any gentlemen who are single, or under the age of sixty, the opportunity is unlikely to arise.'

'Oh, Nell, should I perhaps have taken Albert Haywood's advances more seriously? For he is young, and single, and certainly well able to support us both in comfort... only...'

'Only! Only he is but seventeen, and acknowledged even by his mother to be a fool! No, indeed, no one could wish you to make such a sacrifice; how can you think of it? But you have given me an idea. I shall visit Lady Haywood in the morning.'

'Lady Haywood? You do not mean... Nell, you couldn't, you wouldn't!' Observing that her sister was looking quite ruffled and upset, Eleanor hugged her reassuringly.

'Not about you, you goose! And I am not about to offer myself as a sacrifice, either. Only to ask her advice.'

Amy still looked uncertain.

'Do you think she will be able to help us, then?'

'She may be considered by many to be vulgar,' said Eleanor robustly, 'and she herself would be the first to admit that she has never moved in society circles, though

Sir George was made a baronet. But she is very kind, and what is more she has a great deal of common sense, and unlike poor Albert she is far from being a fool. At least she would be able to give us a reference if we required it.' She rose to her feet. 'It is already getting dark. I will go and help Annie with the supper.'

Amy exclaimed in distress. 'That is another thing—poor Annie. What is to become of her? She has no one in the world but us, and no one understands her as we do. She loves us as her own, and I know she feels her life belongs to us, since it was in visiting her family that Mama took the cholera. We cannot abandon her. Her family could not have her back, even if they wanted to, and she has nowhere to go.'

'Mama visited many families at that time, and the cholera killed thousands in '32. It is not even certain that it can be caught just by visiting people who have it. Some people say that it is only spread by infected water. She could have contracted it anywhere. But, as for abandoning Annie, we could not of course do such a thing. With her disability, she would undoubtedly end up in the workhouse, for with her palate the way it is we are almost the only people who can understand her way of speaking, and nobody else is likely to make the effort. But we must first settle how we are to care for ourselves, before we are able to look after Annie. I shall visit Lady Haywood in the morning. Even if she can suggest no way of helping us, she might be able to help Annie to a place.' She left the room, and with this Amy had perforce to be satisfied.

The morning dawned bright and clear, and Eleanor set off in good time to walk the mile and a half to where Lady Haywood's imposing new house stood near the factory that had made the late Sir George his fortune. Of all the nearby mill owners he had been the most sympathetic to her father's aims, and his factories had been run on what were, for the 1840s, reasonably humane lines. A kindly, bluff man, he had risen through a mixture of hard work and shrewd investment, so that on his death he was accounted 'a warm man'. His business interests had been left in the hands of managers until his only child and heir should be of an age and an ability to assume his responsibilities. There were those who thought that, while the age might be achieved, the ability never would be, for the young Albert, though well-liked, was singularly lacking in the business sense that had characterised all his father's dealings.

Eleanor paused only to turn and give a wave and a smile to Amy, who was watching her from the window, before she started to walk briskly. Looking around, she reflected on how strange it would be to leave these streets, whose pavements she knew as well as she did the inside of her own home. As a very small child she had lived in the country, and she had distant memories of fields and huge cows. Her father had been a curate then, but the move to the city had soon followed.

The sunlight shone cheerfully on the mean houses, brightening the faces of the ragged children who played in the gutter. Only the very smallest were there—the rest had been hard at work for hours among the machinery of the busy mills. The cold air was comparatively fresh after the stench that the summer's heat always brought from the overflowing drains and piled-up middens. She felt a pang of sadness at the prospect of leaving these familiar streets, ugly and wretched though they were. Here Papa had toiled, and she had helped him as much as he had permitted, and here she was of at least some use in the world.

Her journey passed quickly, and, gaining admittance to the house, she soon found herself seated in Lady

Haywood's sitting-room. Her walk had warmed her and, accustomed as she was to the frugal fires and draughty rooms of the vicarage, she found the place almost oppressively hot. All the furniture and hangings were very comfortable, very rich, and very new, and while some might have objected that there was rather too much of everything, and that there were rather too many bright colours, Lady Haywood regarded it complacently. She herself had not yet abandoned the styles of ten years previously, and her more than ample form was made even more imposing by the wide sleeves and skirts of that day. Her round face was flushed with the heat of the fire next to which she sat, but her small eyes were shrewd and kindly.

'Well, my dear,' she was saying, when Eleanor was comfortably disposed in a chair which seemed to her almost sinfully soft, 'how are you? It has been a sad time for you both, and you have lost one of the best men who ever lived.' She saw that Eleanor was unable to reply, and nodded understandingly. 'This is not the moment for sympathetic words—your sorrow is too new. I am very glad to see you. You know I was thinking of you both yesterday.'

'I know you were, and we were so grateful for the lovely flowers you sent. The funeral was very well attended, and it was most kind of Sir Albert to have come.'

'Well, he's a biddable enough young man, and he had a great respect for your father. He told me there were many people there.'

'Yes, one might even say it was crowded. I was surprised how many people came to pay their respects.'

'It's always the same, my dear. They don't realise how much they need someone until it is too late. But what of you, and your pretty sister? What are you to do?'

'That is why I am here, ma'am, to ask your advice. We must of course leave the vicarage before long, as the new incumbent will be arriving.'

'There is no family at all to whom you can turn?'

'None. Both Papa and Mama were only children, and we have no close relatives in the world. And even if we had I should be reluctant to be dependent on them. I had thought I might obtain a post—as a governess, perhaps. What do you think?'

'I think that you are too proud for your own good. What of Miss Amy?'

'I must keep her with me; I had hoped she could be employed as a companion in the same house. I do believe her to be well fitted for such work, for you know no one could be more amiable.'

'No, she's a good girl. But far too lovely. No wife would risk having such a beauty under the same roof as her husband. Oh, you may think that coarse, but you think as I do, for you have enough sense for two. Look at poor Albert, making a spectacle of himself over her!'

Highly discomfited, Eleanor murmured something indistinct.

'Don't mind me, my dear. Speak as I find, that's my motto. I am delighted that Albert's first fancy should have been for a well-brought-up girl of principles, for I need hardly tell you that in his position he is in constant danger of being trapped by some scheming hussy. If he had been older, and she had been of a mind to return his feelings, there is no one I should have been happier to welcome as my daughter-in-law.'

Slightly overcome by this display of plain speaking, Eleanor murmured her thanks.

'All this is no use to you, however. It is a crying shame that you have lived so quietly. Your dear father was so unworldly, but so much beauty should be given the chance it deserves. Oh, I am not criticising the dear man, but his duty to you as his daughters should have included more socialising. How did he expect you to make good marriages?'

Eleanor smiled, but shook her head sadly. 'Papa was blessed with a very deep faith. He believed that God knew what was best for us all, and to him the saying that "the Lord will provide" meant quite literally that.'

'Husbands as well as daily bread? And you shared his views?'

'I would never have gone against my father's wishes and beliefs. Not because he would not have allowed it—he was the most indulgent of parents, and indeed always encouraged us to make up our own minds about things—but because it would have caused him pain. I suppose I had hoped, as he did, that my sister's looks and virtues would in time attract a suitable husband, and no doubt in time they would, but time, my dear ma'am, is precisely what we do not have! Papa's illness was so sudden; he had always enjoyed good health and had no expectations that he would not live for many more years. No, I do not expect a husband to fall like manna from the heavens; I only wish I had made more efforts in the past to see that we had a wider acquaintance.'

'The Lord helps those who help themselves, in fact.'

'Exactly so.' Eleanor laughed. 'Though I could scarcely have besieged the great houses of the area, I should have accepted more of the invitations that came our way. The trouble was that Papa was so immersed in his work with the mill families, and Amy was always content to stay at home. She has no desire to shine in society, as you well know, and positively shrinks from going among strangers. However, that is all in the past, and cannot be changed now.'

They were silent for a few moments.

'If it were not for poor Albert, I should ask you to make your home with me; I have always been fond of you girls. But at the moment I do not think it would do. Albert is by no means over this calf-love of his, and to have Miss Amy staying in the house would try his patience—and hers, no doubt. It is time he set his mind to learning his father's business. It is only a few years before he must take charge. At any rate, you would not widen your acquaintance with me. There was a time when I should have liked to have been accepted into society, but though money may make me tolerated, I know full well that my birth and manners are such that I should never belong. No need to look so embarrassed, my dear! I am too old and too fat to care what the fashionable world may think of me, and to be having to watch every word and worrying about which fork to use next would drive me mad. Can't teach an old dog new tricks.'

Eleanor rose and crossed the room to kneel on a small stool by Lady Haywood's chair. 'No one who knows you would wish you to change one jot, ma'am,' she said warmly.

'It is like your kind heart to say so, my dear. Since I may not offer you a home with me, will you allow me to help you in some other way? My late husband's money is tied up in the business, but he left me more than comfortably off. I dare say I could make you an allowance without so much as noticing it.'

Eleanor took hold of the pudgy, beringed hand that was stretched out to her, and said with heightened colour, 'I could not accept it, as I am sure you understand. I would never have come here if I had thought . . . I only wanted to ask your advice . . .'

Lady Haywood patted Eleanor's cheek with her other hand. 'There, now, I have upset you, and I never meant to. I know very well you are not the sort to come and beg, no matter how discreetly. I knew you would say no, but I had to do it, if only for your dear father's sake. He was a great help to me when Sir George passed on. But you must promise me this, for Amy's sake—if ever you should come to real want, or have any trouble that I could help with, you must come to me. Promise, now, or I shall not be able to sleep at nights, thinking of you two girls starving in an attic!'

'I promise, then, and thank you from the bottom of my heart, though I hope it will not come to that!'

'So do I, but I am glad I have made you promise.' She was so obviously disappointed that she could not help them that Eleanor felt quite badly. She remembered something else.

'There is one way you could help us, if you would be so kind. We are both very worried about our servant, Annie. You know that she was born with a deformed palate, and does not speak clearly? Of course, if it were at all possible we would wish her to stay with us, but if not we cannot bear to think of her with nowhere to go, after all the years she has been with us.'

'Bless you, my dear. I can find her a place in this house any time. It's no hardship, for I know she's a good servant, and goodness knows they're as rare as hens' teeth nowadays! Don't give it another thought, but send her along to me if you cannot keep her with you. This does not advance your present prospects any further, however. Are you set on your plan to seek employment?'

'I can think of no other way of supporting Amy. I am glad to say that she is much stronger than she was a few years ago, but she is still delicate. We cannot afford to rent even one room that would be dry and warm enough for her. The only kind of place we could afford would be certain to be damp and unhealthy.'

'Then I will do my best for you, of course. I can at least give you good references. In such matters a ladyship's word might carry more weight, especially if you are in a part of the country where I am not known!'

'Anyone who knows you must respect your judgement, and I admit I should be more than grateful for your reference.'

'I am not very hopeful, however. Finding work for one is bad enough, but for two... Is there really no relative, no connexion, even, who might be inclined to offer you a home?'

'Only distant ones, and my sister has written to inform them of our father's demise. But I cannot expect anything—they are for the most part only slightly related, and I cannot recall that I ever met any of them.'

'No help from that quarter, then. We must do what we can. I am glad to have had that promise from you— let me tell you I shall expect you to hold to it.'

Eleanor rose to her feet and kissed the florid cheek that was proffered to her. 'I am more grateful than I can say. I must go back—Amy will be anxious. I will put an advertisement in the newspapers right away.'

'Do not accept anything without telling me of it first. There are many unscrupulous people in the world who might try to take advantage of your orphaned state. As well to let prospective employers know that you have friends who take an interest in you.'

'You can be sure that I will do nothing without consulting you. Goodbye, and thank you.'

'Goodbye, my dear. My kind regards to your sister, and do not worry. We will contrive something.'

Something, yes, but what? Eleanor wondered as she stood on the steps buttoning her black gloves. For a moment her heart misgave her, then she drew in a deep breath of the chill, smoky air, and set off briskly towards the vicarage.

In her opulent room, Lady Haywood frowned at the fire, deep in thought.

'The name I can remember, and the address should not be too hard to discover. They will not like it, of course, but I must take a chance on that. Too proud to ask for help, so I will ask for them.' She gave a brisk nod that set her ample chins quivering, and rang her bell briskly.

CHAPTER TWO

THE advertisement duly appeared, but the results were disappointing. By the end of October only two replies had been received. The first was from a far from inconsolable widower, who wished for a governess for his two motherless children and companionship for himself. He did not specify the form this companionship was to take, but, from the glint in his small eyes as they looked her up and down, Eleanor felt it to be both unnecessary and unwise to enquire, and left precipitately. The other reply was from a Mrs White. Eleanor had set off in high hopes, but returned later in the day looking much dashed. She crouched on the hearthrug, warming her hands.

'Really, from the way she looked at me you would think she was buying me at a much-reduced price from a pawnbroker's shop! I could see her calculating just how much work she could get out of me. Moreover, she did not wish for a companion, but would be willing to have you as a sewing-maid—'

Amy laid down the stocking, which she was darning with small, careful stitches, and clasped her hands before her.

'A sewing-maid? I should not mind that, you know. Beggars cannot be choosers, and at least she is respectable and willing to take us.'

'I was about to say, as a sewing-maid and a housemaid, the two duties to be fitted into one day. I rather suspect she would prefer you to perform the first by night, so as to leave your days free to be the latter. I am sure she would grudge the time spent in sleep, if she were paying the sleeper.'

'Eleanor, surely you exaggerate?'

'I think not, dear. You never saw such a calculating eye. The little maid who opened the door to me looked half-starved. And the house! I did not see below stairs, but I saw the nursery floor. The reception rooms, though very chilly—she told me she makes it a rule never to light a fire before November, or after April, unless there is company—were showy in the extreme, but once the nursery floor was reached I could have thought myself in the poorest of houses. Bare boards everywhere underfoot, broken-down furniture, curtains that made ours look positively cosy, and so cold! There were four children—poor, shrivelled things they were, and no wonder, in that place. If that is how she treats her own children, think how her servants must fare! You would not last a month, and nor, I think, should I.'

Amy again took up her needle, and looked sadly at her mending.

'Poor little things! I almost wish we could go there and give them some love, for it sounds as if they need it.'

'My dear Amy! A housemaid may not love the children of the family she works for! I dare say you would never see them. And I am sure Mrs White would frown on any affection from their governess. She would dismiss us within a week.'

'You must be right, dearest, but what is to be done? There are only a few weeks remaining to us in this house. Already it is November, and the new vicar must be here by Christmas.'

Eleanor rose reluctantly from the rug before the small fire, and went to her own work-basket to take out her needle and thimble.

'I do not know how I manage always to be tearing my petticoats! Here is this flounce half ripped off, and I have no recollection at all of doing it.'

'You have walked so far, and so fast, Nell. And besides, the stuff is worn and tears easily. I wish you might have some new.'

'So do I. And those stockings have more darn than knitting in them.'

'They will keep me just as warm. Besides, I enjoy darning. It is no hardship to me.'

For a few moments they sewed in companionable silence. The noises from the street below were so familiar as to be unheard. The fire hissed and sighed as the coals settled in the grate, and there was a rhythmic click of thimble on needle as Eleanor sewed. Amy glanced at her sister's troubled face.

'You have not answered my question,' she reminded gently.

'I have not, because I cannot. I do not know what to do. There is Lady Haywood's kind offer, of course, and I know she would be happy to help us, but I cannot bring myself to take charity from her.'

'No, no, we cannot think of it. Well, we have a few weeks still here. There may—there must—be more replies to our advertisement. I am sure something will turn up.'

'You sound like Papa.'

Amy smiled reminiscently.

'Yes, I suppose I do. Do you remember, when we were short of money or had some other problem, how he would always say there would be a knock at the door?'

'How could I ever forget? And yet, how often that knock did come. Things always arranged themselves, and then how pleased, how triumphant he would be. "There you are," he would say, "help has knocked at our door again.'' If he were here now, he would tell us to have faith. Perhaps, even now, help is knocking at our door.'

Any answer that Amy might have given was forestalled by a loud rapping at the front door, which was immediately below the room in which they sat. Eleanor and Amy looked at one another in wild surmise, then fell into helpless laughter at the sight of each other's expression. Through their laughter they heard the loud tones of a gentleman's voice in attempted communication with Annie.

'Oh, hush, Nell,' begged Amy, stifling her laughter. 'It is surely a stranger, and he will hear us. Whatever will he think?'

She could say no more, for at that moment the door was opened and a flustered Annie ushered in their visitor. His tall frame filled the doorway as he regarded them unsmilingly. Eleanor's first, unbidden thought was that he was the most handsome man she had ever seen. Well above average height, and well-built, he had dark hair, and the skin of his clean-shaven, finely moulded face had the healthy tan of a man who spent much of his time in the open air. His frock-coat was of impeccable cut and cloth, his trousers held straight and smooth on his long, well-muscled legs by the straps under the instep that the newest fashion dictated. Her second thought was that he was the most disagreeable. His cold blue eyes beneath the strongly marked dark brows surveyed her, and she was immediately conscious that the hem of her gown was spattered with mud, and her hair ruffled by the wind. He regarded Amy, and while she was quick to see the flash of admiration in his eyes, it was overlaid with something that looked inexplicably like contempt. Eleanor's blood boiled. How dared he stand there, in his elegant, expensive clothes, and despise them? Ill-dressed and, in her case, untidy, they might be, and reduced to darning their own stockings, but their position as daughters of a clergyman entitled them to a degree of respect. Her late father, himself the most gentlemanly man she knew, had never failed to treat even the least of his parishioners with scrupulous politeness.

He spoke in coldly neutral tones.

'You must forgive me, ladies, for my abrupt entrance, but I was unable to make myself understood by your servant, and so I am forced to announce myself. I am Charles Wyckham.'

Amy put her darning, which in her confusion she had kept in her hand when she rose to greet him, carefully and without haste into her work-basket.

'I am Amy Hunter, and this is my sister, Eleanor.'

He gave a small formal bow to each.

'Miss Hunter. Miss Eleanor.'

There was a momentary pause. Amy's mind searched for a possible reason for his visit.

'Have you perhaps come in answer to the advertisement?'

'The advertisement? I know of no advertisement, Miss Hunter. I am here by my uncle's request. Sir Ambrose Hammond.'

He seemed to place some emphasis on the name, and looked sharply at them as he spoke. Eleanor was disappointed. The name was familiar, but she could not recall that she had ever met Sir Ambrose Hammond. She could not quite abandon the hope that he might be a prospective employer.

'Then does he, perhaps, require a governess, or a companion for his wife?'

He frowned.

'My uncle is a widower, and no, he does not require a governess—'

'I think you have forgotten, dearest,' broke in Amy, 'that the late Lady Hammond was my godmother. I remember seeing her when I was very small, but I believe she died not long after Mama.'

'That is correct. My aunt died twelve years ago. I have come, as I said, on my uncle's instructions. I had thought to offer you his, and my, sympathy.'

His eyebrows were dark and heavily marked. He raised them slightly as he spoke. His sardonic tone made Amy blush, and Eleanor leaped to her defence.

'Because you heard us laughing, do you think we mourn our father any the less?'

'It is not for me to judge, ma'am. I understand that ladies can become hysterical when overwrought.'

'I am never hysterical, nor is my sister. And no, it is not for you to judge. You cannot have known Papa, if you do not know how much he is missed by all, and how especially by us.' To her annoyance she felt the tears rising in her eyes, and lowered her head so that he should not see them.

'Naturally you miss him. And you are about to be turned out of your home, are you not?'

Tears forgotten, Eleanor raised her head furiously.

'How dare you, sir? How dare you imply that we have no other feeling, no other reason for missing him?'

Amy, deeply shocked, moved to Eleanor's side and took her hand, speaking with gentle dignity.

'I must thank you, Mr Wyckham, for your visit, and for the offer of condolence. Please convey our thanks to Sir Ambrose. For now, as you say, we are both a little overwrought, so I wish you a good afternoon.'

For the first time the cold, assessing look left his face, and he spoke more kindly.

'I apologise for my ill-considered speech. Please believe that I have heard nothing but good spoken of your father, and I do sincerely feel for you in your loss. I would be glad if you did not dismiss me yet. My uncle asked me to bring him news of you.'

Eleanor spoke before her sister could reply.

'I cannot think that it would benefit him in the slightest! You know nothing of us, and what you do know you seem to have taken in the greatest dislike. Your lips may frame apologies, but there you stand, calling us ma'am in that—that contemptuous way, and looking at us like a—like a woodlouse...'

'Eleanor!' Amy whispered in horror, but their visitor suddenly smiled. His face was transformed.

'I stand here only because I have not yet been asked to sit, and as for looking at you like a woodlouse, I had no idea I resembled such a creature! I must consult my looking-glass more carefully. Do woodlice stare at you a great deal?'

Against her will, Eleanor gave a gurgle of laughter.

'That is not what I meant, as you well know! I beg your pardon for my incivility, sir. Please, sit down, and let me take your hat and gloves. Our servant, Annie, is not used to formal calls, and is easily flustered by strangers. She is afflicted with a malformation of the palate, and while *we* can understand her, very few others can.'

'Thank you. Hardly the ideal person to be answering the door, perhaps?' He spoke with the carelessness of one used to a houseful of servants, and Eleanor felt her previous dislike of him return.

'Annie is our only servant. She has been with us for many years, and we think of her as one of the family. The fact that she cannot speak clearly does not mean that her brain is impaired, or her heart, and no one could ask for a more devoted servant.'

He said nothing, but handed her his hat and gloves with a little bow, and waited for Amy and herself to be seated before sitting down himself. His face was still reserved, but his look was friendlier than it had been, and lacked the touch of suspicion that had been there before.

'You spoke of an advertisement, Miss Eleanor?'

'Yes, I am seeking a post as a governess in some household where my sister can be a companion to the lady of the house.'

'And you have not, so far, been successful?'

'Not so far. But there is some time, and the advertisement appeared only two weeks ago.' Eleanor forced herself to reply easily. Not for anything would she reveal her anxiety to him. He paused, looking down at the floor.

'My visit,' he said at length, 'is the result of a letter received by my uncle.' He looked at them searchingly, and Amy replied with tranquillity.

'Yes, I wrote to him to tell him of Papa's death. His name was on a list of correspondents in Papa's desk, and it seemed civil to inform him. I believe they wrote to one another occasionally after Mama and Lady Hammond died.'

'That is so, but it is not to your letter that I referred. This was signed by a friend of yours, a Lady Haywood.'

'Lady Haywood? I did not know she was acquainted with your uncle.'

'She is not. She wrote on your behalf.'

More quick-witted than her sister, Eleanor was already springing to her feet. 'How could she? On our behalf, you say? And you thought, of course, at our instigation!'

He smiled again, but she was not to be disarmed.

'If I wondered, it is not altogether surprising. Consider that I knew nothing of her, of you, or of your father. But I do not think it now, so come off your high horse, my girl.'

'I am not your girl! Oh, how humiliating! How could she do such a thing?'

Amy, though pink with embarrassment, spoke more calmly.

'Lady Haywood acted out of the kindness and simplicity of her heart, dear, as you will acknowledge when you are calmer.'

'I am sure she did. Please sit down again, Miss Eleanor. The way you are looking at me makes me fear that I do indeed look like a woodlouse.'

Eleanor, too upset to smile at this modest sally, pressed her hands to her burning cheeks and turned away from him. She could not speak, and if she had been able to, did not know what to say.

'I think,' said Amy, 'that we should all have a cup of tea. Will you tell Annie, Eleanor? We do not ring for Annie, as a general rule,' she explained to their guest, distracting his attention from her sister. 'She works so hard, we like to spare her too many journeys up and down stairs.'

Charles Wyckham rose courteously to his feet as Eleanor left the room. The attention, which would have pleased her in any other man, inexplicably enraged her. The creature was opening the door for her. Well, he should not get round her as easily as that. Eleanor lifted her chin haughtily as she swept from the room.

Outside the door, she stood still for a moment. Her hands, icy with shock, were still pressed to her burning cheeks. Never had she been so rude to a stranger, and never had she felt so out of control of a situation. Her position as the daughter of a well-liked local vicar had ensured the respect of the local people, and in their small circle of friends she was accustomed to meet only with kindness. Never had anyone looked at her, still less at her gentle sister, with such a critical, despising eye. A drunken mill-worker she could face with equanimity, but this man's look of contempt had shaken her to her bones, and his apology had only half appeased her.

Shivering suddenly in the cold of the landing, she ran downstairs to the kitchen. The light was already dimming. In the parlour upstairs some daylight remained, but in the basement kitchen the lamp was lit, and the glow of light and warmth from the smouldering range made it homely and welcoming. Since her mother's death, Eleanor had spent more time in the kitchen than most young ladies of her class. She and Annie between them saw to all the cooking and running of the small household, with the help of an older woman who came in for the heavier cleaning and washing. Often, in the winter afternoons, the girls would bring their needlework down to the kitchen—it was hard to find enough coal for two fires, and that way Papa could have a fire in his study, and the parlour could remain unheated until the evening. Recently, too, they had taken to eating their simple meals together in the kitchen. Annie did not like it, but they were all tired and sad after nursing Mr Hunter, and it did save work.

Annie rose from the chair by the range where she had been knitting and rocking. At the age of fourteen she had been found by Eleanor's mother, and was the neglected child of a large mill family who assumed that because she could not speak she was witless. Half-starved and in rags, Annie had been brought to the vicarage and given care and kindness, the first she had ever known. When Mrs Hunter subsequently took the cholera, Annie nursed her devotedly, and after Mrs Hunter's death transferred her whole-hearted love to the two daughters. By the time she was twenty she was able to take over the running of the household when the elderly housekeeper died, and to all of them she was more a friend than a

servant. Constant use had accustomed them to a method
of communication involving such sounds as she could
make, and gestures, and she had quickly learned both
reading and writing. Such visitors as they usually had
were accustomed to hold one-sided conversations with
her, to which she would contribute only a nod or a shake
of the head and a shy smile.

The kettle was already humming on the side of the
range, and Eleanor swiftly laid a tea-tray with the few
pieces of fine china and the silver teapot that had been
one of Mama's cherished wedding gifts. Annie bent to
open the range, and took out a tray of fresh scones.

'Scones! How clever of you, Annie, for we have so
little in the house to offer a visitor. How fortunate that
he did not call at a time of day when we would have
been obliged to offer him a meal. As it is, I suppose it
would be usual to offer him wine and cake in the afternoon, but I hear that tea is much drunk in fashionable
circles at this time of day, so, as we have no wine to offer
him, we will have to let him think we are followers of
fashion! These will do very well; I will fill them with
some of our apple jelly, and there is the rest of the ginger
cake, too.' She began to lift the tray, but Annie exclaimed and took it from her. 'I suppose I must be a
young lady and not carry things,' Eleanor responded.
Annie gave a laugh and laid down the tray, taking
Eleanor's hand and leading her to the small square
looking-glass on the kitchen wall. Eleanor laughed
herself as she saw her reflection.

'You are right, I look more like a wild woman than
a young lady! Our guest has a low opinion of us,
however. He is not to be won over by tidy hair.' Annie
gave her a sharp, inquisitive look, and made a swift
gesture. 'You think he is handsome, Annie? Well, I do
not! Handsome is as handsome does, as the saying goes,

and his behaviour so far has been very—very un-handsome.' Nevertheless, she allowed Annie to smooth down and rearrange her hair. Then she lit the way with a lamp, while Annie followed her with the tea-tray.

Conversation was kept to a trivial level while they took tea, but Eleanor had the feeling that they were constantly being judged, and that their replies and even their expressions were being weighed. It was a strangely oppressive feeling and she preferred to say little, being unused to watching her tongue and unwilling, in any case, to do so.

Charles Wyckham laid down his cup and rose to his feet. Amy and Eleanor waited for him to take his leave, but he did not. He walked to the fireplace and stood, one hand on the mantelshelf as he stared down into the glowing coals. Then he turned abruptly to face them, and fixed his eyes on Amy's face.

'Miss Hunter, I said when I arrived that I came on my uncle's behalf.'

'Yes, and we are much obliged to you and to him for the kindness.'

'More so than you know. He has charged me to offer you a home with him at Oaklands Court.'

For a speechless moment they looked at him. Then Eleanor drew breath to speak, but Amy forestalled her.

'It is a most generous thought. Please thank him for his kindness, but I am afraid it is out of the question.'

Eleanor applauded silently.

'Out of the question? I do not understand you.'

It was Eleanor who answered him, for Amy, who had for once in her life spoken on impulse, was appalled, and could only sit blushingly silent.

'Sir Ambrose is in no way related to us. We have no claim on his generosity, and we would not like to be so beholden to him. If it had been a question of employment, it would have been a different matter. I do not know what Lady Haywood may have said in her letter, but I can assure you that we are quite able to take care of ourselves.'

'As a governess and a companion? You must give me leave to doubt that. It would be next to impossible to find such a household. You can have no idea how your life could be in such a situation, or how unsuitable it would be for you.'

'We are not afraid of work, and you can see that luxury is something we do not expect or want. Also, we are not entirely friendless. Lady Haywood, though in this instance she has acted ... unwisely ... is still determined to help us. Oh, if only I were a man, I could work for us both. I do not want to be a poor relation, an object of charity!'

'It is indeed unfortunate that I mentioned Lady Haywood's letter. I can assure you that I do not wish to stand here in the guise of a wealthy benefactor. Nor would my uncle wish you to think of yourselves as poor relations. The obligation would not all be on one side.' He sat down again, leaning forward earnestly. 'Sir Ambrose, as you know, is a widower. He is also a very lonely man. You may not know that my cousin Richard, his only child, was killed six years ago.'

Amy gave a soft exclamation of pity.

'Poor Sir Ambrose. Does he live alone now?'

'For a while he did. Richard was very dear to him, and after hearing of his death my uncle became ill, and remained so for a long time. Even now, though physically improved, he is withdrawn, subject to periods of severe depression. Two years ago he invited my widowed mother, his sister, and myself, to share his home, and we have lived at Oaklands Court ever since. Sir Ambrose was anxious that I should learn all that I could about the running of the estate, as after my cousin's death I became the heir.'

'You are to be congratulated, then,' said Eleanor coldly. She spoke out of the bitterness of her own spirit, that had not forgiven him for thinking of her sister and herself as beggars, eager to ingratiate themselves with a wealthy old man. He looked at her bleakly.

'By no means. Richard and I were like brothers. There was only a year between our ages. The small estate I inherited from my father was all that I had ever wanted or hoped for. Do you not think I would give anything— anything—to have my friend, my childhood playmate, back again, and to see my uncle young and merry as he once was?' He fell silent, and Eleanor, abashed, hung her head. She felt instinctively that this was a man who did not speak easily of his inner feelings, and she was deeply ashamed that her pettiness should have led him to open his heart to strangers in a manner which she felt sure was repugnant to him. How often Papa had implored her to curb her impulsive tongue, and how right he had been.

'Please forgive me. What I said was unpardonable, and I beg you to forget that I uttered it. I did not mean to imply...' She paused, not knowing how to continue.

Unexpectedly, his face lightened with a slight smile.

'I think you did, you know! I mean,' he answered her surprised look, 'I think you meant to imply it, but you did not really think it.'

'I did not...' Eleanor replied hotly, then her voice trailed off as she acknowledged that he was in fact right. 'Oh, dear, you are quite right. How well you understand the female mind. I can only apologise again.' She looked directly into his face, too honest to prevaricate, and caught a look of surprised approval.

'There is no need. I am now amply repaid for my suspicions of you, which were equally unfounded and equally damning. Shall we cry quits, and be friends?'

He stood up and held out his hand to her as he spoke, and her own love of plain speaking responded to his forthright openness. Taking his proffered hand, she smiled without reservations for the first time. He turned back to Amy.

'I hope, Miss Hunter, that you will reconsider my uncle's offer. My mother is something of an invalid, and the house is much in need of those touches which only a woman's hand can give. I am out and about a good deal, for the full running of the estate devolves upon me, and since I have much to learn it takes me all of my time. The housekeeper is devoted but elderly, and there is a lack of direction in the household affairs that I feel sure you could help with. At the same time, the house is too empty. There are too many memories for us all. In helping you, I believe that my uncle will himself be helped, distracted by new faces, new ideas, new conversations that can have no painful connections.'

Amy looked helplessly at Eleanor. It was a persuasive picture that he painted. To be of use, to have a home, and one that was obviously more comfortable than any they had known. Such a tempting offer was hard to refuse, and Eleanor had for some time been stifling the knowledge that a position such as she had hoped for was unlikely to be found. She shrank from putting herself in the position of a poor relation, but, for Amy's sake, could she afford to refuse?

She had no idea that most of this was clearly to be read in the expressions that moved across her face. Charles Wyckham had a very good idea of what she was thinking, and, being himself a proud man, found himself much in sympathy with her quandary. Once again she

was surprised to see a glint of amusement in his eyes as
he watched her, and she was annoyed to find her cheeks
growing hot.

'It would be unwise as well as ungrateful to refuse,
Miss Eleanor,' he said gently, and she knew that he was
right. One final trump card occurred to him. 'My uncle
would, I feel sure, wish me to say that you would be
welcome to bring your girl—Annie, isn't it?—with you,
as your personal maid, perhaps. He would naturally want
you to have your own maid, and you might find it pref-
erable to having a stranger wait on you.'

Amy's face lit up.

'It does seem providential, dearest, and if Annie could
share our good fortune, too! Do you not think we should
accept Sir Ambrose's generous offer?'

Looking at her sister, Eleanor knew that she must say
yes. Amy was so fragile, so much in need of the comfort
and security that Oaklands Court seemed to offer. She
must swallow her pride. And as she looked at her sister's
lovely face as Amy smiled dazzlingly at Mr Wyckham,
Eleanor wondered if fate had indeed knocked at their
door that afternoon.

'Yes, we should be happy to accept, though naturally,' she continued firmly, 'we should wish to pay
Annie's wages ourselves.'

'Naturally,' he agreed solemnly.

'And if we should be too much of an imposition I can
still look for a position.'

'Yes, indeed. You could ask my mother to give you
a reference. But I hope things will not come to such a
pass. You can anticipate a happy and peaceful future at
Oaklands Court.'

Eleanor hoped that he was right.

So did Charles Wyckham, as he walked away down
the ill-lit street. When his uncle had first suggested taking

in the two girls, he had been against the idea. He had used all the arguments that Eleanor herself had brought up: that the girls were strangers, not relatives, and had no call on them. He had been quite sure that they were, if not gold-diggers, at least trying to take advantage of Sir Ambrose. The only thing that had persuaded him to come on this errand was that it had brought some signs of a return to normality to his grief-stricken uncle, by giving him something new to think of. He had been sure, however, that the visit would be pointless, and was quite prepared to return with the news that the Hunters were not suitable objects of generosity.

He had been both surprised and pleased by his reception. Of course, the initial introduction had been awkward, but, in spite of the laughter he had heard as he came in, he had quickly dismissed his first idea of them as grasping or designing. Eleanor's flash of temper had done her no disservice in his eyes, and he liked the candour which led her to admit her fault so quickly and openly. Her pride, too, he found perfectly proper under the circumstances, and he had sincerely felt for her as she struggled to make herself accept what was, after all, the charity of a stranger.

From Lady Haywood's letter he had been prepared to find them good-looking, but he had not expected to find such a beauty as Amy. Not only beautiful, but gentle and good, if he was any judge. He felt himself strongly drawn to her quiet dignity. His lips twitched as he imagined his mama's reaction to welcoming two such girls to Oaklands Court. She was fondly looking forward, he knew, to his making a brilliant match now that he was the heir of Oaklands, and he had found himself much amused by her transparent attempts to find him a suitable wife. She would not be best pleased, but Miss Hunter was a modest girl who would not be likely to push herself forward, and, while she might scheme on her son's behalf, Mrs Wyckham would never be unkind to one in need.

He looked forward to describing the meeting to his uncle, hoping to see him smile, and to distract him from the gnawing grief that burdened all his waking moments. The sudden death of his cousin had laid heavy burdens on Charles Wyckham. At the age of twenty he had suddenly found himself responsible for the running of a large estate and household. He was distressed by his uncle's grief and illness, and determined to do his best to be worthy of the trust placed in him. In the years since that time, he had thrown himself body and soul into the business of the estate. The experience had made him mature beyond his years, which, coupled with a serious turn of mind, had limited his inclinations to take part in the social life of the neighbourhood. Now he had the estate running smoothly, and it was time he looked around him for a wife. The beautiful but penniless Miss Hunter might not be his mother's idea of a suitable match, but he was wealthy enough not to need a rich bride, and he knew that if ever the time came he could handle his mama. All in all, he was well satisfied with the day's work.

CHAPTER THREE

ELEANOR climbed wearily from the carriage, grateful for the support of Charles Wyckham's arm as she negotiated the steps. Her legs ached with fatigue, she was stiff from sitting for so long, and her feet, in spite of the hot bricks that had thoughtfully been placed on the floor when they set out, were so cold that she could hardly feel the ground. She turned anxiously to Amy, who looked alarmingly pale. They had spent the whole of the previous day on the journey, taking the train to Birmingham and then to London. A night's rest at a hotel had done little to refresh them, for, although worn out with the physical and emotional claims that the journey had made, they had both found it impossible to do more than doze in the strange surroundings, and with the knowledge of more to be faced on the morrow.

There was sadness, too, in leaving the familiarity of the only home they could remember. Most of the contents of the vicarage had been given away, and a few of the better pieces sold. Papa's desk, which it had been hard to part with, had been left with Lady Haywood, leaving only a few boxes of pictures, ornaments and other belongings to follow them. The bare rooms were still full of memories, faded patches on walls a mutely eloquent reminder of familiar objects. It was hard to say goodbye to the place where both their parents had died, and hardest of all to make that final visit to the quiet churchyard where they lay together.

In all of this, Charles Wyckham had helped and advised. After returning to Oaklands Court to tell his uncle that the girls were to accept his offer, he had come back to Manchester to be with them on the journey. The help of a man on such a journey was of inestimable value, and though at times he acted in a high-handed manner that made Eleanor want to slap him, she knew that without him Amy, at least, would have fared far worse.

An icy wind whipped at her skirts, and she clutched at her shawl.

'Go inside quickly, Miss Eleanor. I will help Annie to bring your sister. You must get into the warm as quickly as possible. Evans will see to your boxes.' Charles Wyckham gave her a gentle push towards the step, where a heavy door was opening, spilling a welcoming glow of light into the gloom of a wet November afternoon. He turned back and offered his arm to Amy, who was leaning against Annie's firm embrace. The house loomed huge against a darkening sky, and Eleanor wondered briefly if she would ever learn to find her way about it. She only had time to get a vague impression of old timbering and brickwork, beneath a stone roof of what she later learned to call Horsham stone, before she was through the front door. The entrance hall was correspondingly large, but for the moment her interest centred on the handsome blaze that warmed the room, the scent of which she had immediately noticed on alighting from the carriage. Accustomed, as she was, to coal fires, the aromatic waft of wood-smoke was as exotic as it was delicious.

'Miss Hunter, you are quite exhausted. If you will permit...' And without more ado Charles bent and lifted Amy, carrying her swiftly over the step and into the warmth of the hall. She was very light in his hold, and his arms tightened protectively. A scent of orris reached him, even through the heavy overlay of coal-smoke that the travelling had left on her clothes. Before she had time to do more than utter a soft exclamation of distress, he had deposited her gently in a large chair by the log fire that burned in a huge grate. She was stricken with embarrassment—no man but her father had ever held her in so close an embrace. He had found the experience distinctly pleasurable, but continued to talk in a matter-of-fact way, giving her time to regain her composure.

'You must forgive my rough and ready manners, Miss Hunter, but you really must get warm as soon as may be. It would never do for you to spend your first days at Oaklands Court laid up with a putrid sore throat or a fever. Why, it would give Miss Eleanor such a disgust of the place that she would be out looking for a position as governess in no time! Thank you, Browning,' Charles said as the butler silently took his coat and hat. 'Is all well here?'

'Yes, Mr Charles. Mrs Wyckham fretted a little about the cold weather, and worried that you would be impeded by ice. Sir Ambrose asked me to welcome the young ladies, and to inform them that he would meet them at dinnertime. Mrs Wyckham is resting in her boudoir, and Sir Ambrose thought that they would prefer a little time to rest before meeting everyone.'

Amy smiled her relief, and Eleanor answered for them both.

'Thank you, Browning. We are very grateful to Sir Ambrose for his thoughtfulness. I, for one, certainly prefer to have time to make myself more respectable before meeting our kind host. Of course, we were very lucky to have Mr Wyckham to escort us.' She smiled at Charles as she spoke. 'It was most kind of you to take the trouble, for the journey must otherwise have taken much longer, and as you see my sister is already very tired. We have never made such a long journey before.'

Charles bowed a formal reply to her thanks, and Browning relaxed. No more than Charles had he liked this sudden idea of his master's, and he had been deeply, though silently, distrustful of the two strangers, coming as they did from a place of which he had heard little but bad. He was relieved to find that, in spite of their appearance, they were undoubtedly gentlewomen. Eleanor's well-modulated voice had also banished the fear that they might speak with what, to him, was a foreign accent. He prided himself that he knew a lady when he saw one, no matter how she was dressed, and these two were certainly ladies.

'Does Mrs Martlett know we are here, Browning?'

'Yes, Mr Charles. I sent a message directly I heard the horses in the drive. She has been overseeing the final preparations of the young ladies' rooms, and will be here at once.'

'Yes, I hear her coming now. Miss Hunter, Miss Eleanor, you will forgive me if I leave you now with our Mrs Martlett, who will show you up to your rooms.'

Amy thanked him in her soft voice, and Eleanor was pleased to see that some colour had returned to her cheeks. Mrs Martlett came forward, a small, brisk figure in rustling black. Eleanor found herself surveyed by a pair of shrewd blue eyes that looked as though they would miss very little, and stifled a smile as she remembered Charles Wyckham's persuasions. If there were indeed a lack of direction in the household, it could not have anything to do with Mrs Martlett. She glanced at Charles, who gave her a rueful grin. The housekeeper watched them impassively.

'I am sure you are very welcome, miss.'

'Thank you, Mrs Martlett. We are very happy to be here. This is our maid, Annie. Mr Wyckham will have told you that she was to come with us?' His nod conveyed to her that no explanations were necessary. Mrs Martlett looked sharply at Annie, who bobbed a small curtsy but who looked, Eleanor was glad to see, remarkably self-possessed. It would not be easy, Eleanor knew, coming to a household of this size, where the indoor staff would be numerous. They would, she knew, have their own customs, and life below stairs would be run on strictly laid-down lines, which Annie would have to learn to fit in with. Eleanor could only hope that the obvious kindness of the master of the house would be reflected in the attitudes of his servants. The housekeeper nodded as if satisfied with what she saw.

'I will show you where you are to sleep, Annie, when the young ladies have finished with you. Then I will take you to the servants' hall for tea, and you can meet the rest of the staff. You'll soon find your feet. Now, miss, if you are ready?'

Amy stood up.

'Thank you, Mrs Martlett. I feel much better now.'

'This way, if you please, miss.' The housekeeper led the way to a fine staircase, its shallow oak treads worn by generations of feet, and polished, as were the heavy carved banisters, to a rich gloss. 'You will want to change out of your travelling clothes, and there is time for you to have a nice lie down before you have to come downstairs. Mr Charles suggested to Sir Ambrose that you might prefer to have a little time to rest and tidy yourselves before you meet him and Mrs Wyckham. A very thoughtful boy, Mr Charles.'

'Yes, indeed. He understands a lady's feelings remarkably well.'

'He always was very considerate. Miss Emily, Mrs Wyckham, I should say, is a very sensitive lady. She was a great beauty as a girl.' She said no more, but Eleanor could read between the lines. Obviously Mrs Wyckham was not always easy to deal with.

'You have been in the household a long time?'

'Since I was a girl, miss. I was a housemaid when Miss Emily was a girl. My father was head gardener to Sir Richard, Sir Ambrose's father.'

They reached the top of the stairs, and the housekeeper led the way along a panelled gallery hung with pictures. She gestured towards them, but the light was too poor for the girls to see them properly.

'Portraits of the family, miss. Perhaps another day you would like to see them? I should be happy to show them to you.'

'Thank you, Mrs Martlett. That would be most interesting.'

'Your rooms are along here, in the west wing. Sir Ambrose, Mrs Wyckham and Mr Charles are in the east wing, but we thought you would be more comfortable here, as there are two connecting rooms and a sitting-room at the end.'

Eleanor and Amy looked at one another in amazement. Sir Ambrose was certainly not treating them like poor relations. Mrs Martlett opened a door and stood aside for them to enter.

'What a beautiful room!' exclaimed Eleanor. She looked with delight at the well-proportioned room. The furniture was of oak, a little heavy and old-fashioned, but lovingly polished to a sheen that reflected the glow of flames from the fireplace. The pattern of leaves on the wallpaper had faded slightly to a soft green on an ivory ground, and this colour was repeated in the brocade of the curtains and bed-hangings, and the cushions of the deep window-seats. The housekeeper opened a door to the next room, which was similarly furnished, except that the predominating colour was a deep pink. Mrs

Martlett looked round the rooms, checking that their boxes had been carried up and that everything was as it should be.

'There is hot water in the jugs, and you need have no fear that the beds are damp, for I saw to it that they were well aired. I will send Jane up with a tray of tea, and if there is anything else you require, please ring. The family dines at seven, so I will come back and fetch you at half-past six.'

Amy was already sitting in a comfortable chair by the fire in the pink room, while Annie took off her bonnet and knelt to remove her boots. On impulse, Eleanor bent and kissed the elderly cheek before her.

'Thank you for making us so welcome. I hope we have not made a great deal of work for you. You are all so kind.' Her voice caught in her throat. She wondered if she had made a fool of herself: young ladies did not generally kiss servants, after all. She need not have worried. Mrs Martlett patted her hand.

'Bless you, my dear. I remember your poor mother. She came to stay here once before she was married, and again with your papa when they were newly wed. A sweet, pretty lady she was, and you have a look of her yourself. My poor mistress often spoke of her, and I know Sir Ambrose is happy that you have come. This has been a sad house lately, and we all hope that having you here will make things better.'

'If it is in our power, you can be sure we will do it.'

With another smile and a pat Mrs Martlett left the room, and Eleanor hurried to help Annie with Amy. Flinging open the trunks, she rummaged for their warm dressing-robes, and before long both girls were out of their travel-creased dresses and snugly sipping tea before the fire in the pink bedroom. On their insistence, Annie drank a cup with them, then hurried to unpack their boxes and bestow their things neatly.

'How very kind Sir Ambrose is! I have never seen such lovely rooms. And a fire in each! We shall be spoiled.'

'You could never be spoiled, Amy,' said Eleanor, looking lovingly at her sister. 'This is more than I had ever hoped for, and I am so deeply thankful that you are here. Are you warmer now? Let me give you some more tea. I am sure I do not know when I have found it more welcome!' She took the cup as she spoke, and refilled it. 'Drink that, and then Annie and I are going to tuck you in bed for a while. It is more than two hours until we need to worry about dressing.'

'Oh, yes. But you must rest too, dear.'

'Well, I will try, but although I am so tired I hardly know whether I could sleep. It is all so exciting.'

'I am a little nervous at the thought of meeting Sir Ambrose and Mrs Wyckham.'

'So am I, but I am sure there is no need. And there will be Charles Wyckham to protect you from them, should they prove to be dragons!'

'Eleanor! You should not speak so of one who is our benefactor. We do not need Mr Wyckham's protection here.'

'I think he would be glad to fight dragons for one of us,' said Eleanor slyly.

'It was not...he did not...' flustered Amy, her cheeks growing pink again at the memory. Eleanor said no more, but she was well satisfied. She felt sure that no man could resist Amy's combination of beauty and goodness, and also that Amy would find him equally attractive.

Their belongings unpacked, Annie left to find her own room, and Eleanor had the pleasure of seeing that her sister was peacefully asleep. She herself, although she was bone-weary, had little inclination to do likewise.

There was so much to think of, to hope for, and there had been little in their life to offer such hopes until now. Suddenly to be so cherished, so lapped in luxury, was almost frightening. How could she every repay it? And if, by some mischance, things did not work out well, if Sir Ambrose or Mrs Wyckham should dislike them, how could she take Amy away from the comfort and security she so badly needed?

Restlessly she wandered round the room, absently stroking the brocade of the bed-hangings, and then moving to the window. The curtains were still open, although little light came from the rain-heavy sky, and she curled up on the window-seat, hugging her robe around her. Suddenly curious, she pulled one of the heavy curtains across, shielding the lights of the room so that she could see outside.

She was looking out, she saw at once, at the other side of the house to that she had seen on arriving. Below her a paved terrace was sheltered and half-enclosed by two wings of the house. A low stone wall set with urns divided it from a sweep of lawn, which dropped gracefully to an area of shrubs and woodland. At this time of the year the trees were bare, their branches moving in the wind and the driving rain. In summer, however, it would be beautiful. In her mind's eye, smiling at her own fancies, she saw Amy sitting in the warm sunshine, saw her strolling on that lawn, saw her happily surrounded by laughing children as fair and lovely as herself. This, surely, was where Amy belonged?

She stiffened, wondering if her imagination were working too well, for at that moment she thought she did see a child. Then she relaxed, smiling to herself for her foolishness. In the uncertain light she must have mistaken one of the urns for a small figure. Then she saw a movement, and this time was sure there was a

child—a little boy—by the wall at the edge of the terrace.
One of the estate children, perhaps, risking a scolding
to play in what must be a forbidden place. He certainly
looked furtive, keeping to the shadow of the wall and
the urns. She raised her hand to tap at the window,
meaning to give the boy a little wave, but at that moment
he looked up and saw her sudden movement. For a
second his face was clearly visible, then he ducked fear-
fully out of sight and was gone. Definitely a case of
someone being where he should not be! Well, she would
not tell on him, she thought. He had obviously not
expected anyone to be in that part of the house. She
dismissed him from her thoughts and stood up, closing
both of the curtains against the chill from the window.
Disdaining her bed, she curled up comfortably on a sofa
near the fire, and, staring into the flames, soon drifted
into sleep after all.

Annie's return awakened Eleanor. She stretched
luxuriously, only half awake. Then, as a maid entered
with a fresh can of hot water for their wash-stands, she
jumped to her feet. They were to meet the rest of the
family, and must be ready.

Quickly she washed, then unpinned her hair and shook
it down in a heavy mass that reached almost to her knees.
It was her one beauty, and secretly she regretted that it
must always be neatly arranged in prim bands. Dragging
her brush ruthlessly through the tangles, she arranged it
again, then slipped into the black dress that Annie had
already laid out on the bed. Annie hurried in to help her
fasten it. She surveyed herself with some dissatisfaction.
The material was cheap, and though the fit of the bodice,
thanks to Amy's nimble fingers, was closely moulded to
her figure, it was very plain, with only a simple frill of
white lawn breaking the unrelieved black. It was, she
supposed, suitable, but it was hardly an evening-dress.

Briefly, she considered putting on another petticoat to make the skirt look fashionably fuller, but dismissed the idea on reflecting that they had economised on the fabric of the skirt, so that it could hardly be made to bell out more. Still, she told herself, it was modest, clean, and tidy, lightly scented with the lavender and orris that Annie had laid between the folds. She went to help Amy.

'How are you, Amy? Did you sleep well?'

'Oh, yes, very well, and I feel so refreshed. Imagine sleeping in a canopied bed! I felt like a princess.'

'You look better too—not so pale. Come, let me help you with your hair. How tightly you have done it—let me loosen it here.'

'Whatever you wish, Eleanor. You know no one ever does my hair as well as you.'

Swiftly Eleanor removed some of the pins, softening the sides of her hair to smooth curves, and allowing a few curls to fall softly on her neck.

'There, that is better. I do not like you to look so severe.'

Amy looked doubtfully at herself in the glass.

'It does look pretty, but do you not think it is a little frivolous? In our situation, I mean?'

'Nonsense,' said Eleanor stoutly. 'You know Papa liked you to look your best. Now your gown—thank you, Annie. What a pity it covers your shoulders, they are so pretty, and these high necks are so unfashionable.'

'Why, Eleanor, I have never known you to take such an interest in fashion before. How do you come to know so much?'

'Oh, Lady Haywood had some copies of *La Belle Assemblée*, and one day when I was there she was called away, and I spent some time looking at them.'

'Well, I think it sounds horridly chilly,' said Amy cheerfully. 'I am sure I would get a stiff neck if I had to sit all evening with my shoulders bared, and anyway, I should feel quite uncomfortable in mixed company. Not that this house is not wonderfully warm, of course, but in the general way I should think it most unwise!'

Eleanor laughed.

'What a practical little person! Don't you remember that *"il faut souffrir pour être belle"*?'

'I thought that was curl-papers and corsets! Fine feathers may make fine birds, but we are not fine birds, so it does not matter. Are we ready?'

'Yes. Two ladylike blackbirds.'

'I think,' said Amy, wrinkling her nose in thought, 'that female blackbirds are brown.'

'You are too pedantic—I am supposed to be the governess!' said Eleanor. She was delighted that Amy was in such good spirits. It had been a long time since she had talked in her old cheerful, inconsequential way. 'We must be crows, then, though that is not very complimentary to either of us!'

There was a knock at the door. The sisters looked at one another, and for a moment their hands met and clasped in mutual comfort. Mrs Martlett came in.

'I came just a few minutes early, to see that you had everything you wanted.'

'Thank you, Mrs Martlett. We are both rested, and everything is perfect. We are looking forward to meeting Sir Ambrose and Mrs Wyckham.'

'I will take you down, then.'

She led the way back along the gallery and down the broad staircase to the hall, where the butler was waiting for them. He opened a door and stepped aside, bowing slightly, and they walked into the drawing-room, where three people sat by the fire, looking towards them. Charles Wyckham jumped to his feet and came to meet them.

'Thank you, Browning. Miss Hunter, you are looking much better now, I am glad to see. And, Miss Eleanor, you have rested? Good. Let me present you to my uncle. Sir Ambrose, here are the young ladies! Miss Amy, Miss Eleanor, Sir Ambrose Hammond.'

Amy and Eleanor made their curtsys, and Sir Ambrose held out a hand to each of them. Looking at him, Eleanor thought that she had never before seen such a sad face. Even smiling, as he was now, his eyes held depths of pain and bitterness such as she had seldom witnessed, even in the poorest and most miserable areas of her father's parish. His face was thin and pale, with lines etched deeply between his eyebrows and around his mouth. He greeted them warmly, however.

'I am very glad to see you, my dears. Welcome to Oaklands Court. I hope you will be very happy here.'

Both Amy and Eleanor tried to express their deep sense of obligation for the kindness he had shown them, but he held up a hand, disliking to be thanked.

'My late wife, your godmother, Miss Amy, was deeply attached to your mother. I have often regretted that I could not do more for your father, and now that you girls are alone in the world I am happy to do what I can for you, in her memory. One of the last things she asked me to do, in her final illness, was to take over her responsibilities towards you. I regret that I have not done something about this sooner, but your father was most reluctant to accept any help that I could have given him.'

Amy's eyes filled with tears.

'I hope you will always find us worthy of your great kindness, Sir Ambrose. We will always strive to be so.'

'I am sure I shall, my dear. Now here is my sister for you to meet. Emily, you will be glad of the company of these two young ladies, I think!'

'Yes, to be sure. How do you do? You will forgive me if I do not rise, but I am a sad invalid, I fear. The doctor has warned me against the least exertion!'

Amy and Eleanor curtsied again, surveying the vision before them in some fascination. Mrs Wyckham was very plump, even fat, and her large form reclined with surprising grace on a sofa. The remains of her beauty were still to be seen in the fine, delicately tinted skin, and in her hair, which was still a determined shade of gold that Eleanor suspected owed not a little to art. Her gown, of fine lilac silk, was cut as low over her shoulders as any that Eleanor had seen in Lady Haywood's magazine, and its wide skirt was richly flounced and trimmed with lace and ribbon bows. As Mrs Wyckham looked them over, Eleanor was once again conscious of the shortcomings of their wardrobes. Soft-hearted Amy came to her rescue.

'I am so sorry you are not well, ma'am. Have you been out of sorts for long? I am sure you have not, for you look lovely.'

Her sincerity was obvious, and Mrs Wyckham was clearly torn between pleasure at the compliment and a desire to claim long-standing ill health.

'As to looks, I cannot now make any great claims,' she said complacently, 'although when I was a girl I believe I was passably good-looking...' She paused, hoping for another compliment, which Amy good-naturedly supplied. 'I am not precisely ill, you know, it is my nerves. I am so very sensitive, the least little thing upsets me. The doctor has said that he has never known anything to equal my nerves.'

'Very true, Mama. Nor have any of us,' interrupted her son with a look of loving amusement. 'But you will not be wishing to discuss them now, when our guests have just arrived. May I pour you a glass of sherry?'

Mrs Wyckham looked as if, on the contrary, she would have liked to discuss them at some length, but agreed that she would like a small glass as a tonic. He poured the wine and served her, taking a glass to Sir Ambrose, and, with a lift of his eyebrows, offered it to Eleanor and Amy. Feeling very daring, they accepted the small half-glasses he poured for them, for although Papa had been by no means against moderate drinking, his habitual shortness of purse had meant that such things were seldom to be had at the vicarage. Sir Ambrose called Eleanor to sit beside him and she complied, while Amy settled in a chair between Mrs Wyckham and her son. Sir Ambrose was obviously putting himself out to set her at her ease, and Eleanor found him both pleasant and easy to talk to. Out of the corner of her eye she could see that Charles was talking to Amy about the journey, and drawing his mother into the conversation very skilfully. A few moments later Eleanor saw a look of displeasure pass over Mrs Wyckham's face, and saw that the older woman's eyes were fixed on Amy's pretty face as she looked up at Charles. Then Sir Ambrose asked her a question and she returned her attention to him.

Dinner was announced, and they went through, Sir Ambrose offering his arm courteously to his sister, and his nephew laughingly offering both of his to the girls, so that they walked in semi-formal procession to the dining parlour, a pleasant, smallish room that was used, Sir Ambrose explained, when they dined *'en famille'*, as the dining-room proper was too large and cold for so small a party. The food was delicious, with many more courses than the girls were used to. Even Eleanor, who had a healthy appetite, had to refuse several dishes, though she noticed that Mrs Wyckham ate heartily of everything, bemoaning all the while that in her invalid state she could manage only a taste, just to please Cook!

After a dessert of cherry tartlets, velvet creams, and a dish of pippins cooked in wine syrup, Mrs Wyckham nodded to the girls to accompany her from the room.

'Mind you do not sit too long over your wine, brother!' she enjoined archly. 'We must not keep these young ladies too long from their beds after their tiring journey.'

They returned to the drawing-room, where she subjected them to a minute examination of their family, their prospects and their financial means that was as artless as it was impertinent. Eleanor could not help smiling as she then enlarged on her son's elevated position and prospects, and her hopes that he would marry well.

'For in his position, my dear girls, he may look as high as he pleases! I suppose he might have married ten times these past three years, if he had wished, but he is so nice in his choice. My son, I have said to him, when you come to take a wife it is your duty to think of the family. That must be placed above every other consideration. For my sake, for your uncle's sake, indeed for your own sake, marry a lady of breeding and wealth, who will be fitted by her upbringing and education to take up the dignities and responsibilities which her position as your wife will bring her.'

She paused impressively. Amy was blinking heavily in a sleepy haze of good food and tiredness. Eleanor nodded solemnly.

'Quite so, ma'am. I am sure he must have been very much obliged to you for your good advice.'

'I think he was, though at the time he only laughed. Such a sense of fun he has always had. I have had to scold him for it, sometimes. Charles, I say, you must not go on in this joking way with everyone. With me, with your uncle, it is perfectly permissible, but there have been those, Miss Eleanor, who have read more into it than they should. Young ladies, for instance, have been known to think that what was in him mere kindness and fun was something more. Hopes have been raised—you understand me, I am sure.'

'Of course, ma'am,' Eleanor replied with civil indifference. 'A gentleman such as Mr Wyckham would never knowingly raise such hopes. I am sure he would not do anything to cause you a moment's anxiety.'

Eleanor understood her only too well. Mrs Wyckham, alarmed at the prospect of a girl living under the same roof as her son who, however young and lovely, was to all intents and purposes penniless, and whose family background, though perfectly respectable, was by no means elevated, was issuing a warning. Although inwardly seething at the slight to her beloved sister, Eleanor could well understand a mother's anxiety that her only son should make a good, or even a brilliant marriage. At the same time she felt sure that, while Mr Wyckham would not wish to marry to disoblige his mother, neither was he the type to submit himself tamely to a marriage without love merely to please her. She must hope that closer acquaintance with Amy would soften Mrs Wyckham's prejudices. If love should grow between them, how could any mother refuse her son his chance of happiness?

At that point the gentlemen rejoined them, and such thoughts were forgotten in the bustle of rearranging seating and pouring coffee from the tray brought in by Browning. Soon after, seeing that Amy could hardly keep awake, Eleanor made their excuses and they retired to bed.

Amy was soon in bed, asleep almost before Eleanor could kiss her goodnight. Once Annie had helped her to remove her gown and unlace her corset, Eleanor sent her to bed, since she, too, was yawning. The room was pleasantly warm, and Eleanor sat for a moment by the fire in her nightgown, slowly brushing her hair and listening to the unaccustomed sounds of the countryside. Town-bred as she was, she was both surprised and amused by the number of hoots, screeches and rustlings that came from the garden and from the woodland beyond it. So this was the peace of the countryside! It was as noisy, in its own way, as the streets of Manchester. Being both sensible and down-to-earth, she did not bother herself with thoughts of ghosts or other unearthly manifestations, but correctly assigned the assorted calls to owls, foxes, and other creatures of the night. Laying aside her hairbrush, she tied her nightcap firmly under her chin and knelt at her bedside for her customary prayers, feeling that she did indeed have many blessings for which to thank her Creator. Her devotions completed, she blew out the candle, then went to the window for one last look outside.

The rain had stopped, and a rising wind blew the clouds across the sky. Moonlight gleamed on the wet stones of terrace and wall, and on the tossing branches of the distant trees. Tomorrow, she promised herself, she would walk to those trees and explore the garden. Drawing the curtains closed over the window, she jumped into bed. The fine linen sheets were cool and slippery, scented with lavender. She snuggled her head into the softest pillow she had ever felt, and in a few minutes was fast asleep.

CHAPTER FOUR

ELEANOR awoke the following morning to the sound of clinking fire-irons and the crackle of a newly lit fire. Opening her eyes, she saw the housemaid sweeping the hearth.

'Good morning, Jane. Is it late?'

'Good morning, miss. I hope I didn't wake you. Mrs Martlett said to let you have your sleep out today, but I knew the fire would be out. No, it's not late, miss, it's only eight o'clock.'

'Then I must get up!' Eleanor was accustomed to rising at a much earlier hour, and started to push back the covers.

'No, no, miss! You stay in bed until the fire has warmed the room. I'll ring for Annie, there's plenty of time.'

'I would not like to be late for breakfast,' Eleanor demurred, subsiding obediently into the warmth of the bed. Her body no longer ached as it had done the night before, but she felt a delicious languor, and was not unwilling to stay there for a while.

'No need to worry, miss. Mrs Wyckham never leaves her room before midday, and Mr Charles rides out every morning. He and Sir Ambrose take their breakfast together at nine. I looked in on Miss Amy, and she's sleeping like an angel; didn't even stir when I made up her fire.'

Annie came in, nodding a greeting to Eleanor. Jane looked uncomfortable. Obviously she did not know quite how to communicate with Annie, and was embarrassed to speak to her in case she did not understand her reply. Annie herself solved the problem by gently touching Jane's arm and indicating the ewer, then pointing questioningly towards herself. Jane smiled with relief.

'I'll fetch the hot water right away, Annie, that's not properly your job, but if you'd like to help?' The awkward moment over, they went out together. Eleanor stretched luxuriously in the comfortable bed. Being so pampered was a pleasant feeling, she decided, at least for a while. She hoped she would soon find something useful to do, for she was not cut out for a life of endless needlework and gossip. For the moment, though, she would enjoy it to the full.

Snuggling her head into her pillow, Eleanor thought about the previous evening. Sir Ambrose had been everything that was kind, and as for Mrs Wyckham— well, allowances must be made for the mother of an only son, and Eleanor did not blame her for wishing him to make a splendid marriage. She herself would never breathe her hopes to anyone, except perhaps Amy, for it could not be denied that by making a home at Oaklands Court they were setting themselves up as targets for the kind of gossip that Mrs Wyckham's friends, if they were like her, were likely to manufacture. Nevertheless, they made such a handsome couple...

She closed her eyes, and the feel of her head on the pillow suddenly brought back the dream of the previous night, which crept up from some depth of her unconscious and caught her unawares. In her dream, she had been arriving at the house, only this time it had been not Amy but herself whom Charles had carried into the hall. It was so vivid, so real, that she could still feel the strength of his arms holding her, the roughness of his greatcoat against her cheek. And, in her dream, he had bent his head and kissed her. For a second she lived again the flood of feeling that had coursed through her body; then, her cheeks burning, she flung back the bedclothes and jumped out of bed, welcoming the chill of air that the newly lit fire had not had time to warm.

Resolutely she pushed the memory from her. It was a dream, no more, and dreams were notoriously fickle. She let her mind dwell on the times when Charles Wyckham had insulted her and Amy, on the dislike she had felt on first seeing him. Ignoring the jug of hot water Annie had set out, she splashed some cold into the bowl on her wash-stand, and scrubbed her face with it until it was tingling. Then, to distract herself, she went to the window, where a gleam of sunshine came in since Annie had opened the curtains.

The wind had died in the night, and the cleared skies had left their legacy of frost on the garden below. In the daylight, she could see the rising slopes of what must be the South Downs behind the woodland, the clear air making them look so close, that she felt she could have reached out and touched them. There was the gleam of water, too, through the trees at the far end of the garden, where there must be a pond, or even a small lake. The chill from the window banished the last traces of her dream, and she found herself suddenly impatient to be up and doing.

Her morning *toilette* was soon made, and, after checking that Amy still slept, she left Annie to look after her and went downstairs. Browning was crossing the hall, and he stopped to bid her good morning.

'Sir Ambrose is already in the dining parlour, Miss Eleanor. Mr Charles has not yet returned from his ride, but we expect him at any moment. Will you join Sir Ambrose?'

'Yes, thank you, Browning.'

He hesitated for a moment, as if there were something he would like to say, but did not know how to say it.

'Is something the matter, Browning? Does Sir Ambrose prefer to breakfast alone, perhaps, or to discuss estate business with Mr Charles?'

He looked relieved.

'Oh, no, miss, nothing like that. It is only that you must remember that my master has been very unwell. Sometimes he—well, he forgets things. I would not like you to be alarmed, miss, if he should say anything a little strange. It is best to humour him at these times, miss, for if he is argued with it upsets him.'

Eleanor was touched by his obvious concern.

'I quite understand, Browning. Thank you for telling me. You may be sure I will do nothing to upset your master.'

'Thank you, Miss Eleanor.' He bowed her into the dining parlour as if she had been the Queen of England.

By daylight it was a pleasant, friendly room. She had learned the night before that the house was of different periods, centring on the oldest part that was of Tudor origin. The wing where she and Amy slept had been added during the reign of Queen Anne, and the other a little later in the time of the Georges. This room was obviously part of the oldest portion of the house. The walls were panelled, the wood not dark with age, but with a silvery gleam to it, and the fireplace, like the one in the hall, was large and deep, with a handsome stone surround. The table was once again covered with a snowy cloth, but this had been taken off the previous evening when the dessert had been put on the table, and she knew that it was of oak, like the heavy, comfortable chairs. Outside the windows, with their narrow casements and old, distorting glass, she could make out the carriage drive, bordered by neatly trimmed grass.

Sir Ambrose stood courteously as she came in, but she saw that his face had a curiously empty, listening look. The sideboard held several hot dishes as well as ham and beef, but he had taken nothing. He asked kindly after her health, and whether she had slept well.

'Thank you, sir, I slept exceedingly well. I must thank you again for our comfortable rooms. My sister is still asleep, but I know she would wish me to do so.'

'I am glad to hear that they are comfortable, but there is no need to thank me. There are too many empty, unused rooms in this house.' He sat down again, and the look of withdrawn melancholy settled on his face once more. Eleanor moved briskly to the sideboard.

'May I not serve you something from these dishes, Sir Ambrose? Here are eggs, and kidneys, and sausages, or will you take some ham? I must warn you that my carving should more properly be called hacking!'

'Thank you, my dear, but I believe I will just wait . . .' His voice tailed off, and she had the impression that he was once again straining his ears to hear something. She paused for a moment, listening, but the house was silent.

'It is a shame not to eat some of these good things while they are freshly cooked,' she said persuasively. 'However carefully they are kept warm, they cannot be the same when they have been standing. Browning told me Mr Wyckham is not yet returned from his ride, so you might have a long wait for him.'

'Mr Wyckham? Oh, yes, Charles. He would not expect me to wait for him. But I should wait for—wait for . . .'

Her throat tightened with sympathy and concern, for she knew that the one he was waiting for would never come again, but she kept her voice light and cheerful.

'If he does not expect you to wait, then you should not, for how uncomfortable he would feel to think that he had delayed you! Besides, you know,' she added slyly,

'I cannot myself sit and eat if you do not, and I am very hungry!'

This appeal to his gentlemanly instincts won the day, as she had hoped it would, and he allowed her to serve him some kidneys and bacon. She took some scrambled eggs and a little ham, and hurried to sit beside him. Enquiring into his preferences for tea or coffee and exactly how he liked them occupied a few more minutes, and when he had his cup before him she commented on the delicious flavour of the ham without giving him time to withdraw again into his thoughts, and learned that it came from their own pigs. By dint of judicious questioning, she was able to keep him talking on such safe subjects while he ate, and was pleased to see that he was growing more animated. Suddenly, however, he dropped his knife and fork on to his plate and jumped to his feet.

'What is it, sir? Are you ill?'

'Hush, let me listen!' His hand grasped her arm painfully, but obediently she listened, though she could hear nothing.

'Did you hear it? I heard a child calling.'

'I heard nothing, sir. Would you like me to go and look?'

He sighed, and let go of her arm.

'No, no need. It was only a passing fancy.'

They sat down again, and at that moment she heard footsteps coming across the hall. More shaken than she would have cared to admit by Sir Ambrose's behaviour, she felt a momentary thrill of fear, and was relieved when the door opened and Charles Wyckham came in. The relief was strong enough to banish the flush of embarrassment she had thought she must feel on first seeing him that morning. She knew that no one could possibly know of her disturbing dream, yet the memory of it was still so vivid, when she allowed it to surface, that it was hard to believe that it had not really happened.

He was still in his riding clothes, and carried a perceptible aura with him, a pleasantly masculine blend of fresh outdoor air and horses. He looked surprised to see Eleanor, and pleased when he saw that Sir Ambrose had eaten.

'Good morning, Miss Eleanor, you are up with the lark! I had not expected you to be downstairs for some while yet.'

She found herself unexpectedly irritated by his assumption that she would stay in bed late.

'Like you, I am accustomed to rising early, Mr Wyckham,' she said frostily. 'My sister is not as strong as I, but I can assure you that it takes more than a few hours of travelling to confine me to my room.'

'You are to be congratulated,' he said coolly, turning to his uncle. 'I am glad to see, sir, that you have not waited for me for once.'

'You have Miss Eleanor to thank for that! She assured me that she was famished, but would not eat unless I did. Then she gave me such an excellent cup of coffee, just as I like it. How pleasant it is, Charles, to have a lady at the breakfast table to minister to us like this. You must let her pour you one, too.'

'Thank you, I prefer tea.' He carried his heaped plate back from the sideboard, and Eleanor eyed it with awe.

'That, too, is within my powers,' she said with awful politeness, turning up the flame of the little lamp under the kettle and measuring some tea into the pot. 'You will have cream in it, I suppose?' She eyed the rapidly diminishing pile of sausages, bacon and eggs that he was enjoying, and he laughed.

'Yes, cream as well. There is a great deal of me to nourish, you see.'

'If you eat like that there will be even more!' she retorted, and regretted it instantly as he raised his eyebrows. 'I beg your pardon, I spoke without thinking.
Naturally your morning ride has given you an appetite.'
She schooled herself to silence, nibbling at a piece of
toast as the men talked. Eleanor was amazed at the difference in Sir Ambrose now that Charles was there. The
absent, listening look was gone from his face as he and
his nephew discussed estate affairs and debated the merits
of a new mare.

'Do you ride, Miss Eleanor?' asked Charles, turning
to her politely. 'I am sure we could find a horse in the
stables for you, and one for Miss Amy, of course.'

'We have never learned,' said Eleanor rather regretfully. 'Living as we did in the town, and my father's
circumstances as they were, we had no opportunity.'

'That is easily remedied, is it not, Uncle? Evans can
teach you both, as he taught—me—when I was a boy.'
He hurried on to cover the momentary hesitation. 'You
need have no fear with him, Miss Eleanor, for he is a
capital teacher, and I believe he would enjoy it. There
is a mare in the stables; she is not young, but she is very
kind—a good ride for a lady. You would both benefit
from the exercise, for you will not be wanting to walk
in this mud.'

'I am not afraid of mud,' began Eleanor indignantly,
remembering the filth on some of the streets she had
been accustomed to visiting, and thinking that clean
country mud would be a pleasant change. She did not
want to appear too eager, but inwardly she was excited
at the prospect of learning to ride. 'I do not want to
cause any trouble,' she added more temperately.

'Not at all, my dear,' said Sir Ambrose kindly. 'Naturally, living in a town it was not possible, but here you
might feel yourself a little isolated if you do not ride.

Not that you would not be welcome to take the carriage, if you wish to go out, but you will be more free on horseback, and it is very good exercise, as Charles has said.'

'That is settled, then,' said Charles, without giving her the chance to say anything else. This annoyed her so much that she felt strongly inclined to say that nothing would induce her to learn to ride, but that it would have been so ungrateful and impolite to Sir Ambrose. Besides, she was longing to learn. A genuine objection did, however, occur to her.

'I have no riding habit!' she exclaimed in dismay. 'Could I perhaps alter one of my old gowns?'

'I do not think so,' said Charles dubiously. 'It would not be comfortable. We can send for the dressmaker in the village that Mama uses sometimes, but that would take some time.'

'No need, no need,' said Sir Ambrose. 'I am sure Mrs Martlett would be able to find some of your aunt's habits, for they were all put away carefully when she was ill. Should you object, my dear, to wearing them? They will not be in the latest fashion, of course, but such things do not date as quickly as gowns, I believe. You can always have a new one made later.'

'How could I possibly mind? It is so good of you, and nothing would please me more, if you are sure, my dear sir, that you do not mind?'

'I should be glad to think that they are being used, and so would she have been. They will need some alteration, perhaps, but I think you would have been much of a height.'

Obviously the memory of his late wife did not upset him in the same way that other memories did.

'Excellent,' said Charles Wyckham in his habitual decisive fashion. 'I will speak to Evans. Now, if you will excuse me, Uncle, I promised Roberts that I would spend the morning at the farm. I want him to use some of this new guano on the six acre field, but he is a hard man to convince! Miss Eleanor, I wish you a good morning.' He was gone before Eleanor could reply.

'I must see whether my sister is awake,' she said. 'Is there anything that I could do for you, sir?'

'No, thank you, my dear. I generally spend the morning in my study. I have some letters to write, and I like to see to some of the bookwork of the estate.'

'Please do not fail to ask me if I can be of any use. I always helped my father with his work, and I am so accustomed to be busy that I shall feel strange if you make me feel too much a guest. We both want to be "useful rather than ornamental", as Papa used to say.'

'I am sure you will be both,' he said with a slight smile, opening the door for her. As she went upstairs she heard him walking slowly towards his study, and wondered whether he worked there, or just sat and listened. There was something infinitely pathetic in the thought of this kind man, endlessly listening for the voice of a child who had grown into a man, and would never return to gladden his father's heart again. His refusal completely to accept what had happened was obviously the only way he could live with the loss of his son. It seemed a harmless enough foible, though she could see why Browning had been at pains to warn her.

Amy was awake, though not yet out of bed. She looked a little guilt-stricken at seeing Eleanor up and dressed, and confessed that she had allowed Mrs Martlett to order her breakfast in bed.

'Tomorrow I shall be up earlier, and breakfast downstairs, but since you tell me everyone else has eaten I suppose it does not make much difference. Oh, Eleanor, this bed is almost sinfully comfortable. What would Papa have said?'

'Papa would have been delighted for us, little Puritan! You know how much he liked for us to be comfortable. We will soon find some way of being useful in the household, and then you will not feel obliged to atone with a hair shirt, or peas in your slippers.'

'As if I would! You are teasing me again. It is not respectful to your elders.'

'And betters, dearest; I freely acknowledge it, for you are much better than I. I am afraid my conscience is behaving lazily on the subject of soft mattresses and a fire in our bedrooms. And we are to be pampered still more!' She told her sister about the plans for riding lessons. Amy looked gratified, but a little nervous.

'Do you think we could? They are such very large creatures, I should be afraid of falling.'

'Nonsense,' said Eleanor bravely. 'Mr Wyckham assures me that we will be completely safe with Evans, and you may be sure he would not let any harm befall you. Only think, Amy, of the outings we can take together. From what I have seen of it, the countryside round here is beautiful, and in the warmer weather we will be able to explore it properly. There is a line of hills beyond the garden which I am sure must be the South Downs. Only think, if we were to climb to the top, we would see the sea!'

This agreeable prospect soon allayed Amy's fears, and Eleanor kept her other reason to herself; namely, that since Charles appeared to spend much of his time on horseback, it was only sense for Amy to learn to ride also. Mrs Martlett returned and readily agreed to hunt out her late mistress's riding habits and see about altering them.

'Now that is one thing I can do,' said Amy firmly. 'I am not clever, like Eleanor, but I can sew. I feel like spending a quiet day, and I should enjoy doing it.' Mrs

Martlett soon returned with her arms full, for the late Lady Hammond had been fond of riding. The only black habit had unfortunately been attacked by moths, in spite of the careful way it had been put away in brown paper and camphor, but they chose a dark blue for Amy and a green for Eleanor. They were found to be only just too big, requiring so little in the way of alteration that Amy declared she could have them finished that very day.

She was soon happily settled in the sitting-room that adjoined their bedrooms, which they had been too tired to explore the previous evening. It was a charming room, at the end of the wing, so that its windows faced both west and south. It was furnished with the delicate, spindly furniture of the turn of the century, its walls papered with silver-grey stripes, and the upholstery and curtains a soft blue that exactly matched the shade in the faded but beautiful Aubusson carpet. Altogether feminine, it suited Amy as if it had been made for her, and she exclaimed in delight as she examined the inlaid sewing-table and the small pianoforte. They spent a cosy morning together, joining Sir Ambrose and Mrs Wyckham for a light luncheon, Charles having sent a message to say that he would eat at the farm.

In the absence of her son, Mrs Wyckham was most gracious to the girls. Once again she was splendidly attired in a dress of pink silk, very ornate, which she stroked with absent-minded complacency as she looked at Amy and Eleanor in their simple mourning gowns.

'I should like to have the use of the carriage this afternoon, brother, to pay some morning calls. This is the first fine day for a week.'

'Very good, my dear.' Sir Ambrose's voice was calm and friendly. The occurrences of breakfast might never have happened. 'Perhaps our two young guests would care to accompany you? They should be meeting our neighbours, and it would be company for you.'

Mrs Wyckham looked a little dismayed, but she was not an unkind woman, and repeated her brother's offer, looking in concern as she did so at their dresses. Eleanor took pity on her plight.

'It is so kind of you to offer, Mrs Wyckham, but perhaps we may accompany you some other day? I, for one, have certainly had enough travelling around to last me for a while. I can still hear the sound of the train at the back of my mind, that endless clackety-clack! Then, too, our recent bereavement makes it unsuitable for us to be doing too much in the way of socialising.

Mrs Wyckham was gracious. 'I know exactly what you mean, Miss Eleanor. I had occasion to visit London a few months ago, and I thought my poor head would never stop pounding! But then, I am remarkably susceptible to the least thing, as my doctor can tell you. When you are more settled, however, I must make you known to our set. It is a small enough circle of neighbours, but most agreeable people. You need not feel in the least shy of them!'

Eleanor, who had never felt shy of anyone in her life, thanked her. She was amused to see that Mrs Wyckham was torn between a certain amount of shame at their shabby appearance, and her wish to introduce them to people who would distract their attention from her son. She turned to Sir Ambrose.

'Did you finish your letters, sir? Is there perhaps anything I can do for you this afternoon?'

'Nothing, my dear, for today.'

Eleanor finished the apple she had been eating, which he had earlier been happy to tell her was one of a very good crop they had had that year. She looked at him earnestly. 'You must not be too kind to us, Sir Ambrose.

You know that we cannot be happy merely to be your guests. You must let us be useful to you.'

He patted her hand kindly. 'There is plenty of time, my dear. You have only been here for a day, after all! Give yourselves time to settle in, and get over your journey. You will soon find many things that you can turn your hands to.'

With that she had to be satisfied, and the girls returned to their sewing. One of the habits was already done, and was being sponged and pressed by Annie, and Amy was working on the other. She sat in a comfortable chair near the window, the sunlight gleaming in her hair, humming a little as her needle flashed in and out of the blue material. As always, her posture was gracefully upright, her straight back showing no sign of strain, and Eleanor, who always felt stiff and irritable if she sewed for as long as an hour, wondered how she managed it. She went to the window, looking again at the rolling downs, their flanks shaded in greens and browns.

'It is a fine day, Amy, and the terrace is very sheltered from the wind. Will you not come down and take some air?'

Seeing that she was longing to go out, Amy obligingly agreed, and soon, shawled and bonneted, they found their way through the hall and outside. The sunlight was warm on the enclosed terrace, and Eleanor and Amy walked slowly up and down. The air was as delicious as wine to them, untainted by the smoke of the countless houses of a town. Everything was bare, but the gnarled rose-bushes in the beds that flanked the wall, and the tiny green snouts that already pushed their way through the earth in the urns, gave promise of delights to come. Eleanor would have liked to explore further, but Amy confessed that she was tired.

'I will go in now, but there is no need for you to come, if you do not want to. I know very well you have been longing to walk further. You keep looking down the garden!'

Eleanor laughingly agreed, and, promising not to stay out too long, she ran down the broad flight of steps that was set into the retaining wall of the terrace. There she hesitated for a moment, for the grass was very wet, but telling herself that she had good, stout boots she succumbed to temptation, lifted her skirts clear of the wet, and walked briskly down the lawn.

An area of shrubs, criss-crossed with paths, was an ideal place to walk, for the paths were gravelled and therefore quite dry. Never having had anything much in the way of a garden, Eleanor was ignorant of what the shrubs were, but even to her untutored eye the variety was amazing, and she became fascinated by the different shapes and types that grew in such carefully managed disarray.

A sudden chill in the air warned her that the short winter afternoon was drawing to a close. Regretfully she looked towards the woodland beyond the shrubbery. A small stream spanned by a narrow, rustic bridge formed a boundary between them, and fed into the lake she had seen only by glimpses from her window. It was not very large, its banks for the most part overhung with trees that were reflected in the still surface. It was very lovely, and she would have liked to continue, but she could see that the ground was very muddy, and that it was already gloomy in the shadow of the trees. The lighted windows of the house offered warmth and comfort, and she walked swiftly back.

At the foot of the steps she paused for a moment. The glow of the setting sun lit up the face of the terrace wall. It was of smoothly shaped stones, not very high, with

here and there a space left open, and the browned remains of small trailing plants growing from it. They
would make admirable footholds, she thought, and
smiled as she remembered the boy she had seen the night
before. As she thought of him she caught sight of one
clear footprint in the soft earth of the rose-bed. Still
smiling, she bent to smooth it over. It was unexpectedly
small—he could not have been more than five or six years
old. When the incriminating mark was obliterated, she
walked swiftly indoors.

CHAPTER FIVE

AT DINNER that evening Eleanor noticed that Sir Ambrose appeared to be making a great effort to talk and be cheerful. She also noticed, as she had done the night before, how Charles Wyckham watched his uncle, ready with a light word or a question to recall him when his face showed that he was withdrawing into himself. High-handed in other things, he did this with a delicacy that did him credit. She did her best to help, and won a look of approval that pleased her, though she was annoyed with herself for feeling so pleased. Her wish, after all, was to help her benefactor, not to strive for Mr Wyckham's approval.

Mrs Wyckham, meanwhile, chattered to Amy.

'You may be quite sure that our friends in the neighbourhood will soon be paying their calls to meet you,' she said. 'We are fortunate in having several delightful families hereabouts. You must be sure to stay indoors for the next few afternoons. It would be most vexing if they should come and find you absent.'

'Oh, yes, ma'am,' murmured Amy, looking a little nervous.

'Let me see,' said Mrs Wyckham as if she had not spoken, 'the Trehearnes will be sure to come, and the Jenningses. They have two daughters, you know, charming girls, and of course there is plenty of money there, though I believe it did come from trade. Still, that was their grandfather, of course, and that makes all the difference. Augusta and Arabella have been brought up with every advantage, and they dote on Charles!'

'Well, if your idea of doting is to collapse into giggles every time I speak to them, I dare say you are right, Mama,' said Charles. 'But since they do that to every male over the age of ten, I am not inclined to set much store by it.'

'Really, Charles! You must not heed him, Miss Hunter. He has these joking little ways, but I know he must be fond of them, for they are most agreeable and—and cheerful,' she finished defiantly. Eleanor bit her lip to hide her smile. 'The Lutcomes, of course, you will meet on Sunday; our Vicar and his sister. They come from a good family, and he has some money of his own beyond his stipend. They make a pleasant addition to our little circle of friends, for he is very clever, although so very plain.'

Charles turned to his uncle. 'Mama has given me a good idea, sir, with her talk of our neighbours. Would it not be a good thought to hold a small party? Christmas is not far away, and would it not be pleasant to see all our friends gathered under this roof at that time?

Sir Ambrose looked troubled. 'It is a long time since we did anything of the sort.'

'All the more reason that we should do it now——'

'But, my dear boy, you cannot have considered,' Mrs Wyckham broke in. 'It is quite out of the question. These girls are in mourning. For them to be gadding about would not be at all the thing.'

'I did not say anything about "gadding about", Mama. A quiet party, just a few of our neighbours, with no dancing of course, was all I had in mind. That is no worse than paying morning calls, surely? I did not suggest we should hold a ball!'

'It is very soon, and such a sad loss,' objected Mrs Wyckham. Charles leaned forward persuasively.

'No one who meets the Miss Hunters could think that they do not sincerely mourn their father. But I do not believe it can be right to give way too much to their very natural feelings of sorrow. In coming here they are beginning a new life, among new friends. Would it not be for the best for them to put their sorrow behind them? From what I have heard of him, it is precisely what Mr Hunter would have wished.'

Eleanor, who had begun to stiffen at the way he seemed ready to decide their lives for them, caught his eye upon her with an unspoken message in it, and realised suddenly that he was speaking more about his uncle's feelings than theirs. Obviously there had been no entertaining at Oaklands Court since the death of Sir Ambrose's son.

'Perhaps you are right——' sighed Sir Ambrose.

'Nonsense, Charles! I cannot agree that it is suitable!' broke in Mrs Wyckham crossly.

'Come now, Mama. You have said yourself how agreeable it would be to see more of our neighbours. What a pleasure it would be to welcome the Miss Jenningses here!' He paused to allow this thought to sink in, and when he saw from her expression that she was beginning to see the advantages, added, 'It would be pleasant, too, for Miss Hunter and Miss Eleanor to meet some young gentlemen.'

Eleanor could scarcely forbear to laugh at the thoughtful look that spread over Mrs Wyckham's face. She was obviously much tempted by the prospect of marrying Amy off to the first young man who should cross the threshold, thus leaving Charles free to pursue a young lady of fortune.

'We have not asked Amy and Eleanor what they think,' pointed out Sir Ambrose. Eleanor threw him a look of gratitude. It would never have occurred to Mr

Wyckham, she was sure, to consult their wishes on the subject.

For herself, and even more for Amy, as she knew, the idea of appearing in public among strangers, at however small and select a party, so soon after Papa's death, seemed vaguely shocking. She would undoubtedly have declined at once, had she not realised that Mr Wyckham was more interested in distracting his uncle's grief than theirs. As he said, they were starting a new life at Oaklands Court, and if by submerging her own scruples she could in any way repay the debt of kindness owing to her host, she did not see that she could refuse. She glanced at Amy, who said only, 'Let Eleanor decide. She knows more about such things.'

'Well, Miss Eleanor? What do you say?' Charles's eyes were fixed on hers, as if he were trying to bend her will to his. She looked at Sir Ambrose.

'If you feel that it shows no disrespect to Papa's memory, then I am sure it would give us both great pleasure. But only,' she continued firmly, 'if you truly wish it, and if you will let us do all the work for it, as far as that is possible.'

Charles laughed out loud. 'Independent and self-willed woman! I am sure no one would wish to deny you that duty! You may report to Mama in the morning, and plan your work.'

Mrs Wyckham smiled graciously. 'Yes, for my nerves, you know, would not permit me to do a great deal, much though I should wish to. But with Miss Amy as my amanuensis, and Miss Eleanor to oversee the domestic arrangements, I am sure we shall do very well.' Eleanor was glad to notice that Mrs Wyckham had reverted to calling Amy by her given name, instead of the formal 'Miss Hunter' that had signalled her earlier disapproval.

'I hope you will not be kept too busy,' put in Charles. 'Do not forget your riding lessons. Evans assures me he is looking forward to teaching you, and he has been hunting out ladies' saddles for you. Has the problem of the habits been solved?'

Amy was pleased to be able to tell him that she had finished altering one for Eleanor, and that her own was ready but for a few stitches in the hem.

'Very good! We shall soon have you out with the hunt,' he teased, laughing at her horrified expression. Eleanor engaged Mrs Wyckham in conversation, so that Amy was free to talk to Charles. While the surface of her mind was occupied with talk of who should be invited, a subject on which she could necessarily have little to say since she was acquainted with none of the people being mentioned, the rest of her thoughts were pondering the problem of their clothes. For herself she did not mind, but she was determined that Amy should be seen at an advantage. She passed the contents of both their wardrobes under her mental eye, only to reject everything as unsuitable. No wonder Mrs Wyckham had given in so easily to the scheme. Her heart sank as she thought of the rich Miss Jenningses, and she determined that she would find something new, at least for her sister. She had a little money in hand from the sale of their things at the vicarage; the problem would be to persuade Amy to allow her to spend it on such a frivolous object.

The following morning Eleanor had her first riding lesson. Amy, who made the excuse that her habit was not quite finished after all, came out to watch for a while, but the wind was cold and Eleanor soon sent her indoors as she was not moving about enough to keep warm. Evans settled Eleanor into the saddle, showing her how to hook her knee over the pommel and smiling quietly at her inclination to clutch at the mare's mane.

'Sit up straight, miss, and keep your hands down. That's good. Don't look at the ground, now, just keep looking ahead, between her ears. I'll lead her for this morning, just until you get the feel of the saddle and get your balance right.' They set off slowly across the cobbled yard around which the stables were built. Eleanor concentrated fiercely, feeling at first very insecure and very far from the ground, but gradually, as the mare did nothing more alarming than maintain a steady walk, she found herself moving more easily with the motion.

'Very good, miss! Keep that back straight, now. We'll have you riding in no time. How do you feel?'

'Surprisingly comfortable, thank you. It is very high, but not as bad as I feared. I feel quite happy.'

He grinned at her.

'Not tomorrow, you won't be! Stiff as a board you'll feel, I'm afraid, for the first few days. But that'll soon pass.'

His dire forebodings were quite right, Eleanor soon learned. Charles laughed when he saw her gently lowering herself into her chair at breakfast the following morning.

'I believe Mama has one of the new inflatable cushions, that she sent off for when she was buying a rubber hot-water bottle. Shall I ask her if you may borrow it? I am sure she would not grudge it.'

'I am perfectly comfortable, thank you,' she lied coldly.

'I should not dream of contradicting you, but if you could see yourself! You look like an arthritic duck.'

'How pleasant to be receiving compliments so early in the morning,' she announced to the world at large. 'My head will be quite turned.' Amy gave a soft giggle. 'Perhaps, Amy, you would be so kind as to pass me an

egg? This chair is so comfortable I feel quite disinclined
to move.'

'Of course, dearest,' Amy hurried to comply.

'You may laugh today, Miss Amy,' said Charles, 'but
if you are to have your lesson today, you will feel every
bit as uncomfortable as your sister tomorrow. Do not
look so cross, Miss Eleanor. I am not really so unsym-
pathetic. To prove it, I will give you some excellent liniment. It is a little pungent, to be sure, but I can assure
you that you will feel more comfortable if you rub it
into your afflicted limbs. The main thing is, you must
carry on with the lessons and get those muscles working
again.'

Eleanor opened her mouth to say that she did not want
any liniment, when a twinge made her think again. 'Must
I really ride again today?' she asked in piteous tones.

'He is quite right, my dear,' said Sir Ambrose kindly.
'The liniment will help you, and I promise that in a few
days you will have no pain at all. And Evans tells me
you have the beginnings of a good horsewoman in you.
Well done!'

The liniment did indeed have a powerful fragrance,
but both Eleanor and Amy were glad to put up with it,
since they found it did much to alleviate the pain of
muscles that had been put to unaccustomed use. As the
days went by the stiffness subsided, and both girls began
to feel more confident. Trotting was the worst, but, once
they had learned the trick of adapting to the rhythm of
the horse, they found that cantering was surprisingly
easy. Evans was very satisfied with their progress, and
they themselves felt the benefit of the air and exercise.

Eleanor had not forgotten the problem of a new gown
for Amy, but her tentative suggestions had met with a
flat veto. Amy, usually so docile, was not to be moved
on a point of principle, and this time she felt that their

small store of money should not be spent on finery. She refused downright to consider a new gown for herself only, and since they could not, in any case, afford one for each of them, she was resolved that they should appear in what they already had.

'There is no shame in our poverty. People should not think any the worse of us because we have no fine clothes.'

Eleanor kept to herself the certainty that, though people should not do so, they almost certainly would, and resigned herself.

They were together in their sitting-room one morning, composing a long overdue letter to Lady Haywood, when Charles Wyckham came in.

'Miss Amy, Miss Eleanor, can you spare me a few minutes? My uncle wished me to ask you something. Since Christmas is approaching, he would like to offer you some new gowns, as a Christmas gift.' He saw that Eleanor was about to protest, and held up his hand. 'One moment, if you please, Miss Eleanor. He understands your feelings very well, and knows that you would dislike to be any more beholden to him. Nevertheless, I hope you will swallow your pride and allow him the pleasure of making this gift.' He walked abruptly to the window, and spoke while looking out. 'You have seen, I think, how deeply his son's death has affected him. In asking you to come and live here he has, I hope, made the first steps on the road to recovery. He told me, not long ago, that everything and everyone around him reminded him of Richard. That is why I think your being here is such a good thing, and it is also why I hope you will accept his gift. You have agreed, and I know it went against your feelings to do so, to attend the projected party, and I beg that you will also agree to have some new clothes made up that are not strict mourning. You will not mourn your father any the less in clothes that are not black. It is just that the visible signs of your sorrow remind him every day of his own.'

Eleanor and Amy looked at one another.

'Papa did not let us wear black for Mama,' Eleanor reminded her sister.

'We were children then. I should not like to cause any talk.'

'If you will agree, I will undertake to speak to Mrs Trehearne on the subject,' offered Charles. 'She is both kind and sensible, and I am quite sure that she would be willing to quell any gossip. Her opinion is valued in the neighbourhood, and a quiet word from her would soon set things right.'

'Yes, she called yesterday. I liked her very much.'

Eleanor seized the chance to ask a question that had been puzzling her for some time. 'Mr Wyckham, it is now more than six years since your cousin died. Surely such excessive grief as Sir Ambrose displays should have worn itself out by now? You said the other evening that it could not be right to go on grieving forever. Sir Ambrose seems in every other respect a sensible man.'

Charles sighed. 'You are quite right, of course. He has never spoken to me about his deepest feelings, but I believe that it is not only sorrow, but a strong sense of guilt, that still clouds his mind. Let me explain the circumstances of Richard's death.'

He stayed at the window, sitting himself on the window-seat and talking with his head half-turned away from them, his eyes not seeing the room at all, but looking inward to his memory of his cousin and friend.

'As an only child, Richard was idolised and petted, especially after my aunt's death. At the same time Sir Ambrose, fearing I think that he might be injured, protected him a great deal—probably too much. He was never allowed to do anything that might be remotely dangerous. By nature a high-spirited boy, Richard rebelled against this cosseting, particularly as he began to grow up. While there was still a great deal of love between them, there grew up a lack of understanding, of sympathy, between them, which hurt them both, though neither was prepared to give in.

'As a result, Richard became more and more headstrong, and when he was eighteen he began to get involved with a local group of smugglers. Smuggling, you may know, is common in these coastal areas, and, if not respectable, is at least not particularly frowned upon. Richard was not the only young man of birth to enjoy the risks and excitement of running a few kegs of brandy. I have been out with them a few times myself, at that age, but I am afraid I am such a poor sailor that I quickly tired of the sport.

'Richard, however, did not. Sir Ambrose heard of it and, deeply alarmed, forbade his son to have anything to do with the smugglers, which of course had the effect of making him keener than ever. He asked his father to let him join the Army, which might have provided a healthy and honourable way of using his youthful energy and high spirits, but Sir Ambrose, fearing once more for his safety, refused.'

He paused. Eleanor and Amy had sat in silence, listening to his tale, but now Eleanor stirred. 'What a pity!' she exclaimed. 'It would have been just the thing for him, and after a year or two he might have been happy to sell out, and come home again.'

'It is not for us to criticise,' murmured Amy in her gentle voice. 'As an only son he was of course very precious to his father.'

'I do not want to appear to criticise Sir Ambrose, but surely a parent's truest love is seen not in shielding the child from every wind that blows, but in allowing him to learn to use his own judgement? A cage made by love is still a cage, and harder to escape from than a barred room.'

Charles Wyckham looked at Eleanor.

'You understand very well how he felt, it seems.' His voice was grim, almost critical. Eleanor lifted her chin and returned his look.

'I think I do, a little. We were lucky, for our father allowed us to join in his life and work, but most girls are kept in just such a cage as I have described, and never have the chance to escape it.'

'Surely, when they marry?'

'Then they only exchange one jailer for another, very often. How many young ladies in these parts join the smugglers on their runs?'

Amy looked shocked, but Charles laughed.

'None, then! Am I to understand that you would like to? If so, I have to tell you that I would not permit it!'

'No, I do not, though if I did I regret that I would not ask your permission first.' Once again his manner set her temper rising. Why was it that she could never talk to this man without wanting to argue with him? Eleanor realised that she was being both childish and rude, and bit her lip.

'Please go on with what you were telling us, Mr Wyckham,' put in Amy. 'We would both like to hear it.'

He glanced at Eleanor, who kept her eyes lowered, and continued.

'At about this time Richard met a girl, a farmer's daughter. She was only seventeen, and very lovely. Richard, who was only a year older, fell wildly in love with her, and declared his intention to marry her. He and his father argued bitterly and long, and the upshot was that Richard stormed from the house, vowing never to return. He had already arranged to take part in a run that night, and as far as I know he fetched the girl, intending, I suppose, a runaway match. Unfortunately, the smugglers' luck ran out that night, for they were challenged as they were unloading the barrels. Richard, still wild with rage after the quarrel with his father, did not run, but drew his pistol and shot at the Excisemen. He was an excellent shot, and one of them was hit, and died almost instantly. In a panic, the smugglers loaded Richard and the girl, Lucy, on to the boat, and took them over to France, where they had contacts and friends who would hide them.

'When Sir Ambrose heard the news, he collapsed, and for a while his life was despaired of. Messages were sent to France, through the smuggling network, and Richard must have decided to come back and see him. He may have hoped to slip in and out under cover of darkness, and make his peace with his father.'

He paused again, striking the palm of his hand with his fist, his face twisted with remembered anguish. 'He was betrayed.' He brought the words out with difficulty.

Amy and Eleanor uttered exclamations of distress. 'Who could have done such a thing? I know little of smugglers, but surely among themselves I understand there is great loyalty?' said Eleanor.

'You must understand that I do not know any of this at first hand. I can only repeat what I have heard, for I was away in Switzerland. I had been there for some weeks, and, as I was moving around more or less as the whim took me, it was some time before the messages reached me. By the time I returned, it was all over. The smugglers would not talk freely to me, but it seems sure that someone knew that he was coming in that night. They were waiting for him, there on the beach. There was a fight, and he was wounded, but escaped. He managed to make his way, God knows how, to my house, fearing, I suppose, to be caught if he came here. He arrived, weak from loss of blood, and I—I was not there.'

'You could not have known,' said Amy gently.

'No, and if I had there is little I could have done,' he said bitterly. 'He was already at the point of death. But I would have seen him. He could have spoken to me, sent at least a message to his father. If only I had not gone away, maybe I could have prevented that fatal quarrel in the first place.'

'You must not blame yourself. You cannot have been so very old yourself. If your cousin was as angry as you say, he would not have listened to you. Whom did he see, that night?'

'Mama was there, but she was so shocked and frightened by the sight of him that she was unable to do very much. She could not stop the bleeding, and she dared not send for a doctor, for he was a wanted man.'

Eleanor could imagine the scene, and could picture only too easily Mrs Wyckham's probable reaction when confronted by a bloodstained, moribund figure.

'But who could have betrayed him? Who knew of his coming?' she asked again. He paced restlessly down the room.

'Only the other smugglers, and I could have sworn none of them would have betrayed him. They are a close-knit, loyal group. They have been operating in this area for a long while, and in the last few years their activities and their profits have increased. I believe they have a new leader, but I do not know who he is. The reward for Richard's capture would have brought them less gain than the profits they would receive on the run.'

'It was not just more bad luck?'

'No. The soldiers called out to him by name, though he was well disguised. No, they knew he was there. And

one day I will know who brought him to his death.'
Looking at his face, Eleanor could quite believe him.
She shivered. After a moment he brought his attention
back to them.

'Now, you see, my uncle can never forget that he
parted from Richard in anger, and can never forgive
himself. He is now morbidly convinced that he, and he
alone, is responsible for Richard's death. He cannot bear
to think of it, and yet he cannot put it out of his mind.
Sometimes, when the memory is insupportable, he goes
back in his mind to the days when Richard was a child,
when they were happy. Sometimes he thinks he hears the
child Richard calling to him.'

'I know. He did it one day at breakfast,' said Eleanor.
'I did not understand altogether at the time, but I was
so sorry for him.'

'You must not think him weak,' said Charles with difficulty. 'He and his sister—my mother—were the only
survivors of ten children. Their own childhood was
overshadowed by their parents' sorrow at the early death
of their other children, and I think they both grew up
with the knowledge that life is, at best, an uncertain
thing. My mother, as you will have noticed, is still
preoccupied with her own health, and, combined with
my aunt's death, it is why my uncle was so protective
of his own only son.'

'It is very natural. We will do whatever we can to help.'

'Then you will accept his gift? Planning such things
distracts him, and gives him such pleasure. If you will
agree to wear some quiet colours, rather than black, I
am sure it would help.'

'We should be very happy to accept,' said Amy, and
he gave her a look of real gratitude.

'That is excellent. We must plan a trip to Lewes, so
that you may choose some materials. May I offer myself

as an escort? My taste is probably execrable, but I should
be happy to act as footman, or porter, and later perhaps
as guide. Lewes is a pretty town, and has much of
interest. Shall we say tomorrow, if the weather permits?'

He was already going towards the door. They guessed
that the conversation had been painful to him, and were
quick to give their assent before he was gone.

Amy turned to Eleanor.

'Do you think we have done the right thing?'

Eleanor frowned.

'I hope so. I do not like to accept so much, and yet
what could we do? It would have been churlish to refuse
what was offered with such kind intentions. I do believe
that Sir Ambrose is better since we were here; he seems
much less withdrawn, more relaxed, when we are together
in the evenings. I hope that soon I will be able to persuade him to allow us to help him with his work in the
daytime. I have to admit, as well, that I was worrying
a little about what we could wear for the projected party.
I am so glad that Mr Wyckham will see you looking
your best.'

'Mr Wyckham? What has he to do with it?'

Eleanor felt her cheeks grow pink. Once again her
unruly tongue had betrayed her.

'Only that he is single, and eligible, and you are a very
pretty girl. Oh, Amy,' she threw caution to the winds,
'it is such a chance for you, if he should fall in love with
you.'

'And what kind of a return would that be to Sir
Ambrose, for all his kindness to us?'

'If he were worried by such a thing, he would never
have invited us to make our home here in the first place.
He is not a mercenary man. I am sure he would not
stand in the way of your happiness, if you loved one
another.'

'But I am not in love with him, Eleanor.'

'Of course you are not. You have hardly had time to get to know him yet.'

Amy looked troubled.

'You would surely not wish me to marry him just because he is suitable and—and wealthy, would you?'

Eleanor stared at her.

'Of course not, dearest. I know you would never do such a thing. But if he were to fall in love with you, I am sure you would quickly learn to care for him. He is everything I could have wished for you: kind, and sensible, and handsome too.'

'Oh, yes, a very paragon! But we should not be talking like this. I am sure Mrs Wyckham would say it is not proper.'

'I am sure she would—but I cannot believe that most girls do not do so!'

'I suppose you are right. But I do not know...I like him very much, of course, but I cannot imagine loving him...I have never been in love, so I don't really know how it would be...'

Amy still looked worried, and Eleanor wondered at it. She simply could not understand how Amy could fail to be attracted by Charles Wyckham. She had no expectation of being swayed by such tender feelings herself, of course. All her plans centred on Amy, and getting her happily settled for life. It had never occurred to her to wonder what *she* would do if Amy married Charles. The thought caused a little pang, which she suppressed firmly. She had been sure, with an almost superstitious feeling, that when Charles Wyckham had knocked on their door that day he had been sent as an answer to all her problems.

Obviously it was too soon, and, as she reassured her sister and coaxed a smile back on to her face, she de-

termined that the subject would not be mentioned between them again, at least for a while. Time and
propinquity would, she was sure, do all that was necessary to awaken her Sleeping Beauty sister.

CHAPTER SIX

THE visit to Lewes was accomplished the following day. The weather, though cold, was fine and sunny, and Charles put himself out to be an amusing companion, pointing out landmarks and objects of interest as they went. The girls were quite unused to riding in a carriage, and for them that was already a treat. In Manchester they had gone everywhere on foot, and consequently it was not often that they had left the confines of its streets, for though the outlying countryside was not so very far, the journey was considered too tiring for Amy to make, though the fresh air might have done her good. They had, one September, by the good graces of Lady Haywood, been out to the river at Kersal Moor, to watch the regatta there, though never of course to the Whitsun horse-races, of which Papa could not approve.

The countryside through which they passed, and which they had scarcely seen on their arrival, was quite different from any they had known before. On their rides up to now they had kept within the confines of the estate, for Amy was as yet nervous of her new skills and reluctant to go too far. Now they were able to see and enjoy the little country lanes, bordered and overhung by trees and bushes, decked in places with the silver filigree of Old Man's Beard.

'They call it Traveller's Joy too, I believe,' said Amy, 'and it is an apt name, for it is certainly very beautiful.'

'Wait until you see the hedgerows in spring, and early summer, Miss Amy! When the banks are full of primroses and violets and celandines they are truly lovely.

Our lanes may be badly surfaced, and indeed they always seem to be either mud or dust, but they are very pretty.'

'I can imagine. You have seen our Manchester streets, Mr Wyckham. How I wish that some of those poor children could see this! Living as they do, they hardly even see a bit of growing grass, let alone a tree or flowers. There was some talk of getting up public subscriptions to buy land for parks. I do hope it will happen, and that there will be somewhere for the mill people to go.'

'What of the countryside outside Manchester? What little I saw seemed very fine.'

'Oh, yes, it is, but most of the children are too tired, on Sunday, to walk very far. They work such long hours, you see, and they are so young. However, I do not mean to spoil our enjoyment of today by harking back all the time. Have we far to go, Mr Wyckham? This journey is so pretty, I shall be quite sorry to arrive.'

'Not very far, but I think when you see our town you will not regret that the drive is over. I may be partial, of course, but I have always thought it very beautiful. There are some fine buildings, as well as many quaint old ones which will interest you. Do you care for such things?'

'Yes, I dearly love to look at old buildings. Are they of brick or stone?'

'Ah, that is where I shall puzzle you. What if I should say that they appear to be of brick, but are not?'

'I think you must be teasing me! I have never heard of such a thing.'

'No, no, on my honour! It is a process which I believe is unique to this area. We call them mathematical tiles, for they fit together exactly, giving the impression of bricks as the gaps between them are filled with mortar. I have given you the clue—now I challenge you to say which houses are brick, and which are not.'

'Well, if they are mathematical, you had better not ask me! Eleanor is the mathematician in our family.'

Eleanor did her best to be quiet, and withdraw into the background, so that Amy would be forced to keep the conversation going. It went against her usual habits, but she succeeded well enough, and was able to congratulate herself on her self-control when she even heard Amy venture this mild joke. The short journey passed quickly, and soon the girls were exclaiming in pleasure at their first sight of Lewes. Used, as they were, to the contrast in Manchester between the poor, working-class streets where their father had worked, and the more spacious, grand areas where such as Lady Haywood lived, they were delighted with the little town, nestling in the fold of the downs, with its main street sloping steeply downhill, lined with elegant houses. The carriage was left in the stables of the White Hart Hotel, where they were to have luncheon, and Charles promised them a guided visit of the town once their shopping was concluded.

Having decided to accept their host's offer of new gowns, they gave themselves up to the pleasure of choosing. Never before had they had such an opportunity, and soon the shop was festooned with lengths of stuff as bolt after bolt was unrolled. They fingered, exclaimed, and at last had trouble in choosing. They were not helped by Charles, who obligingly suggested such unsuitable items as heavily figured brocades, and solemnly expounded the merits of a brilliantly vulgar glacé silk of cherry-red, shot with orange.

'So cheerful!' he enthused. 'And think how you would stand out in a crowd—you would never be lost, we should be able to see you at once.'

'Yes, I always wanted to appear in public as a tomato,' agreed Eleanor with spurious enthusiasm, unable to endure her self-imposed silence any longer. 'You are not being very helpful, Mr Wyckham!'

'Miss Amy,' he said at last, 'we must be decisive. Much as I am enjoying the entertainment, I fear that our luncheon will be spoiling, and that if I do not soon eat it I shall lack the strength to walk you to the inn, and you will be forced to carry me between you, like Jack and Jill with their bucket.'

'Yes, for we shall even be going up a hill, and quite a steep one at that! I wonder what became of the bucket, when they had their mighty fall? The streets of Lewes are as steep as that famous hill, I believe.'

'Oh, dear, I am so sorry,' said Amy, ignoring her sister's flight of fancy. 'We are certainly being very slow. But what to choose? You must help me, Eleanor.'

'I do not think that Mr Wyckham will faint from lack of proper nourishment just yet, Amy. He prepared himself for the coming ordeal with admirable foresight, for I sat opposite him at the breakfast-table and saw how much he ate! Nevertheless, we have already been too long, and Mr Bance will be wanting to be rid of us.'

The shopkeeper replied imperturbably that the young ladies must not trouble on his account, for he was used to waiting for ladies to make up their minds.

'I should think you must be,' said Charles with some feeling. 'I know when you send patterns to Mama, it takes her days to choose. How fortunate that she is not with us today!'

Mr Bance murmured that Mrs Wyckham was a lady of exquisite taste, exquisite taste. Eleanor, mentally reviewing the number and style of that lady's gowns, thought to herself that she must indeed be a valuable customer.

'I have the answer,' said Charles. 'Since you are unable to choose for yourselves, you must choose for one another. Being such modest young ladies, you will be better acquainted with one another's appearance than with your own, and therefore better qualified to choose.'

This excellent idea was adopted with enthusiasm. Eleanor had been studying the periodicals that Mr Bance had so helpfully produced, and now exclaimed, 'Here is the very thing! That blue paduasoy is just right for you, Amy, and this style, with the jockey sleeves and the little frill of lace at neck and cuffs, would be so becoming, and quite simple.'

'Without the rosettes at the front, dear. They would be too frivolous,' said Amy firmly.

'Yes, I agree. And for the evening, what do you say to the pale lavender sarsenet, with the bertha trimmed with matching ribbon?'

'Yes, that is just what I would like. How clever you are! Now it is my turn. I like that golden-brown grosgrain for you. It is just the colour of the autumn leaves. Do you like this style, with the buttons and the frogging? You could have a darker brown braid, and it would look very well.'

'Yes, but not the little cape. I should feel so restricted.'

'As you wish,' Amy agreed. 'What about the evening-gown? Do you like a bertha?'

'No, not for me. Look here, these horizontal pleats, following the neckline, look graceful and comfortable, and I like the tiered skirt, though not these great bows.'

'Yes, it is better kept simple. But the colour?'

'What about that silvery stuff?' suggested Charles, throwing in his pennyworth of advice.

Mr Bance shook out the length of lustring so that the fine silk shimmered, the soft grey turning to silver where the light caught it.

'The very thing for Eleanor! Well done, Mr Wyckham, you have earned your luncheon.'

Charles had taken a private room at the inn, and they enjoyed a fricassee of chicken and some mutton cutlets, followed by some baked apples, and a junket fragrant with brandy and nutmeg, topped with cream. Their conversation, free from the constraint imposed by the presence of Sir Ambrose and Mrs Wyckham, ranged widely, and this time Eleanor found it impossible to keep too much to the background. For one thing, Amy had never been as much interested in public events as she, and it was soon obvious that Charles had a wide-ranging interest in the world around him. Edward Hunter, unusually for a man of his time and his profession, had encouraged Eleanor to read such newspapers as came their way, and had frequently discussed with her the implications of what she read.

From an enquiry by Charles into the machinery used in the Manchester mills, the talk had broadened out into the wonders of modern inventions that seemed to be appearing so thick and fast in all aspects of life.

'When one considers what changes have occurred since the Queen came to the throne, and that is less than ten years! What will life be like by the time the next monarch comes to the throne, I wonder?'

'It rather depends how long she remains Queen,' put in Amy. 'After all, as a married lady there are dangers...' She hardly liked to mention the fact of confinement in front of Charles, and yet the incidence of women dying in childbirth was always high.

'Very true. We should be left, then, with a child King and a Regent, I suppose. The name does not carry altogether happy memories with it. I suppose Prince Albert would stand as Regent, though not alone, of course. As a foreigner he would be most unpopular.'

'I know very little of him,' said Eleanor. 'Certainly the Queen seems very devoted to him.'

'Completely so. I was fortunate enough to meet him when I was in London. I was very impressed, and I had not expected to be. He is a very serious, thoughtful man, and I believe he has the good of the country very much at heart. He is the kind of man we need: prepared to examine new ideas, not dismiss them out of hand just because they are new.'

'Everything is new now,' complained Amy. 'I suppose I have seen the bad side of it, in Manchester, but there is something dreadful about the machinery in use there. It is so—so inhuman. It runs and it runs, and seems to eat up the lives of those who work with it.'

'What about the steam-trains, do you find those dreadful too? They talk about railway mania sweeping the country, and certainly there have been so many lines built in the last few years, but surely that is a good thing?'

'I suppose it must be. But the railways cannot go everywhere. I am glad of that—I would not like to see them take the place of our beautiful horses!'

'There was talk of a steam-omnibus, about twelve or thirteen years ago, to run between Paddington and the Bank. I know I was wild to go on it, for as a boy of eight I went on Shillibeer's omnibus. It seemed very grand to me, carrying all of twenty-two inside, and drawn by three horses. The steam-omnibus was never given a licence, though.'

'I should think not, indeed! The danger, having a thing like that on the open streets!'

'Oh, Amy, don't be so stuffy! After all, people laughed at the first railways, too. And now look at them! We were glad enough to travel by train on our journey here. Only think how long it would have taken by stage-coach, and how cold and uncomfortable it would have been. Then, with Mr Gladstone's parliamentary train, even the poor can travel, at only a penny a mile in the third class.

Think what a difference that will make to them, to everyone. Nobody but the rich have ever been able to travel other than on foot, until now.'

Amy looked unconvinced.

'Did you read of the launching of the big iron ship, the *Great Britain*, last year?' asked Charles.

'Oh, yes!' Eleanor could not hide her enthusiasm. 'It has a screw propeller instead of paddle-wheels, doesn't it? And only fifteen days to cross the Atlantic!'

'It is very silly of me,' admitted Amy, 'but I can never really understand how a ship made of iron can float.'

Eleanor decided that the conversation was not showing Amy to advantage, and turned the subject.

'I know you have travelled a great deal in Europe, Mr Wyckham. Have you visited America also?'

'I have not—though if circumstances had not forced me to return home I should certainly have done so. It sounds an extraordinary and fascinating place.'

'How I envy you the chance to travel! Papa often said I should have been born a boy, not a girl, for I should dearly love to visit all these faraway places. Amy is more dutiful than I; she is content to stay at home.'

'I do not like changes and upsets. To be busy at home is just what I like, among the people I care for.' Amy blushed, embarrassed at having spoken out so freely.

'Then you are very fortunate,' said Charles kindly, and Eleanor was pleased to see how softly his eyes rested on her sister's lovely face.

After their meal they explored the town, admiring the remains of the castle and delighting in the steep, narrow lanes that ran between the houses. Charles teased them by refusing to say which houses were tiled, but they soon learned the tell-tale signs to look out for. They were able to do a little extra shopping for trifles such as embroidery silks and some ribbon. Returning home in the

twilight, they were both tired, but happy at the con-
clusion of a successful day. A dressmaker from the village
was to come the following day to make a start on the
new gowns, and she had promised to do her best to have
them finished by Christmas, now not much more than
three weeks away.

Their life had quickly settled into a routine. They rode
nearly every morning, if the weather was fine, and each
day found them more confident. They were riding further
each day, exploring the countryside with Evans in at-
tendance. Eleanor was glad to see how the exercise in
the crisp, clean air was bringing a glow of health to her
sister's cheeks. Usually, in Manchester, she had been
obliged to spend most of the winter months indoors, as
the smoky air and the cold winds combined to give her
numerous chest complaints, which the dread spectre of
tuberculosis always made more worrying than they
already were. Now Amy was eating and sleeping well,
and Eleanor had never seen her in such good looks.

Eleanor did her best to help with the running of the
house, for she soon learned that Mrs Wyckham was but
a token head. Mrs Martlett deferred to her as a matter
of course, but, having taken the rambling and frequently self-contradictory instructions, she carried on
and did things as she thought they should be done. Hes-
itating to put herself forward, Eleanor asked Mrs
Wyckham if she could relieve her of the burden of the
daily conferences with the housekeeper. Mrs Wyckham
was happy to let her, providing she remained nominally
in charge. Though unused to running so large a
household, Eleanor had a great deal of common sense,
and was willing to learn from Mrs Martlett. As time went
by she was amused to find how often her opinion and
advice were not only sought, but acted upon.

Amy, for her part, preferred to concern herself with village and church activities. Attending Divine Service on the first Sunday of their stay, she had met and liked the sister of the local vicar. They had been at the vicarage for some five years, since the death of the previous vicar who had died in his ninetieth year, much loved for his kindness to his flock. In his last years his memory had become increasingly confused, and his parishioners had become accustomed to finding him wandering the village, mumbling happily to himself, and with no idea whether it was morning or afternoon or why he had come out. As a result, parish affairs had been left in a muddle, which the present vicar, Mr Lutcome, was still dealing with. He was, as Mrs Wyckham had remarked, a distressingly plain young man, being very tall, very thin, and afflicted with a long nose and very protruding ears. While Eleanor privately concurred with the description of his appearance, she was quick to appreciate both his intelligence and his goodness. Being of a scholarly turn of mind, he depended upon his sister to help with the practical side of running the vicarage and the parish. Some years older than he, she was in fact his half-sister, her mother having died when she was a young girl. Kindly treated by her stepmother, she had devoted herself to that lady's children, and worked uncomplainingly as his housekeeper and unpaid curate.

They were a pleasant couple, and Amy soon made friends with Miss Lutcome, and enjoyed helping with the small school in the village, which Miss Lutcome supervised. She spent many quiet afternoons in the vicarage, sewing clothes for village children in need, while Mr Lutcome composed his sermons companionably in the same room. He was aware that, if he was left to his own devices, his love of scholarship would make his sermons well nigh unintelligible to his listeners, so he formed the habit of trying them out on 'the girls', as he called them. At first abashed, Amy soon found herself able to advise and suggest, and the simplicity of her faith made her an admirable foil to his learned quotations. At home, Amy made it her business to keep Mrs Wyckham company whenever that lady wished it. Eleanor was glad to see it. She herself had little taste for the idle, gossipy conversation which was that lady's favourite way of passing the time, and she was pleased that Mrs Wyckham should become fond of Amy. Her initial distrust of this beautiful stranger was soon allayed by Amy's retiring habits, and by the fact that she made no effort to interest or attract Charles.

In no time at all Christmas was upon them. Eleanor was determined to make the season as festive as possible, and had coerced the elderly gardener into bringing several barrowloads of assorted greenery to decorate the house. Sir Ambrose expressed his pleasure at the sight, and, much encouraged, Eleanor planned to bring a small fir tree indoors, a custom newly introduced from Germany by the Prince Consort, which had all the charm of novelty. Charles was admitted to the secret, and helped her to smuggle the tree into a curtained alcove in the drawing-room.

'We will never keep this a surprise,' complained Charles, rubbing his hands which were sticky with sap. 'The fragrance is so strong, they will smell it the moment they walk into the room.'

'Never mind, as long as they do not see it yet,' replied Eleanor. 'They will not know how it is to be decorated. Look! Mrs Martlett recalled that when the damaged chandeliers from the dining-room were replaced, the old ones were stored in the attics. She has found all the lustres, and now that I have washed them they shine almost like diamonds. When the candles are lit I really think it will look quite magical, don't you?'

'Yes, if it does not burn the house down first,' said Charles. Eleanor looked worried, but refused to be daunted.

'I am sure it will do no such thing. All that is needed is a little care and attention. I have found two long-handled snuffers that will be just the thing.'

'And I suppose I am to be one of the lucky snuffer wielders?' His long-suffering tone brought a flush of anger to her cheeks.

'Mr Wyckham, if you dislike the idea of this tree so much, I wish you would have told me straight away! It would have saved a lot of time, and you would not have had to give up this afternoon to helping me. It is certainly no pleasure to me to have such an unwilling companion. We may still take it away, and forget the whole thing.'

He was contrite. 'I am sorry, Miss Eleanor. I do not dislike your little tree at all. It will certainly look very pretty.'

His instant apology disarmed her.

'I am sorry too, Mr Wyckham. I spoke very abruptly. Only I was afraid that perhaps you thought I was taking too much on to myself, and interfering with the usual arrangements for Christmas. I do not want to be pushy.'

'Please don't think of such a thing! This is exactly the sort of thing I had hoped from you—a bit of new life and some fresh ideas.'

'That is all right, then. Be careful, Mr Wyckham! I think you have not secured it adequately—it seems very wobbly. The lustres are quite heavy, so with those and the candles, and the gilded walnuts, it needs to be very firm.'

'The wretched thing bites! I shall be scarred for life.'

'Let me see. Nothing but a scratch. How is it that men can be brave about real injuries, and yet make such a fuss over tiny ones? You do not complain if you are thrown from your horse.'

'I,' replied Charles with dignity, 'am never thrown from my horse.'

'Oh, what a fib! You forget, sir, that Evans taught you to ride, just as he is teaching me!'

Charles groaned. 'Now, I suppose, all my childish follies are to be thrown in my face.'

'Not at all, I would not do anything so unladylike.' With deft fingers she continued to hang the lustres, which she had strung with pieces of silk, on the lower branches, while he obligingly reached up to the higher ones. In the silence she found herself suddenly very conscious of him; he was standing so close to her that their bodies frequently touched as they worked. Once they both reached into the box of decorations at the same time, and their hands met. Eleanor felt a thrill pass through her at the touch of his hand, and turned away in some confusion. For a moment her head spun. She could feel the warmth of his touch on her fingers, smell the aroma of Russian Leather with which his clothes were impregnated.

She shifted away from him, shocked at her own reaction. Her life, she supposed, had been a sheltered one, and she had never before come into close contact with such a young, attractive man. Nevertheless, she was horrified that she should find herself feeling this way about a man whom she generally found more irritating than attractive. Dreams of love and romance had never been part of her life; she had thought herself immune to such sentimental thoughts. Was she, perhaps, more susceptible than she knew? She hoped she would not find herself with these uncomfortable feelings with every young man with whom she came into contact.

Dismissing such an idea as absurd, she forced herself into calmness. She was not to know that Charles, too, had felt that sudden shock as their fingers touched, and was also examining his own feelings. Up to now he had scarcely thought of the two girls as more than incidentals, less than sisters, but with the kind of unattainability that a sister would have. Amy he admired for her beauty and her goodness, but she did not move him, and his mother would have been happy had she known with what indifference he could contemplate her. For Eleanor he felt some respect, for her independence and intelligence, but at the same time those very qualities he admired in her also caused him annoyance. He had no very clear idea of how his perfect woman should be—he was only very sure that she would not be as meek as Amy, nor as headstrong as Eleanor!

The tree was finished, and Eleanor stepped back to admire it. Even with the candles unlit, the glass lustres caught such light as was available and sent it back in splinters of rainbow colours as they swung and turned gently against the dark green of the branches. The round golden balls of the walnuts made a perfect contrast, and the little white candles clipped so carefully on to the ends of the twigs held their promise of glory to come.

'There. How pretty it is! May we invite the children to see it on Christmas Day?'

'The village children? It is a long way for them to come, and I thought they were to have their own celebration. I am sure I have heard Miss Amy mention it.'

'Not the village children, exactly, but those of the estate.'

'As it happens, there are none. Most of the servants are elderly, and the estate workers that live near the house are mostly unmarried, or elderly also.'

'But I thought . . .' said Eleanor, then changed what she had intended to say when he looked at her questioningly. 'Are there no children living nearby, within walking distance?'

'None that I know of. And if there were, they would not come here. You have seen how my uncle is. I have given orders that children should be kept away from the house, so that he should not be caused any distress. The sight of a boy, or the sound of children's voices, is more than he can bear. All the villagers know this, and understand it.'

'I am sure you have done it for the best, and yet . . . he cannot be protected for ever. He sees children when he goes to church, for instance.'

'That is not so bad. It is here, in this house or in the garden, that he minds about.'

'Would it not be better to confront the problem, once and for all?'

'We are not all blessed with your strength of character,' Charles replied drily. She felt the implied criticism, and turned away to draw the curtains across the alcove.

'I beg your pardon. I do not mean to interfere,' she said stiffly. Before he could answer they were interrupted by Amy.

'Why must you beg Mr Wyckham's pardon, Eleanor? How is it that you two cannot spend more than a few minutes together without disagreeing?'

'No disagreement, Miss Amy. Merely a slight difference of opinion,' said Charles smoothly. Eleanor could not bring herself to speak, and hurried from the room.

CHAPTER SEVEN

CHRISTMAS DAY arrived, and the household met in the drawing-room before church to exchange gifts. Eleanor and Amy had put a great deal of thought into theirs, wanting them to be as good as their limited means would allow. For Mrs Wyckham they had embroidered a flounce of fine cambric, Eleanor scalloping the edges and Amy embroidering it with rose-buds and garlands of leaves. For the first time she embraced the sisters with some warmth.

'Such pretty work! I shall trim my new summer gown with it, my dears.' She, in her turn, gave each of them a shawl of Norwich silk, which Eleanor guessed had been chosen with Charles's help since the colours complimented their new gowns, which they were wearing for the first time that day.

For the gentlemen they had chosen two of Papa's books, finely bound in calf, which they had kept when the vicarage was cleared. They had also made a pair of gloves for Charles, and a pair of embroidered slippers for Sir Ambrose. By a coincidence, Charles's gifts to them were also gloves: a pair for riding and a pair of fine kid for evening wear.

It was a happy day, and if several of them had memories of earlier years, and people who would never celebrate with them again, they kept their sad thoughts to themselves. The Christmas goose, which had been the object of interest and speculation for some months, was served in all its glory, and followed by an equally magnificent pudding and all the other familiar English favourites. After a short interval to recover from this feast, they repaired to the drawing-room, where the candles were lit on the Christmas tree for the first time. Eleanor was quietly delighted by the exclamations of surprise and pleasure from all present, and felt that her venture had succeeded beyond her hopes. The servants came in to receive their gifts, and the remainder of the day passed happily away in the playing of childish games like spillikins, and fox and geese.

It was with the agreeable consciousness of being well-dressed that they prepared to go downstairs a few evenings later for the party. Eleanor was in Amy's room, putting the final touches to her hair, when there was a knock at the door. Annie answered it, and returned with two bunches of hothouse violets.

'Oh, look, Amy, how perfect! The purple for you, of course, and these white ones for me. Keep still, I will put some in your hair.'

Swiftly she tucked a few of the flowers into Amy's hair, just where the smoothly brushed wings ended and the golden curls began, and pinned the rest to the fall of the bertha that hung gracefully from the low neckline.

'There, stand away and let me see you. Oh, Amy, it is perfection! Didn't I say that the low neckline would become you?'

'You are sure it is not—unsuitable?'

'Of course it is not, merely fashionable. You look beautiful.'

'No more than you do, dearest Eleanor. Let me do your flowers. How pretty they are, with that delicate veining of mauve. I have never seen you look so well.'

Eleanor laughed and disclaimed, but was privately delighted. Her dress was simple and unadorned, the only decoration being the fall of soft pleats that formed the bodice and the short sleeves, above which her shoulders shone white against the glowing brown of her hair, but the silken gleam of the lustring needed no ornament. It was so light that her wide skirts seemed to float and flow as she moved, swirling out from her small waist.

The good country food and healthy outdoor exercise that she had enjoyed for the last few weeks had restored the gleaming lights to her hair, and given the rich cream of her skin an added glow. She would never have the brilliance of complexion that Amy enjoyed, but she was happy as she was.

'I wish Papa were here,' said Amy wistfully. 'How he would have enjoyed seeing us dressed up so fine!'

'I know, dearest. But there must be no sad thoughts tonight. Come, we will go down together.'

The evening presented few terrors, for they were by now acquainted with most of the guests. The weather, though overcast, had been dry and mild for some days, and all their neighbours were there. Eleanor was amused to see that the Miss Jenningses, Augusta and Arabella, behaved precisely as Charles had said they would. He caught her eye as she watched them giggling and shaking their curls at him, and winked outrageously, causing her to break into stifled laughter when she should have been listening to General Bridges, who was telling her at great length about the Boxing Day meet.

Amy's first feelings of shyness soon wore off, and Eleanor had the satisfaction of seeing her talking with some animation to a group of their younger neighbours. Glancing round, she saw that Charles Wyckham was standing near her, and was also watching her sister. At that moment he turned and saw her looking at him.

'You look like the cat that had the cream! But you have every right. She looks very lovely, and will undoubtedly cause a stir in the neighbourhood.'

'Thank you. I will take that as a compliment, for I am very partial to cats.'

'Fonder than you are of woodlice, I suppose, though you are so well acquainted with them.' He gave her a quizzical look, and her lips tightened for a moment, before she forced the smile back to her lips.

'How unfair of you to tease me by raking that up! Must I apologise again?' she asked sweetly.

He looked down at her, and raised one eyebrow. 'You do not rise to my bait—how disappointing.'

'It grieves me to deprive you of your entertainment,' she said coolly, 'but it would be most improper of me to be squabbling with you in public, as you very well know.'

'But how much more amusing,' he murmured. She looked up at him in surprise, smiling against her will as she caught the twinkle in his eye. At that moment they were approached by a stranger, and she was surprised to see Charles's face stiffen into the immobility that she guessed masked dislike.

'Will you present me to your companion, Charles?'

The man spoke with the familiarity of old acquaintance, but she felt sure that the dislike was mutual.

'Certainly. Miss Eleanor Hunter, may I present Mr Jeremy Hammond?'

He bowed over her hand in a courtly fashion, and for one horrified moment she thought he was going to kiss it in the continental style. His face was smooth and bland against his dark whiskers, his colouring as dark as Charles's, but with eyes of a curiously light hazel that seemed to reveal nothing. In his dress he was elegant to the point of dandyism: the over-padded chest as rounded as a pouter-pigeon's above the narrow waist, the trousers fitting without a wrinkle and held, as most men's of his age were, by a strap under the instep. His linen was dazzlingly white, and he smelt strongly of some over-sweet perfume, possibly from the pomade that glistened in his hair. His voice was as smooth as his face.

'Miss Eleanor, I am delighted to make your acquaintance. I have heard so much about you, and about your lovely sister.' He glanced at Amy as he spoke. She was smiling up at Charles, who had moved away once the introduction had been made. Eleanor thought that she could see a momentary expression of what looked like anger as he saw them, but it was gone before she could be sure.

'Thank you, sir. Did I hear correctly that your name is Hammond? Are you related to Sir Ambrose?'

'I am connected, yes.' He dismissed the relationship with a wave of his hand, and she caught the flash of diamonds from the heavy gold ring he wore. 'I have a house a few miles away, but I am not often there. I like to travel.'

She asked him civilly about his travels, and he stayed talking with her for some time. He was an amusing companion, with a fund of anecdotes from his adventures abroad that could not but set her laughing, but she could not like him. His amusing anecdotes were frequently spiked with malice, with a sharpness of observation that looked for the worst in everyone, and usually found it. Also, she had the feeling that he was deliberately setting himself out to charm her. He made no attempt to circulate, or to make himself agreeable to anyone else, and once when another young man tried to join in the conversation he sent him off with a snub that was devastating in its effect, though spoken in a lazy voice.

All the time he was talking, she had the impression that his mind was working on two levels. On the surface he was the entertaining conversationalist, but beneath that he was assessing and appraising, coldly and analytically. He asked her about her family, questioning her perhaps a shade more closely than necessary, and all the time those disquieting hazel eyes were studying her, and Amy, too. At length he left her side, and when he did so she found she was exhausted, her shoulders stiff with tension and her knees shaking so that she was obliged to sit down. A few minutes later she saw him talking to her sister. He spent most of the rest of the evening in Amy's company, turning the pages for her when she played the piano, and fetching her supper. Eleanor would have thought that he was captivated, had it not been for that first half-seen look of anger and dislike.

The evening was to finish with the Christmas tree, which had been decked with fresh candles for the occasion. The other lights were extinguished, and the guests exclaimed in delight as the curtains were opened to reveal it. Eleanor was very satisfied with the effect, and stepped back towards the windows to make room for the people who were crowding round to admire.

It was because she was watching the guests rather than the tree that her eye caught a flicker of movement outside the window. The day had been mild, and with so many people in the room it had become too warm, and several of the heavy curtains had been opened. Without moving her head, she turned her eyes towards the blackness of the window.

At first she saw only the glitter of the candles and the prisms, which, as the only lights in the room, were brilliantly reflected in the glass. Then, as her eyes became less dazzled, she saw the whiteness of a face, low down, looking in. For a moment her heart lurched in fear, but then she saw from the height and the size that it was a child.

The face was close to the window, so that the breath clouded the glass and was impatiently wiped off with what looked to be a rather ragged sleeve. This was the movement that had caught her eye. It was a boy, a handsome child, and for the moment he was so absorbed in looking at the tree that she was able to study him. He looked thin, there were hollows in the cheeks, and the dark eyes, open wide in wonder, looked too big for the face. His roughly cut hair was also dark, but there was in his face something familiar, so that she felt she ought to know him. She realised that he must be the child she had seen on her first day at Oaklands Court. Where had he come from? Charles had been quite sure that none of the local children would come here.

His face was filled with longing, and her heart went out to him. Involuntarily, she made a movement with her hand towards him, and he looked at her. She would have held out her hands in welcome, and beckoned him to come to the door, but with one look of fear he was gone. Swiftly she stepped to the window, cupping her hands against the glass to see out, but he was not to be seen.

'Miss Eleanor.' A voice behind her made her jump. She whirled round, instinctively putting her body between the man who had addressed her, and the window.

'Mr Hammond, how you startled me!'

'Is anything the matter? Are you looking for something? I thought I saw something move out there.'

Suddenly she did not want him to know about the child. He was watching her closely, his hand on the sash as if he were about to lift it up and look outside. She gave an inane little laugh and stepped away from the window, so that he must perforce turn to follow her as she spoke.

'Oh, no, Mr Hammond. I was only looking to see if there were any stars!'

'It has been cloudy all day, Miss Eleanor.'

'Yes, so silly of me. I just thought, you know, that the sky might have cleared. I do so love to look at the stars, don't you?'

She was prattling to distract him, and was revolted to hear herself sounding just like the flirtatious Jennings sisters. She could scarcely be surprised when he looked down at her under slightly lowered lids, a look so blatantly of invitation that she nearly recoiled.

'Perhaps, Miss Eleanor, you might care to come and look for the stars with me? I, too, love to look at them, particularly in the company of such a delightful young lady as yourself.'

The words were flirtatious, but his eyes were coldly lascivious. She shivered.

'Oh, no, I don't think we ought to do that! It is December, after all, and so unwise to go outside from such a warm room as this. Besides,' she gave another silly giggle, 'whatever would people say?'

'I never care for that.' There, at least, she thought, he spoke the truth. She did not seriously believe that he wanted to inveigle her outside, he was merely testing her. She pretended a look of doubt.

'Well, perhaps...' she said coyly '...if it were just for a few minutes...' She assumed as inviting an air as she could, and had the satisfaction of seeing him withdraw.

'Perhaps, as you say, it would not be wise. Another time, maybe.' She was right, he had been testing her. He had seen some kind of movement, maybe even the child's face, and wanted to know whether she was hiding something. When he thought she might actually take up his suggestion, he had withdrawn at once. He certainly did not want to put himself in a compromising position with a young woman of no fortune and little beauty. She hid her amusement and chattered on, watching the bored look grow on his face, and before long he was taking his leave.

The other guests were going home also, and soon they were alone. Mrs Wyckham sank into a sofa with the appearance of one who has, however painfully, done her duty, though as far as Eleanor could see she had enjoyed herself more than anyone. Sir Ambrose sat in his usual chair, and accepted a small glass of brandy from his nephew. He beckoned the girls over to him.

'I think we may say that was a most successful party,' commented Mrs Wyckham, accepting a similar glass and sipping it with the air of one taking a necessary, but unpleasant medicine. The level in the glass dropped rapidly. 'Several people remarked on how pleasant it was to be in this house again. It was more than time that we started entertaining, Ambrose. It was quite like the parties when we were young—only not so gay, of course!'

'I expect you are right, sister. Certainly our young guests were a credit to us. You looked very pretty, my dears, and your decorated tree was as much admired as you were.'

'If we looked pretty it was only thanks to you,' said Amy, leaving her chair to kiss him. 'You have been so very kind to us, Sir Ambrose. I do not know how we can ever thank you for all you have done for us.' He took hold of her hand, and kept her close to him.

'I hope you are beginning to feel at home here?' They were both quick to answer that they were. 'In that case I should take it very kindly if you would consider yourself part of the family. I want you to think of me as an uncle. The time for formality is passed. Do you agree?'

There were tears in the girls' eyes as they came to kiss him in answer. They clung round him for a moment in happy confusion.

'Thank you—Uncle Ambrose.'

'The name sounds all the sweeter on your pretty lips, my dears. I never had daughters, but if I had, I should have wished them to be like you.' He looked across the room. 'I suppose I should have discussed this with you first, Charles, as things are, but I think I know you well enough to believe that you will not dislike it.'

Charles Wyckham bowed to each of them, kissing their hands ceremonially. 'Cousin Amy, Cousin Eleanor, I salute you and welcome you to the family.' The words were almost joking, but there was a warm look in his eyes.

It occurred fleetingly to Eleanor that she did not dislike it, as she had shuddered at the thought of Mr Hammond doing the same thing. She stifled the urge to lift her hand to her cheek, and glanced at Amy, who was looking almost irritatingly composed.

Eleanor glanced at Mrs Wyckham. That lady had risen from her reclining posture with a jerk, and was looking alarmed, a feeling which she tried to hide with a flood of words.

'My dear girls, this makes me very happy! You have quite won your way into our hearts. Already I think of you almost as daughters. Charles, my dear, you have welcomed them as cousins—perhaps you had been better to think of them as sisters!'

'Obedience is the first duty of a son, Mama,' said Charles, and before they were aware of his intention he had bent and kissed each of them on the cheek. On any other occasion, Eleanor would have laughed at the expression of chagrin on Mrs Wyckham's face.

'My dear Charles! You mistook my meaning entirely! You go quite beyond the bounds of propriety. You must not allow him to tease you, girls. It is all in fun, you know. He will have his little jokes. You will take no notice of him, of course. It is all high spirits.'

Amy said composedly, 'I am sure we can take Mr— that is, Charles, just in the way that he means. I am very happy that he can think of me as a sister, for I am sure I have often wanted a brother on whom I might depend. It is such a comfortable feeling.'

She spoke so openly and guilelessly that Mrs Wyckham relaxed, but now it was Eleanor's turn to conceal her chagrin. How could Amy speak so contentedly, so quietly, about being a sister to Charles? He was everything that Eleanor had always wanted in a husband for her sister, and although he could undoubtedly be irritatingly overbearing in his ways, she was sure that this would not annoy Amy half as much as it did herself.

'I hope that you will always feel comfortable here, as you put it,' said Sir Ambrose. 'I am not as young as I was, and one must be prepared for the future. I would not like you to think that your home depends solely on me. I intend to leave you provided for, so that in any event you would be able to have a home of your own, should you not wish to stay here after my death. Of course, I expect you will be married before then, and already in homes of your own!'

They thanked him as best they could, for such talk could only make them sad. It pleased Eleanor to see that Mrs Wyckham was quite unmoved by this further offer. Her brother was a wealthy man, and could well afford to leave enough to the girls to see them secure without seriously affecting Charles's inheritance. Though pretentious and a little foolish, she was at heart a kindly woman, and as long as she was sure that her cherished son was still free to make a great match, she was quite happy to have the girls settled there.

Eleanor's head was whirling as she went upstairs, and it was long before she could settle to sleep. So much had happened in one short evening. Long after Amy lay

peacefully slumbering, Eleanor sat by her fire in her
nightgown and robe. She could not believe that her sister
was so unmoved by Charles. Surely Amy could not be
so foolish, so blind, as to have lived for all these weeks
in this house without developing some warmer feelings
for him than sisterly affection? Her own pulses had
quickened almost unbearably at the touch of his lips on
her cheek. Half dozing as she sat, she relived that embrace, and in her dreamy state those warm, strong hands
that she had touched that afternoon held her to him,
clasping her close, and she lifted her face so that he could
kiss not her cheek, but her lips. She woke with a start.
This was the second time she had dreamed like this! It
was madness, insanity! For her to think of him like that,
when all that she wanted in the world was to see him
married to Amy. Apart from anything else, she told
herself briskly, he was hardly likely even to notice her,
with Amy in the house.

She fidgeted around the room, reluctant to go to bed,
fearing a return of that dream and feeling, illogically,
that it was disloyal to her sister to have such fancies. At
last she laid her now aching head on the pillow.

'Don't think of him, my girl,' she told herself firmly,
'for you may be sure he will not be thinking of you.
Now, or ever!'

At last she slept, and though she dreamed, it was not
of Charles. Instead her subconscious reverted to the other
startling event of the evening, and she saw again that
white face staring in at the window. This time, however,
he did not run away, but stayed, the mouth working
frantically as he tried to speak to her. No sound came
through the window, however, though she strained her
ears, and in the end his small fists were beating silently
on the glass, his eyes pleading with her. She tried to reach
him through the window, but though it gave way to her

touch as though it had been made of silk, it clung to her, impeding her movement, as though she were trapped in some monstrous spider's web. She could move forwards only slowly, step by painful step, as though her feet were clogged in quicksand, and when she tried to speak no sound came out. As she moved forwards he retreated, as if pulled irresistibly backwards by some invisible force, his face to her and his hands reaching out. Struggle as she might, he receded from her, smaller and smaller, until at last his white face whirled off into darkness, and she sank to the ground unable to stir another step, and weeping bitterly because she had failed him.

She awoke before it was light with tears on her cheeks, and a sob still catching in her throat. Half awake, she struggled from her tangled sheets and went to the window, half expecting to see that white, desperate face. There was nothing but darkness, so complete that the window was nothing but matt black, the only light in the room provided by the dim glow of the dying fire. She fell to her knees by the window-seat, and sent up a fervent prayer for all the souls lost in that terrible darkness, and especially for the one child among all the others that she could not forget. For him, most of all. Then, comforted a little, she crept back to bed and slept dreamlessly until late the following morning.

CHAPTER EIGHT

ELEANOR awoke with a heavy head, and for once was
glad to be able to breakfast in her room. Somehow, after
her dream of Charles, she could not face the thought of
seeing him across the breakfast-table. She knew that she
must see him soon, but that short respite was a help.
With luck, he would be busy about the estate for most
of the day.

Amy was also tired and languid after the party, and
the two girls spent a peaceful morning together in their
upstairs sitting-room, for Mrs Wyckham was keeping to
her bed all day, and Sir Ambrose had shut himself in
his study. Eleanor told Amy about the child, though not,
of course, about her dream. Amy was distressed.

'Poor little boy! What a shame he should have run
away. I am sure, under the circumstances, that Sir—that
is, Uncle Ambrose,' she corrected herself with a smile,
'would not have minded.'

'Mr Wyckham says that he cannot bear to see a child
in the house, particularly a boy,' said Eleanor. She could
not quite bring herself to call him by any less formal
name, and Amy did not notice it.

'Even so, something should have been done,' she said
with unusual decision. Where the welfare of others was
concerned, Amy was a different person from the meek,
biddable girl she usually was. 'For a child to be out so
late at night, at this time of year, and so far from home!
There are no other houses nearby—he must have travelled for some distance. And you think you have seen
him before?'

'Yes, the first day we were here. I almost thought I had imagined him, at first, but I saw his footprint in the flower-bed the next day. He was obviously trespassing, and I did not say anything for fear of getting him into trouble. Then, when I learned of Uncle Ambrose's wishes, I was all the more willing not to mention him.'

'He must have heard about the party, and come to see for himself. You are sure you did not recognise him?'

'I don't know. There was something familiar about him...'

'Then he must have been one of the village children, and you would have seen him when you visited the school with me.'

'No.' Eleanor was quite positive. 'I am sure he is not. I had never seen him before. I could not have forgotten that face; I can see it now. A handsome little fellow, he would have been, if he were clean and better fed. When I said he was familiar, I only meant that he reminded me of someone.'

'Dark-haired, you say? Could he have been a gypsy child?'

'I don't know. I have not heard of any gypsies round here, and I am sure we should have heard of it, for Mr Wyckham keeps a close watch on that sort of thing.'

This time Amy noticed. 'Mr Wyckham? You are very formal!'

'Cousin Charles, then. I am not used to it yet.'

'It is not like you to be so forgetful. But to return to your little boy—he cannot be a gypsy if you saw something in his face you recognised. Perhaps he is related to one of the servants or something?'

'If you mean what I think you mean, they are surely rather old, most of them! Still, you may be right. If you do not feel like riding this morning, shall we walk in the shrubbery for a while? The air will do us good.'

'Yes, if you like. I will get my things.'

At Amy's suggestion they first walked round the outside of the house. Coming to the window where Eleanor had seen the boy, they surreptitiously examined the ground, but to no avail. A gravel path ran along the wall at this point, and beyond it were well-tended lawns. Neither of these surfaces showed any marks, and Amy, who had hoped at least to get an idea of the direction the boy had taken, was disappointed. Keeping to the gravelled paths, they sauntered through the shrubbery, for the air was still mild with that unexpectedly springlike feeling that sometimes came in December, and fooled one into thinking that winter was coming to an end before it had properly begun.

'I suppose he was watching from the garden, and could not resist coming nearer to have a look at the tree,' said Eleanor. 'I am surprised no one heard him—it is impossible to walk on the gravel without making a noise.'

'He would have been careful, if he was as frightened as you say. Besides, everyone was exclaiming and talking—enough sound to drown out what was coming from outside.'

Not taking much notice of the gathering clouds, they were surprised by a few heavy drops of rain.

'Oh, dear, see how dark it is suddenly! We are in for a downpour. Come on, Amy, we must run!'

They picked up their skirts and hurried back, ignoring the paths and taking the most direct route across the lawns to the nearest door. They were not a minute too soon; the raindrops were falling ever faster, and as they stood breathless in the back hall they could see and hear that the rain was now falling heavily.

'It was not much of a walk,' said Eleanor, 'but I suppose we had some air. Are you all right? You did not get too wet?'

'No, only my bonnet, and it is an old one. I had been meaning to reshape it for some time, for it was quite out of shape. Now it is damp I will do it straight away, and yours too, if you like. I know you hate such work!'

Eleanor sighed. 'I am afraid I do. There is something so depressing about steaming this dismal black straw, and it looks so dingy it hardly seems worth the trouble.'

'Poor Eleanor! I will do it for you, and have it looking like new. Leave me to do it, for I have a little surprise in mind.'

Amy bustled off with both their bonnets, and Eleanor took her old shawl off, and hung it on a hook in the lobby where the family kept such garments, ready for use in the garden. She did not know what to do, and dawdled up the stairs after Amy, wondering where to go.

Passing along the portrait gallery, she amused herself, not for the first time, by mentally bringing the various people portrayed there to life, and putting words in their mouths. They were for the most part undistinguished pictures, painted by local artists and of little value except to the family. Mrs Martlett had given the girls a little tour of them soon after their arrival, and held forth at length about the different characters. Like most families they were a mixture: a few saints, a few sinners, and a great many ordinary people who had lived quiet, uneventful lives in this very house.

As she passed along the line, mentally greeting her favourites, Eleanor's eye fell on a small portrait, not very well lit, and she stopped in her tracks. It was, she knew, the picture of Sir Ambrose's grandfather, made when he was a young man. The figure was stiff and wooden, but the artist had somehow captured in the face what must have been a good likeness—at least, it had a character and life that many of the other portraits failed to achieve. Eleanor had often seen it before, but this time she examined the face more closely, and with a thrill of recognition knew why the child had seemed so familiar. Allowing for the differences of age, dress, and nourishment, they bore a strong similarity.

For one short minute Eleanor felt a thrill of superstitious fear. She remembered Mrs Martlett stopping before this very picture.

'Just the image of Master Richard, this one is. He would have been his great-grandfather, but the likeness is uncanny. My master had it taken down for a while, after Master Richard died, but Mr Charles persuaded him to put it back.'

Eleanor found that her skin had gone cold and tingly, and gave herself a little shake. She, the daughter of a vicar, to be believing in such things! Besides, no ghost that she had ever heard of left well-marked footprints behind it, nor did its breath mist up window-glass. Her down-to-earth mind soon came up with a much likelier explanation. It was not uncommon, in such places as this where the same families had lived for generations, to see the facial characteristics of the leading family occurring in the village. This child could well be descended from an illegitimate child of the Hammond family. Young Richard, by all accounts, had been interested only in his Lucy, and she found it hard to believe that Sir Ambrose...but then, he had been a young man once, she supposed, and it might still not be his responsibility. The striking dark colouring that both Richard and Charles had shared could well surface in a descendant after several generations.

Her head full of conjectures, she returned to her room, deciding to say nothing as yet to Amy of what she had discovered. Her sister was more easily shocked than she.

She returned to a scene of busy activity. Both the bonnets had been stripped of their simple trimming and steamed back into shape. Now Amy was standing near the fire and brushing something on to one of the hats from a bottle that stood nearby in a pan of hot water.

'Oh, I did not want you to see until I had finished it. Wait a moment, it is nearly done. Now, what do you think? Be careful, it is not quite dry yet.'

Eleanor examined the bonnet. The black straw, which had been so dingy, was beautifully stiff and a glossy black.

'It is wonderful! How did you do it? Was it black ink and oil, like before? This looks much better than the last time.'

'No, I heard of a new way. It is black sealing-wax and spirits of wine, heated together. It should make it more waterproof, too.'

'How clever you are! It really does look like new. I have plenty of scraps from my new gown to line it with, and trim it, too.' She was glad to have this distraction, for the thought that the sad child she had seen could be a distant relation of her benefactor had made her feel worse about him than before.

Two days later Eleanor awoke with the feeling that something about her room was different. The light coming in round the edges of the curtains was both brighter and clearer, and the air felt colder, in spite of the fire that already burned brightly. Jumping from her bed, she huddled a shawl round her and flung back the curtains, to find that the lowering clouds of the previous day had covered everything with a thin blanket of snow. Snow in the city had meant icy streets or, worse, muddy slush, but this was quite different. She could hardly wait to be out in it.

At breakfast she was surprised to see that Amy was not wearing her riding habit.

'Do you not ride this morning, Amy? It looks like a fairyland outside, and now that the skies are clear you will not be at risk from getting wet.'

'I think you have forgotten that there is to be a meeting today at the vicarage to discuss the provision of winter comforts for the poor in the village. You know we have been able to collect quite a sizeable sum, and it is most important that it should be spent to the best possible advantage, and on those who are truly in need.'

'But, Amy, it is so beautiful...'

'You would not wish me to put my own pleasures above the needs of my fellow creatures, Nell.' Amy's voice was gently reproving. 'Hannah particularly asked me to be there, for she was kind enough to say that my experience, through Papa's charitable schemes, is very useful.'

Eleanor was repentant. 'Of course, if Miss Lutcome depends upon you, you must be there, only I wish you were not so very good, Amy! You make me feel like the most selfish creature on earth. Would you like me to come to this meeting? I should be happy to be of assistance.'

'Selfish? You? It is no such thing, and I will not have you say it!' Amy cried out indignantly. 'I do these things because I like to. There is no need for you to give up your ride. Evans can accompany you, and you will enjoy it far more than I would have done, for I feel the cold so much more than you do.'

'Evans will do no such thing,' interrupted Charles decidedly, 'for he will be driving you into the village.'

'Oh, no, it is not worth the trouble of putting the horses to. I can perfectly well walk. It is not far, and I do it often.'

'Not in the snow, you don't. And you have just now said how you feel in the cold. You will support me in this, I am sure, Eleanor.'

For once Eleanor was glad to hear him laying down the law. 'Naturally I will. You must not think of doing such a thing, Amy, it would be most unwise. Evans must take you, and I can very well ride out on my own.'

'You will do nothing of the sort,' said Charles firmly.

Eleanor stiffened. 'And why not, pray? You do it all the time.'

'I, my dear Eleanor,' said Charles in the patient tone of one explaining the obvious to a backward child, 'am not a young woman, and I have been riding for considerably longer than two months. Moreover, I have lived in this area all my life, and I know the countryside well.'

'I may be only a young woman, but I am not a fool!' she retorted with some warmth. 'I cannot see what danger there could be in riding Lady, who as you must know is the quietest horse in the stable, in the immediate vicinity of the estate. In any case, you cannot forbid me to go. You have no authority over me.'

'I cannot,' he said with a steely glint in his eye. 'I can, however, forbid Evans, or any of the stable-boys, to saddle a horse for you.'

'You would not dare humiliate me like that!'

'I would dare, my dear girl. Motivated, I need hardly add, by my brotherly concern for your well-being.'

'Of all the overbearing, aggravating...' Words failed her.

'Pray do not distress yourself,' said Amy gently. 'I am sure Charles means things for the best.'

'Your sister is right, Eleanor,' agreed Sir Ambrose, 'and so is Charles, although I can quite see that he must appear overbearing. It would not be safe, my dear, for you to ride out unaccompanied, particularly in this weather. What if Lady were to slip, and you be thrown? We should all be worried about you.'

'I would not worry you for the world, Uncle,' said Eleanor contritely. 'Of course I will not ride, if you do not wish it. I am sorry if I have distressed you with my want of temper. I am not used to being ordered, but your wishes must always be laws with me.'

'Your conduct needs no explaining,' said Charles airily as he stood up. 'Such behaviour is commonly found in those who are too much used to having their own way. Good morning, Uncle Ambrose, Amy, Eleanor.' And before Eleanor could do more than gasp her indignation, the door had closed behind him. Her state of mind was not improved by noticing that both her sister and Sir Ambrose were stifling laughter at the sight of her face.

Not wishing to upset Amy, Eleanor said no more on the subject as they went upstairs after breakfast, but privately she was determined not to allow Charles Wyckham to order her around. Accordingly, once she had seen Amy safely bestowed in the barouche, she changed into one of her oldest dresses, with an extra flannel petticoat, a thick shawl and her old, stout boots. Her old bonnet, refurbished and trimmed by Amy, was now too good to wear on such a day, so she pulled an old woollen comforter from her chest and wrapped it round her head and neck. Thus warmly, if unbecomingly, attired, she let herself out of the house and walked towards the woods.

Picking her way through the trees, she found that she did not altogether regret being on foot, for it permitted her to take paths that would have been too small for a rider. Entranced by the beauty of the snow-laden branches, she walked on, and eventually found herself on a path which she had never taken before, which led up on to the lower slopes of the downs.

Once she was clear of the trees, she stopped and looked around. From where she stood the house was still hidden by the wood through which she had just passed, but further away she could see the spire of the village church, and she spared a thought for Amy at the vicarage, sorry that her sister was not there to share the beauty. Around and behind her the sides of the hills rose steeply, the usual dappling of green and brown turned to glistening white, shadowed with blue and violet. Only a few sheep, their white fleeces looking suddenly drab and dirty against the snow, moved in the frozen landscape.

Rather than struggle up the steep hillside, she took a diagonal path that followed the contour of the slope. As she slowly climbed higher, she began to feel a breeze, sea-scented and stingingly cold, but she only pulled her shawl and comforter a little more tightly round her and walked on, taking a childish delight in the sight of her own clear footsteps in the unmarked snow. Here and there she could see a delicate tracery where birds had hopped, and several times the track of some small creature. So intent was she in searching for these minute marks of life that she did not at first notice that there was a cluster of buildings ahead of her that had been hidden by a fold of the hill.

The sudden barking of a dog alerted her, and she stopped. There was a farmhouse, with byres and sheds built around a yard, and the barking came from a black and white collie which was tied to one of the sheds, jumping against the rope that held it. The place looked, if not prosperous, at least well-kept and tidy, and she wondered if this was one of Sir Ambrose's tenants.

At that moment the cry of a child, cut off with suspicious suddenness, set her moving again towards the farm, but before she could take many steps the figure of a large man had emerged from a barn and was striding towards her, looking so threatening that she came to a halt.

He was a middle-aged man of imposing stature, dressed in the stout corduroy trousers and frieze coat of a countryman. His face was angry, and although she could not yet hear what he was shouting, she felt that the stick he carried was not intended merely as an aid to walking. Stubbornly, though, she stood her ground. She had done no harm that she knew of, and surely could have nothing to fear.

His long legs carried him rapidly nearer to her, and soon she could distinguish his words.

'Away! Out of here! Private farm, no trespassing. Get away with you!'

She attempted to apologise and to explain, but her voice was drowned out by his.

'There's nothing for you here. I want no extra workers, so be off with you, woman, before I set my dog upon you.'

She drew herself up, and tried to speak with dignity.

'You are mistaken, I am not looking for work, I am merely out walking. Does your landlord know you treat people in this way?'

'There's no landlord here. This farm is mine, and my father's before me. And I'll have no loose, idle women wandering my land, up to no good, frightening the stock, so take yourself off.'

'How dare you, sir! I am Miss Eleanor Hunter, of Oaklands Court, and——'

She had no chance to continue, for at the mention of Oaklands Court he appeared to swell with rage, his eyes bulging and bloodshot. He raised his stick threateningly, and flecks of spittle appeared at the corners of his mouth as he roared, 'You dare to speak that name to me! I'll hang for a murderer before I let my land be fouled by one of that breed again. Get out, or by the Blood of the Lamb I'll have your blood!'

His face was suffused, the hand holding the raised stick trembling with passion. Eleanor turned and ran. Too frightened to follow her own footsteps, she just went downhill, slipping and stumbling as she went. Without warning, she found herself on a steep slope. She tried to stop her headlong rush, but was unable to do so. Inevitably she felt her feet slipping beneath her, and then she was falling. There was a flurry of hoofs and a shout, and instinctively she pulled in her arms and legs, making herself as small and compact as possible. There was an exclamation of surprise, and in a moment the rider had reined in his horse and dismounted.

'Are you hurt? You may count yourself lucky if you are not, for you fell right beneath his feet. It is really... Eleanor!'

Carefully she uncurled herself and stood up, shaking the snow out of her skirts. Charles stepped quickly forward to seize her by the shoulders.

'No, I am not hurt, but Charles——' She had to stop because he was shaking her, his fingers gripping cruelly into her arms, his face white.

'Of all the stupid girls—did I not tell you not to go out? You could have been killed! Whatever possessed you? And then to be running downhill, in the snow! If it were not that Valiant has more sense in one foot than you have in the whole of you——'

She clutched at the front of his coat, reassured by his presence, even by his anger.

'Charles, there's a man, and I think he must be mad! He shouted at me, and then threatened me with his stick, and truly I had done nothing, not ever bothered his sheep, and I heard a child crying, and I was so frightened!'

The words came out in jerks. Abruptly he stopped shaking her, and looked more closely into her face.

'A man? Were you at the farm? A large man?'

'Yes, with a stick, and when I said I was not looking for work but had come from Oaklands Court, he was so angry. I thought he was going to attack me.' She could feel herself trembling, and clung to his coat for support as her legs felt as though they would no longer support her. The anger faded from his face and he put his arms round her, gently supporting her. Gratefully she leaned her face against the broadcloth of his coat. She felt at once safe and strangely elated.

'You are all right now, he has not followed you. He does not like strangers on his land, and when you said you were from Oaklands...what a mischance that you should have gone that way!'

'It was because I was on foot. I took a different path through the woods.'

'You should not have been outside the grounds!'

'You only forbade me to ride, not to walk.' There was a shade of defiance in her voice, but he only laughed and released her, brushing the snow from her clothes.

'Termagant! May you have learned your lesson from today, though I do not doubt you are beyond reclaim. Come, we must go home, for you will take cold in those damp clothes. I would put you up on Valiant, but I think you would be warmer walking. Can you manage, do you think?'

'Oh, yes, I am quite unhurt. But how could I have known I was likely to meet a madman? You should have warned me.'

'It is not a matter one would usually discuss with a young lady,' he said repressively.

'Don't be so stuffy, Charles. You know my life has been far from sheltered. I am not so easily shocked.'

'Take my arm, you will be safer, and I will tell you as we walk. Hargreaves, the man you met, is a proud, puritanical man, as harsh and strict with his own family as with the men who work for him. His only child, a daughter, was hardly allowed to speak to anyone outside the family. He was devoted to her.

'Was? Is she dead?'

'Nobody really knows, but it is assumed so. Do you remember I told you how my cousin Richard had fallen in love with a farmer's daughter? That was she. I suppose they must have met in secret, for neither his father nor hers would have approved. That, I suspect, was half the trouble. If they had been able to meet normally, their emotions would have burned themselves out in no time, as these calf-loves so often do, but the secrecy only added to the romance. As I told you, when he was forced to leave the country Richard somehow persuaded her to go with him. It was madness, of course, and would have been the ruin of both of them. As it was, within a few weeks he was dead, and she was never heard of again.'

'Did no one try to find her?'

'When he heard that she was gone, her father repudiated her utterly. He has never mentioned her name from that day. Her mother was already dead. As I told you, I tried to find her, for Richard's sake, so that she should not be in want. But she had vanished without a trace. No one has ever heard a word of her since.'

'Poor child, what a terrible story. No wonder her father hates the name of Oaklands Court. Would he really have hurt me, do you think?'

He was slow to answer.

'I don't know. He is certainly a strange, solitary man, and even before these troubles he was known to have a terrible temper.'

She shivered, and stumbled with legs that felt weak. He let go of his horse's rein to put the arm she was not holding out to support her, and they both stopped walking. Looking up at him, she found his face was far nearer than she had realised, for he was bending solicitously towards her. She looked into his eyes, and for once they were not teasing, or irritated, but merely intent. They were quite still, and she found herself unable to look away from him. She remembered her dream. All at once she knew that he was going to kiss her, though he had not moved.

They had not noticed the approach of another rider. At that moment he hailed them.

'Wyckham! Miss Hunter! What is this? Has there been an accident?'

Eleanor was suddenly conscious, beneath the appraising stare of Jeremy Hammond, of her shabby, snow-marked clothes, and of the fact that she was still clinging to Charles's arm. He seemed in no way abashed, but withdrew his other arm slowly. The newcomer's eyes were fixed on them; she could scarcely hope that he had failed to see their previous attitude.

'Thank you, Hammond. Miss Hunter has been so unlucky as to take a slight fall in the snow. She is unhurt, however, and we are walking home as fast as may be so that she may change out of her damp clothes.'

'Can I be of assistance? Will you take my horse, Miss Hunter?'

'Oh, no, thank you, we are nearly home. As Mr Wyckham says, I am not hurt.'

'How did you come to fall? Were you up on the downs? They are very steep just up there.'

For some reason Eleanor found that she did not wish to say what had happened, and she was quite sure that Charles did not either. She could not understand why

Mr Hammond should be interested, and yet he undoubtedly was, trying to question her as to which paths
she had taken, and even asking if she had met anyone.

'You were so close in conversation when I met you,
I thought you must be discussing something important!'
His tone was light, but he looked at them sharply.

'Not at all. I was merely remonstrating with Miss
Hunter that she should have been so unwise as to go out
walking alone, in such weather.'

'Of course, and she was properly contrite, I am sure.'

Eleanor managed a creditably demure look. Much to
her annoyance, for she would have liked to talk further
on the subject of Hargreaves, and more particularly
about the child she was sure she had heard there, Mr
Hammond insisted on dismounting and accompanying
them to the door of the house, where common civility
dictated that Charles must ask him in for a glass of
sherry. The invitation was accepted, and she was glad
to escape to her own room on the pretext of changing
her damp clothes.

CHAPTER NINE

As Eleanor walked up the stairs, she wondered what would have happened had Jeremy Hammond not turned up at that particular moment. Had Charles really been about to kiss her? She found it hard to believe. He had never shown any interest in her as a woman, and most of the time she thought he either tolerated her because his uncle wished it, or found her irritatingly headstrong, as he was so often telling her. No, she must have imagined the whole thing, influenced by the dream of the other night. She would think of it no more. Certainly he had been shocked by how nearly she had been hurt in falling under his horse's hoofs, but knowing Charles he could well have been more worried over his horse's well-being than hers. All in all, it was as well that they had been interrupted before she had had a chance to make a fool of herself, by showing too clearly that his closeness disturbed her. All she would regret was that she had not been able to finish their talk.

As it happened, she had no further opportunity of speaking to Charles again that day. It took her some while to change, for when she looked in the glass she found that her hair was half-way down her back and her face was muddy. To add to her vexation, she found there was a big triangular tear in the fine cambric petticoat that she wore beneath her stiffened crinoline to keep the horsehair from scratching. By the time she had washed and changed, it was already luncheon.

Charles was not there. Eleanor was surprised to find how disappointed she felt—somehow she had counted on seeing Charles at once, and being able, when the meal was over, to talk over the events of the morning. Fortunately Amy was so full of her meeting, and what had been decided, that she failed to notice that her sister was unusually silent. After luncheon Eleanor said only that she had been out for a walk, and that she had slipped in the snow. She found herself suddenly tired, and was quite happy to spend a quiet afternoon with Amy and Mrs Wyckham in their little sitting-room. She lay on the sofa, her needlework slipping from her hands as she dozed, and Amy sewed and hummed peacefully at the window, and discussed fashions with Mrs Wyckham in a desultory manner.

As she was changing for dinner, Eleanor asked Annie if she had heard of any children living nearby, or coming to the house. Annie shook her head doubtfully, then glanced at the door of Amy's room, which was ajar. Eleanor looked quickly round the door.

'It's all right, Annie. There's no one there, she must have gone to fetch something. What is it?'

Rapidly, listening all the time for sounds of Amy's return, Annie told her in her usual mixture of speech and gesture that there were no children on the estate, but that one of the younger maids had recently come near to being dismissed when she claimed that the house was haunted.

'Haunted? By what?'

'That's just it, Miss Nell.' Annie's nasal speech was difficult to understand, even for Eleanor. 'She said it's haunted by the ghost of poor Mr Richard.'

'Mr Richard? But what has that to do with this? I was asking about children, not ghosts of young men. Besides, I don't believe it. He didn't even die here.'

'She said he is a child ghost. That he's come back as a child to haunt his father, and that's why Sir Ambrose keeps hearing a child's voice.'

'But that is ridiculous. Sir Ambrose has had these delusions for years. Why should she suddenly start saying that he is haunted now?'

'Because she saw him, Miss Nell. Says she saw him in the hall, all shadowy and misty, and he was the image of that picture of Mr Richard that's in Sir Ambrose's bedroom.'

'And she was in the hall? Where was she standing? Where did she see him? Or think she saw him, rather?'

'I don't know, miss. I could not ask her, but . . . she's been told by Mrs Martlett not to talk about it again, or she'll be turned off without a character. She doesn't understand me too well, either.'

'No, don't worry, Annie. This is better not to be spoken of. Did you believe her?'

'I believe she saw something, but not that it was a ghost. Probably just a shadow, or something. But she's a truthful girl, not given to making up stories. And she was really frightened.'

'Hush, I hear Miss Amy coming back. I do not want her to be worried with all this.'

As she went down to dinner, Eleanor paused in the hall, looking round. She wondered what it was that the maid had seen. Moving swiftly she went to stand by the door that led to the terrace, which was glazed. Looking across the hall, she saw her own reflection in the window by the front door. Surely the misty figure must have been that—a reflection in the glass. If the door had been open, as it often was on fine days, the boy could have ventured up to it, relying on the twilight to hide him. He must have a strange fascination for this house, that he kept coming to it although it must mean a long walk for him.

The following day was again sunny, but icily cold. It had not snowed again, and the original covering, only about two inches thick, still lay. Amy and Eleanor rode out with Evans, enjoying the picturesque beauty, but decided to take a shorter route than usual so that Amy should not get too cold.

They were on their way home, on a broad woodland ride that would take them directly to the house about two miles away, when they heard the thudding of hoofs approaching from the side.

'That'll be Mr Charles,' said Evans. 'He was off to the Home Farm this morning and he usually comes back this way. It's a good place for a gallop.'

'Let's wait for him, and return together,' said Amy. As she spoke the steady thunder ceased, and the cold air rang with the shrill scream of a frightened horse, followed by a crashing thud. Evans at once turned his horse and went off at a gallop, followed by Eleanor and Amy.

They had not far to go. As they rounded a bend in the ride, they saw Charles's bay gelding, Valiant, lying on the ground, his eyes rolling in fear as he struggled to rise. Nearby lay the terrifyingly still form of his rider. A few yards behind them a small tree trunk made a low, natural jump where it had fallen across the ride.

Evans flung himself from his horse and ran to Charles. Eleanor reined in, her heart in her mouth, and saw that he was stirring. Her whole body tingled and prickled with relief, and she drew a breath, only then aware that she had not been breathing. She thought that she would never forget the sight of Charles's long body lying so still on the snowy ground, the whole picture imprinted in black and white behind her eyes.

'Mr Charles! Mr Charles! Don't move, now, stay still for a moment. Are you hurt bad?'

'No.' His reply was between a gasp and a moan. 'Not hurt. See to the horse.'

'I will, but not until I've seen to you. Can you move your legs?'

'Yes.' Charles was struggling to sit up, one arm lifted awkwardly across his chest. 'Broken collarbone, I think. Nothing worse, just a bump on the head that put me out for a moment.'

'Thank God for it. How did it happen, Mr Charles? Did he take the jump wrong? I'd not have thought you could have such a fall from so low a jump.'

'I don't know, I can't understand it. He took the jump perfectly, but he must have landed all wrong somehow, for he couldn't keep his feet under him, and he was down before I knew what was happening.'

Amy and Eleanor had also by now dismounted, and came to help Charles who had managed to sit up, his face drawn with pain. Eleanor snatched off the woollen scarf she had worn tucked inside the jacket of her habit, and knelt to fashion a sling so that Charles's arm was supported, while Amy held the horses. Evans went to Valiant, who had by now got to his feet again and was standing, head down, and trembling. The groom swiftly ran his hands down the horse's legs, talking soothingly. 'There, my old fellow, there now, no bones broken, then? That's good. Come on, now, if you've got your breath back. Just one step. That's the way. Good boy, good old boy, then. All right, now.' The murmuring voice went on as he led the horse gently in a small circle, checking that he was not harmed.

'What was that?' cried Amy suddenly, her face turning even whiter than it had been. They all listened.

'What did you hear?' asked Eleanor.

'Footsteps,' whispered Amy. 'There was somebody there.'

'It was probably only an animal,' soothed Eleanor.

'We've seen no animals all morning. No, this was footsteps. It sounded so stealthy, like someone creeping through the undergrowth. And when we listened, it stopped.'

'A poacher, most likely,' said Charles.

Evans, who had calmed the frightened horse, seemed about to say something at that, but a quick look from his master, and a warning shake of his head, made him subside. 'Valiant has taken no great harm from his fall, sir, though he'll be a bit lame for a while. He's been lucky, with a fall like that. I was sure his leg would be broken. Can you stand, Mr Charles?'

With great care they helped Charles to his feet. His shoulder was obviously painful, but he made no complaint. When he tried to put his right foot to the ground, however, he gave a quickly stifled groan, and would have fallen if Evans had not been supporting him. He gave a wry smile.

'Valiant is not the only one who will be lame for a while, it seems. I must have sprained it when I fell.'

'Or broken it,' suggested Evans gloomily. 'Thank God you fell clear of the horse, and he was not on you as he fell.'

'We must get you back to the house at once,' said Eleanor. 'Your boot must come off as soon as possible, before your ankle can swell too much. As it is I fear it will have to be cut off.'

'I'll ride back for help,' said Evans.

'No,' said Charles. 'No, let the young ladies go.' He and Evans once again exchanged a quick glance, which silenced any objection the older man might have made. Eleanor saw that look, and wondered, but this was not the time for questions or arguments.

'Come, Amy,' she said. 'We must not waste time. Can you use that fallen tree to mount from?'

She would have led the horses to it, but again Charles intervened. 'No, not that. There is a tree stump just over there that will do better.' Looking at him in surprise, she saw an unmistakable warning in his eyes, and did not argue. Amy, too, was looking remarkably pale and shaken still, and Eleanor was eager to get her back to the warmth and safety of the house. For some reason Charles wanted the girls out of the way, and for once she was glad to obey him. In a few moments they were mounted and riding swiftly back to Oaklands Court. As they reached the bend in the ride she glanced back, and saw Charles and Evans deep in discussion. Charles was gesturing back towards the fallen tree, and she just had time to see Evans go where he was pointing before they turned the bend of the ride...

Help was quickly dispatched, and a stable-boy sent galloping for the doctor. Charles was carried back to the house, rather white round the lips, and up to his room. Within a short time the doctor arrived. Eleanor and Amy waited with Mrs Wyckham, who was voluble in her anxiety.

'Nothing can persuade me that it is not dangerous to be setting his horse at every gate and hedge he encounters. And in this snow, too! He really should be more careful. My nerves cannot stand such alarms. What would become of me if he were to be—I cannot say the word, but you know what I mean. An only son has responsibilities, after all. He owes it to me to take care of himself.'

She continued alternately scolding and complaining, but Eleanor and Amy could see that she was very upset, and hardly knew what she was saying. They did their best to calm her.

'My dear ma'am, let me lend you my smelling salts, I have them here,' said Amy, holding the little glass bottle under Mrs Wyckham's nose. 'I am sure it cannot be good for you to upset yourself like this, and you must be strong, for Charles's sake.'

'I can assure you that he is only slightly hurt. The doctor will soon be finished, and then you can ask him yourself. Let me fetch you a cup of tea, and perhaps you should take a few drops of laudanum. You will be wanting to see him as soon as possible, and think how it would upset him to see you like this.'

'That is very true. When he was a little boy, it was always Mama he wanted when he was ill. I must be ready to go to him.'

When the doctor was announced a few minutes later, he found Mrs Wyckham sipping at her cup, while Amy and Eleanor hovered round her with the smelling bottle, and a handkerchief soaked with eau de cologne, with which Eleanor had been tenderly dabbing at the afflicted lady's forehead. His lips twitched.

'This is very good, my dear Mrs Wyckham, very good indeed! Here was I, hastening to your side, expecting to find you ill with anxiety, and I find that the good young ladies have been caring for you better than I could have done myself!'

'Yes, they are good girls, and I do not know how we should manage without them. But how is he, my poor boy? Is he in much pain?'

'You must not distress yourself, ma'am, he will do very well. The collarbone is broken, but it is a clean break and he has not been moved more than necessary. Thanks to the young lady's presence of mind,' he bowed to Eleanor, 'the arm was well supported, and I anticipate no problems in that quarter. The ankle is much inflamed, but not broken, and although he will not be able to walk on it for a while, there will be no lasting harm. He has had a nasty bump on the head, and no doubt has a headache, but nothing that time and sleep will not cure. I am in no anxiety about him, no anxiety at all.'

'Thank God for it. I must go to him, my poor boy.'

The doctor, who had been taking her pulse, patted her hand soothingly. 'Not now, for I gave him a sleeping draught and I think he will be already asleep. Do not forget that you are my patient, too! This excitement is not good for you, and only think how it would distress your son to think that he had made you ill. I want you to let these young ladies give you some of your drops, and then you must rest for the remainder of the day. Yes, I insist. It would never do for my favourite patient to be making herself ill.' With much cajolery he persuaded her to lie down on the sofa, and Amy administered the drops, promising to stay with her as she slept.

Eleanor accompanied the doctor from the room. He dropped his light, bantering tone as he looked at her.

'You and your sister did very well, my dear. Mrs Wyckham likes to think of herself as an invalid, and though in many ways she is not as weak as she likes to think, there is an irregularity in the pulse which I cannot like. Any sudden shock, such as this, could have serious consequences.'

'Will she be all right now?'

'Yes, provided she is kept quiet for a while and has no upsets. I will take a look at her tomorrow when I come to see Mr Wyckham. He may have some fever in the night—I have left something for him to be given if so. At all events, a light diet, no wine or red meats, and as little activity as possible. I have also left another draught to help him to sleep tonight.'

After the doctor was gone, Eleanor conferred with Mrs Martlett.

'He is asleep now, miss. He looks very pale, but Doctor says he will be all right. I shall sit up with him tonight, if there is likely to be some fever. He should not be left alone.'

'But not all night, Mrs Martlett, it is too much for you. Let me help you. I nursed my father in his final illness, and this can be nothing compared to that.'

'Well, if you are sure you wouldn't mind, miss, I must say it would be a help. I will have a bed made up in the dressing-room next door. I can sleep there, and be on hand should you need me.' Eleanor had no difficulty seeing through this transparent ruse, and wondered with a corner of her mind what harm a man with a broken collarbone and a sprained ankle could possibly be thought to have done to her reputation, even if she should spend some hours alone with him. Nevertheless, the rules of conduct must be obeyed, and she assented meekly to these arrangements.

Eleanor and Amy took their luncheon with Sir Ambrose. He, always nervous of illness or accident for those close to him, was anxious and worried, and both girls made a great effort to play down the effects of Charles's fall. In the afternoon Eleanor lay down on her bed, meaning to have a sleep in preparation for a wakeful night. Proper slumber, however, eluded her. Every time she closed her eyes she saw again Charles's still form lying in the snow, her half-sleeping mind conjuring up pools of blood, broken necks, or simply death from exposure or pneumonia if they had not happened to be there. When she drifted into sleep her dreams were troubled, and although she could not remember them she was glad when Annie came to wake her in time to change for dinner.

When dinner was over, Eleanor provided herself with a book and a large, soft shawl and made her way to the east wing. Mrs Martlett met her, and took her into the bedroom. Charles was asleep, and a screen had been arranged so that she could have a light beside her chair that would not shine on his face. The fire was well made-up, and a covered jug of fresh lemonade stood ready to hand if he should wake and be thirsty. Eleanor settled in her chair, assuring Mrs Martlett in a whisper that she was perfectly comfortable, and would call or ring if anything should be needed.

She could not resist casting a curious glance round the room, once she was alone. It was, she knew, formerly a guest bedroom, for naturally enough Charles had not liked to use the room that had formerly been his cousin's, and Eleanor had been told that Richard's old room was still preserved as he had left it. The furniture, like that of the rest of the house, was heavy and old-fashioned, the room somewhat sparse and comfortless compared to the rooms she and Amy had been given. A large bookcase, well filled with volumes both new and old, gave evidence of his wide interests, for it contained not only the latest novels and poetry, but other, more serious works of history and science. Everything was scrupulously tidy, the only ornament a fine piece of glass, Venetian as she guessed, that stood in a place of honour on the chest. The curtains at the windows, and on the old-fashioned bed, were of wool finely embroidered in crewel stitch, very old, but showing signs of loving mending in places. Above the tang of wood-smoke, to which she was now accustomed so that she hardly noticed it any more, was the aromatic fragrance that she had noticed about him. He was not scented, like Jeremy Hammond, but obviously some mixture of spices and Russian Leather was used in his cupboards and chests.

The room was very quiet, and, having read for over an hour, Eleanor felt her eyelids closing. She went and looked at Charles, who had not moved. She laid her hand softly on his forehead below the nightcap that was carefully fitted on his head: it was hot, but not unduly so, and she went back to her chair, making up the fire before settling herself back with her shawl around her. She fell into a light doze.

Some while later she was aroused by a movement from the bed. The fire had burned low, and the room felt chill. Quickly she put some logs on, and lit a fresh candle. She went to the bed. Charles's eyes were closed, but he was moving his head restlessly, and now and then a muttered word escaped his lips. As she stood, uncertain whether to rouse him, he spoke clearly.

'Ice,' he said urgently. 'Ice, under the snow.'

She took his hand, and held it firmly. His skin felt hot, and again she laid her other hand against his face, forehead and then, scarcely aware of what she did, his cheek. It was long enough since he had shaved that morning for the growing beard to show dark against his skin. Abstractedly she moved her hand against it, enjoying the way it felt harsh and bristly in one direction, smooth when she stroked her fingers downwards. At once his eyes opened, and for a moment he stared at her blankly, a tiny frown between his dark eyebrows. She snatched her hand away. Then, before she had time to be frightened, his expression changed.

'Eleanor,' he said, 'you should not be looking after me. Where is Mrs Martlett?'

'She is lying down in the next room, and the door between us is open, so you need not fear I am compromising you! It is time you stopped telling me what I should not do,' she said, smiling to show that she was teasing him. 'Mrs Martlett is not young, and cannot be expected to sit up with you all night. We are sharing the time.'

He frowned.

'I am not ill. Good heavens, girl, I was hardly hurt!'

'You have a broken collarbone, and, if I am not very much mistaken, a fever. Do you want a drink?'

She held the glass to his lips, lifting his head so that he could drink. He swallowed the lemonade eagerly, and thanked her. She went to the wash-stand and fetched a damp sponge and a towel. Expertly she washed and dried his face and hands, then turned and smoothed his pillow.

'Thank you, Nurse,' he said meekly. She gave a slight smile.

'I did most of the nursing when Papa was ill. Amy is not strong enough, so Annie and I did it between us. One soon learns the trick of it. The doctor has left another sleeping draught for you, if you would like it?'

He shook his head impatiently, and winced. 'No, thank you. My head already feels like a block of wood. I am not in pain, only uncomfortable. In any case, I would like to talk to you. Did you hear anything when your sister thought she heard footsteps in the woods?'

'No, I don't think so. Did you?'

'I was not sure. I was confused from the fall, but I did have the feeling that there was someone there.'

'A poacher?'

'Perhaps.' He frowned, thinking, then transferred his gaze to her, wondering how much he should say. Eleanor waited. At length he continued, as if there had been no pause. 'It seems a curious time of day to be out poaching, and in this weather there would not be much to take. I thought perhaps it might be connected...' He paused again.

'With the ice under the snow?' she prompted. He gave her a sharp look.

'How did you know?'

'You were talking in your sleep just now, and that is what you said. What does it mean?'

'Just that. There was ice under the snow, and that is why Valiant fell. I sent Evans to check it after you had gone.'

'Is that so unusual? Surely in this cold weather——'

'Cold, yes, but dry. It hasn't rained for over a week. You forget how well I know these woods. I have ridden in them all my life. There has never been water there before. There has been no thaw, no rain, to make a puddle.'

She stared at him in horror.

'You mean, someone put it there?'

He looked grim.

'I mean just that. The earth had been scooped away and smoothed to make a little hollow to hold the water until it froze. It must have been done yesterday evening, or last night. And then the ice had been sprinkled with snow to hide it. Evans found a lot of footprints in the undergrowth, and a place where the snow had been collected up and taken away.'

'A practical joke? But who...? Charles, you might have been killed! It would have been...murder!'

'Precisely—with the murderer lying in wait to finish the job. Only you two and Evans were there too quickly.'

'Then what Amy heard...there *was* someone there?'

'Yes. Evans saw his footprints, the same as the ones by the fallen tree, and the place where he was hiding. There was a heavy branch lying to hand, too, that had come from that same fallen tree. Evans went back after I was home and followed the footprints. Whoever it was had tried to cover them, but in too much of a hurry to do a proper job. He had a horse hidden about a quarter of a mile away. By the time Evans went back, he was long gone.'

'It was not just mischief, then? It was actually aimed at you?'

'I am sure so. This is the day when I usually go to the Home Farm, and that is the ride I would generally take to come back. Any of the local people would know that. That fallen tree had been cut down. Anyone who knows me at all would know that I would come that way, and jump it. The miracle is that I am alive at all. By rights I should have broken my neck. At the very least he could count on me staying down long enough for him to finish me off. A quick blow on the head, the branch rearranged to look as though I had fallen on it, and nobody would have been any the wiser. Just the sort of unfortunate accident that can occur so easily.'

Eleanor shivered.

'You mentioned the local people. Do you think it could have been that farmer, Hargreaves? He looked mad enough for anything, and he hates us. Seeing me the other day, and hearing the name of Oaklands Court, might have set him off.'

'I wondered about that, but I don't think so. He probably is a bit mad, but not that sort of cold, calculating madness. He might lose his temper and hit out at me, even kill me, if he met me by chance, but I do not think he would come down to the woods, and set this up.'

'Then who? And why?'

'That is what I do not know. But I will.'

Looking at him she had no difficulty in believing him. 'You will not take too many risks? Another attempt might well succeed.'

'I will be careful. But whoever it was clearly wants it to look like an accident, and I would not think he would risk another attempt too soon. But I will be on my guard.'

'Well, you will be safe for some days, at any rate, for the doctor says you will not be able to walk for a while yet. And I think you should sleep, now. You will not get better any faster by worrying in the middle of the night.'

He grimaced. 'You sound like my old nurse. Any minute now you will be offering me castor oil, or Gregory's powder.'

'I might do just that, if you do not try to rest. Do you want any more lemonade?'

'No, thank you.' She turned to go, but he caught her hand and detained her. 'Eleanor, I know that you do not like me to advise you, but for your sister's sake I must ask you not to go out unaccompanied. Take Evans or your maid, but do not go alone, or without telling someone where you are going. It may be that our friend is only interested in me, but who knows? You must not take chances with Amy's safety, or your own.'

She knew that his concern for her sister ought to have pleased her, but somehow it did not. She forced a smile.

'You need not worry; I will take care of her. And it is not your advice that I resent—only your orders!'

'Hussy,' he said cheerfully. And, oddly, this impolite response made her feel suddenly happier. 'All right, I will behave. My eyes are closed, I am resting. And you should do likewise.' He gave her a push towards the chair, but at that moment Mrs Martlett arrived, roused perhaps by the sound of their voices, and Eleanor was sent back to bed. She meant to lie and ponder on what she had just learned, but the warmed bed was too much for her, and she fell into a deep and, happily, dreamless sleep.

Charles stayed awake, although his eyes were closed and he did not move. He was in more pain than he had been prepared to admit, his whole body a mass of grinding aches and complaints at its misuse. Nevertheless, he did not want to take the laudanum that was offered to him. Release it might give, but he disliked the way it removed his mind and body from his own control.

Abandoning the problem of his own accident, about which he could do nothing until he was well, his thoughts ranged back to his cousin's death. In particular, his betrayal by one of the smuggling gang. Charles had some ideas of his own about that group, and about its new leader. If what he suspected should be correct, then the two events were clearly connected. And if that were so, then it followed that Amy and Eleanor might also be in danger. After all these years, Charles thought that the reason for the sudden attack on himself might well be tied up with the fact that two young, lovely and, above all, marriageable girls were now living under the same roof as he was.

A slight frown crossed his face. He wondered whether his warning to Eleanor had been strong enough. He hoped that by appealing to her protective feelings for Amy he would curb her own love of wandering the countryside, but he could not count on it. He could not ask Sir Ambrose to express a wish that she should keep near the house without explaining to his uncle the reason, and he knew better than anyone that even a hint of such a danger might have serious effects on his uncle's health. Damn this injury, that would keep him tied to the house where he could not keep an eye on her! He would have to be a fractious invalid, and see if he could keep her at his side. The frown vanished, to be replaced by a slight smile. The prospect was, he thought, decidedly appealing. Eleanor might be headstrong and argumentative, but she was never boring. He anticipated an amusing convalescence.

Still smiling, Charles fell asleep.

CHAPTER TEN

THE fever proved to be only slight, and within two days Charles was insisting on leaving his bed, and walking with the aid of a stout walking-stick. He could not yet manage the stairs, but spent his days in his mama's sitting-room, or the girls'. He was soon chafing at the enforced leisure, and they did their best to entertain and distract him. The weather continued to be very cold, and it was no hardship to forgo their daily rides in order to keep him company. It quickly became his habit to spend his mornings in their sitting-room, while Mrs Wyckham was still abed. Daily reports of the estate business were brought to him, and they soon realised how important his efforts were to its smooth running.

'Do all landowners have as much to decide and oversee?' asked Eleanor one day, after she had sat quietly through a long discussion of the disposition of various fields on the Home Farm.

'By no means. They employ an agent to do this. But it pleases me to help my uncle by acting as his agent, and I do believe that no employed man can take such an interest in the land and the people as one whose livelihood depends upon it. Sir Ambrose employed an agent for a while, but it was not found to be satisfactory.'

'In what way?'

'I am afraid he took advantage of my uncle's illness to line his own pockets. The temptation was great, no doubt, but he treated the tenants badly, and as a consequence the land was in very poor heart. It has taken a long time to remedy, but most of the farms show a good profit now.'

'It is not just the land that has benefited,' said Amy warmly. 'I know you have done a great deal to improve housing conditions among your workers, for Edgar—Mr Lutcome, that is—has told me, and I have seen some of the new cottages myself.'

'I am afraid my motives are not entirely those of disinterested benevolence,' he replied. 'I have always believed that men who are well treated will, by and large, repay you by working willingly and well.'

'It is not an idea that is held by most men in your position,' said Eleanor drily.

'No, it has not been popular with some of our neighbours. They are beginning to see the results, however. Families who live out their lives in dark, damp, insanitary cottages, however picturesque they may look on the outside, are never entirely healthy. A man who is bent double with rheumatism, or who is weakened by frequent fevers and colds, cannot work as well or as long as a man who is fit. Already I think the signs are there; I believe that the tenants' children now at the school are far healthier than those living in our neighbours' cottages.'

'Yes, they are, and better fed too. And as a result, of course, they learn much faster. Are the parents better off because they can work longer hours?'

'Partly, but also because I pay slightly higher. The other bone of contention with our neighbours is that I mollycoddle the men by paying them ten shillings a week, instead of nine. One shilling more a week is not much, to be sure, but it does help provide a few extras.'

'That is not so high,' objected Eleanor. 'It is eleven or twelve shillings in the north, I believe.'

'The farmers in the north have to compete with factory wages,' said Charles. 'Round here nine shillings is the usual amount. Of course, the older men remember the time when it was nearly twice that, when corn prices were so high during the wars against the French.'

'Bread is still dear,' said Amy sadly.

'Of course it is, and will be until they make an end of the Corn Laws,' said Eleanor.

Charles laughed at her vehemence. 'You would abolish them, then?'

'Of course I would,' cried Eleanor. 'Would not you?'

'As one of the farmers that the law protects, I would not. But,' he went on quickly as she was about to protest, 'as an employer, I would. I, too, have seen the hardship that it has caused. I think it very likely that it will be repealed soon. I have a friend in the House, and he keeps me informed of what is said and done there. According to him, Gladstone has quite turned against it, and now Mr Peel seems to be suffering a change of heart. I gather that as long ago as last March he was unwilling to reply to Cobden, who was holding forth as usual against the Laws. Peel actually crumpled up his notes, and asked Sidney Herbert next to him to answer. I believe he said "You must answer this, for I cannot."'

'Surely the bad harvest, and the Irish potato famine, must have helped him to decide?'

'Yes, a bad harvest was, dare I say, needed, to help push opinion. When the weather was so fine in June it looked as though the harvest would be good, but of course the endless downpour in August changed all that. And, as you say, the potato blight. Of course, the price of corn means little or nothing to the Irish, who live mainly on potatoes anyway—or did, when they could. But I believe that it gave a warning of what could happen if corn stayed at a high price in this country. At present potatoes are grown, but not widely. If bread stays dear, poorer people are bound to turn to potatoes as a substitute, as the Irish have done. Then, should the blight reach here, it would mean not only starvation, but rebellion and insurrection as well. That is a danger that is always with us.'

'Papa brought home an Irishman last year, to give him a meal and some help. Of course, there are so many of them in Manchester—I believe as many as one in five of the working men. He had come over to Liverpool, and, finding no work, had walked through the country, begging as he went. He said all his family, almost all his village, had perished in the potato famine. There was nothing, literally nothing, for them to eat, except the rotten potatoes that smelt so bad they could not force them down. It was most affecting. I believe he found work soon after, building railways.'

'Yes, many of them have ended up there. It is hard work, a hard life altogether, never staying in one place for any length of time, but I believe they are quite well paid. It is true that the Irish have suffered terribly in recent times. From that point of view alone, it is right that the Corn Laws should be repealed. But it will bring about much change, if it happens, as I believe it will soon.'

'Change for the better,' said Eleanor.

'Perhaps. Certainly our attitudes to farming will have to change. Where, before, landowners could to an extent rely on an artificial price to bring in their money, now they will have to make their land support itself. The income tax of sevenpence in the pound has to be found, too, at least for the next three years. I am sorry, I must be boring you.'

'Not at all,' said Eleanor truthfully. 'I had no idea it was so complicated. How must these changes be effected?'

Charles leaned forward in his chair, his face alight with an enthusiasm she had never seen there before.

'The old, out-of-date methods must go,' he said. 'Farmers are, have always been, stubbornly traditional, resistant to change of any sort. But they will have to change! The old ways of their grandfathers and great-grandfathers will not do. When I first took charge here, I found that the old wooden ploughs were still in use, although the Rotherham plough has been available for thirty years!' He paused, and Eleanor, who had not the slightest idea what the Rotherham plough might be, murmured an exclamation. 'Yes, indeed,' he continued, 'and some of the land here is very heavy, clay for the most part, though of course at the foot of the downs it is chalkier. I have almost had to force the tenants to put in drainage. Once they saw the results on the Home Farm they were easier to convince, but of course it was a great deal of labour, and they were unwilling to spend time and energy on it.'

'And I have heard you speak of guano, I believe,' Eleanor dredged up from her memory. 'Have you succeeded in persuading them to use it? It is a fertiliser, is it not?'

'Yes, they will use it, if I am prepared to pay for it,' he said sourly. 'I hope to have some good results from using it on the Home Farm this year, and then they might be prepared to try it. But it is uphill work. Of course, it is not cheap, and one must be careful about the quality, but I am sure it is a good thing. I just have to persuade the tenants of it!'

'Yet you enjoy your work?'

'Of course! What could give more satisfaction than to see a field that was previously waterlogged, good for nothing, producing a fine crop of corn, or hay?'

'And helping to feed the hungry,' put in Amy, her eyes shining. He laughed at her, but kindly.

'You must not attribute your own noble motives to me, Amy. Though the end may be more food, I fear I take more interest in the means.'

'Yet the end is achieved,' she replied tranquilly.

'I had no idea farming was so interesting to you,' said Eleanor. 'I thought you only looked after the estate to help Sir Ambrose.'

'In the beginning, that was so. Oh, I was brought up to farming. My own estate is hardly more than a large farmhouse, and farm. My father had money invested, as well, and his mother had come from a wealthy family and she left much of her fortune to me. I always wanted to travel and see the world, and as soon as I finished university I set off to Europe. There was not enough work for me, running my own small place, and I wanted to do something—oh, I don't know, something great in the world! Do not ask me what. I suppose I intended to come back one day, when I was older, perhaps to settle down with a wife to rear a family of children. But at that time I was free of all encumbrances, and I went vagabonding off to Europe, travelling as the fancy took me.'

'It sounds rather uncomfortable,' remarked Amy.

'Miss Stay-at-Home!' Eleanor laughed. 'I think it sounds wonderful. I am ready to die of envy. How I would have loved to do such a thing!'

'Really, Eleanor, you quite shock me.' Amy was ruffled. 'How could you suggest it? To go off and leave

Papa and me! And travelling on your own! You should not say such things, even to me.'

'I did not mean I wanted to leave you and Papa, Amy. Only that if I had been in such a position as Charles, I would have liked to travel like that.'

'Even so,' Amy was only slightly mollified, 'I cannot think that any properly brought-up young girl would ever wish to do such a thing, now or in the future. Travelling alone, and abroad!'

Seeing that Amy was shocked and upset, Eleanor at once begged her pardon. 'Do not be so vexed with me, Amy. I did not say I would ever do such things—surely you know I would not?—but only that I would have liked to. One may dream a little, after all.'

'Surely it is better to think only of what is possible, and suitable? I sometimes think you allow your imagination too free a rein, Eleanor. It is not right to question the Divine Providence who has doubtless put you here for a purpose.'

It was not often that quiet Amy scolded her sister, and her remarks were received in a respectful silence. Even Charles, who had some sympathy for Eleanor's dreams, refrained from looking at her. He tactfully returned to their previous topic of conversation.

'When I first came home,' he resumed, 'after Richard's disappearance and death, everything was in such a muddle that I did not know where to begin. At first, as I told you, I spent some time in France, looking for that poor girl, Lucy Hargreaves. My uncle was in such a state, he was quite unfitted to see to anything. It was at this time that the agent he employed really did the harm. He had been misappropriating money from the rents for some time, in a small way, but now he really went to town. As soon as he heard I was coming back, he disappeared, taking with him not only every penny he could lay his hands on, but also the records of the previous few years, which were of greater value. I was—pretty stunned, myself. I suppose it was a year before I started to take a proper interest in everything. At first it was just a duty, something I had to do as my uncle's heir, but the more I did the more it began to fascinate me, and now you might say I am just another country squire, wrapped up in his crops and his stock.'

'Will you still run the estate, when you are Sir Charles?'

He looked at her in surprise. 'I shall never be that. The estate itself is not entailed, and my uncle can leave it where he wishes, but the title goes in the male line. I am only related to him through my mother.'

'Who will the future baronet be? It must be a disappointment to him, that he will get the title but not the estate.'

'I do not suppose he has ever thought about it, since there was never any likelihood of him succeeding to the estate, any more than I regret not getting the title. You have met him, I believe, on the night of the party. And on the downs, the day you fell.'

'Mr Jeremy Hammond? He said he was only a distant connexion.'

'A little more than that, although he has never been close to this side of the family. His grandfather, James, was the younger brother of Sir Ambrose's father, my grandfather. We are second cousins.'

'Not a close relationship, perhaps, and yet he lives not far from here, so you must have known one another all your lives.'

'Known, yes, but I am afraid we have never been friends. As children we disliked one another, and the feeling has persisted. We see as little of one another as possible. He does not live down here permanently. He prefers to be in London.'

'He has land down here?'

'Yes, though I believe it is heavily mortgaged by his father, who lost a great deal of money in gambling. I have heard, however, that some of the mortgages have been redeemed in the last few years, though I do not know where the money could have come from, for I have never known Jeremy Hammond to lower himself to work.'

'Perhaps he gambles more successfully than his father?' suggested Eleanor.

'Maybe. He would take a chance, but not, I think, one that might put him at risk. As a boy he would always be encouraging others to mischief, but was never there for his share of the blame or punishment. Richard and I used to hide from him, if he visited.'

His face lightened with a reminiscent smile, and Amy encouraged him.

'Where did you hide?'

'We had our own special places. Here, of course, there are plenty of hiding-places in the shrubbery and the woods, so when he found one place we just changed to another. At my home we had one very special place, an old hollow tree. It was an old oak, very big, and the beauty of it was that it did not look hollow. We only found it by accident, when I climbed up after a bird's nest. I slipped down inside the tree, and it was lucky Richard was with me and went to fetch a rope, for I could never have climbed out on my own. There was space enough inside for both of us to sit down, and we kept a rope with knots in it hanging down the inside, so that we could get in and out easily.'

'What fun you must have had!' said Eleanor enviously.

'Yes, we called it our castle, and never told anyone about it. It used to infuriate Jeremy that he never managed to find out what and where it was. He used to follow us, but we were too careful for him. He never could bear to think that we knew something that he did not.'

'Is the tree still there?'

'I suppose it might be, although it is years since I looked. It belongs to the happy days of childhood.' His expression became sombre, and Amy quickly distracted him with a question about farming to lead his thoughts back to safer, less emotional ground.

Eleanor was very thoughtful for the rest of the day. The knowledge that Jeremy Hammond would inherit the title from Sir Ambrose had come as a surprise to her, for at the party she had formed the definite impression that the relationship between them was very slight. Mr Hammond had, she thought, been at some pains to make her think so. She also felt sure that Charles had not particularly wished to talk about him that morning. She determined to question him further. It seemed to her impossible that a man should not resent inheriting a title without the land and the income that would normally dignify it, more particularly if, as Charles had said, his own estates were encumbered. Accordingly, the following afternoon, she picked a moment when Mrs Wyckham was dozing, and Amy had left the room in search of some silks, to ask him further questions.

'If, for some reason, you were not to inherit from Uncle Ambrose, Charles, who would?'

His look showed her that he had not been taken in by her casual approach. 'If I did not know you better, I should have thought that you were cherishing hopes of doing so yourself.'

She flushed with annoyance. 'You know very well that I would not dream of such a thing!'

He laughed. 'One of the things I find so amusing about you, Eleanor, is the way you jump at every little thing I say. You positively ask to be teased, you know. Now do not be angry: remember that I said, "if I did not know you better". But I do, and you have no need to defend yourself. I know you have no mercenary motives. You mean, of course, if I were to die?' he finished bluntly.

'Yes,' she replied with unusual brevity. He frowned.

'That, of course, would depend on my uncle.'

Recognising this time that he was teasing her, she suppressed her rising irritation.

'Naturally it would,' she said mildly, 'but I cannot believe that you have not any idea. There cannot be that many to choose from.'

'If you cherish hopes, dear cousin, perhaps you wish me to throw myself on my sword, in the Roman fashion. It would be a most gentlemanly act, would it not?'

'You are quite shameless,' she snapped, 'and while the act might be gentlemanly, such a suggestion is most certainly not. I would never expect Uncle Ambrose to leave Oaklands to us, as you very well know. It was you, after all, who begged us to come here!' She saw that he was laughing at her, and subsided.

'I apologise, I apologise, only do not look daggers at me like that! You make me quite frightened, and in my state of health, you know...' He let his voice die away plaintively, and she had to laugh.

'It is most unfair that you can make me laugh, even when I am angry with you. But do not think I have not seen through your tricks, for I have not forgotten that you have not answered me. I will answer myself, then, and say that it seems to me very likely that Mr Jeremy Hammond would inherit the estate as well as the title if you were to die before Sir Ambrose. You may not like him, but he is the nearest relation there is, and there is no actual harm known of him.'

'Nor any actual good. But is it quite likely.'

'And since you tell me that his land is heavily mortgaged, he would doubtless be very glad to inherit.'

'Who would not be?' His reply was mild, but he looked at her sharply.

'So you could say,' she continued, 'that he has a strong motive for wishing you—out of the way.'

'You lay yourself open to serious charges of slander, my dear Eleanor. Such thoughts are better not expressed in public.'

'Of course not, I am not completely hare-brained! But you must admit—'

'I admit nothing,' he said, his voice cold. 'I would thank you not to concern yourself in this. I, too, can see further than the end of my nose, and I also see that there might well be danger in this. It is not women's work.'

Eleanor paled with anger.

'Of all the ungrateful...I was only....oh, you men! Never fear, I shall not meddle in your masculine affairs. And you may go to—to the devil, before I help you! And don't laugh at me!' She ran from the room, just managing not to slam the door behind her, and made her way to her bedroom, where her fury gave way to a burst of tears.

Charles lay on his sofa, and cursed himself. It was true that he was constantly tempted to tease Eleanor; he enjoyed seeing her rise so easily to his bait, and loved to watch the different emotions as they crossed her face, for she was a poor hand at hiding her feelings. This time, however, he realised that he had handled things badly. His own thoughts on the subject of his accident, and Eleanor's guesses, seemed to be the same. If they were right, then Jeremy Hammond was a dangerous customer. Charles was quite clear in his mind that the accident that had befallen him had been intended, not to maim or frighten, but to kill. If help—and witnesses—had not been so close at hand, Charles would have had his skull broken where he lay, and no one would have been any the wiser.

That Hammond feared and probably hated him he was sure. While there had been two heirs for the property, it had possibly not occurred to him that there was any likelihood of his inheriting—or had it? Had he, perhaps, not known that the estate was not entailed? If that were the case, he would have expected to become the heir to everything when Richard had died. It would have come as a nasty shock to him to find that only the title would go to him, and that Sir Ambrose was free to leave the property as he wished. Certainly, since Richard's death, Hammond's attitude to Charles had changed.

Then, too, there had been the scene on the downs, which Hammond had probably seen. Charles thought back to that moment when he had all but held Eleanor in his arms. She had been soft and yielding, and his own fear and anger for her safety had exposed deeper feelings than he had been conscious of. Certainly, in that moment when her face was so close to him, it had seemed almost the natural thing to kiss her. He would certainly have done so, had they not been interrupted. He wondered if she had realised—probably not. Girls, he knew, were not supposed to think of such things, until they were engaged. He wondered, also, how she would have reacted. Conventionally, as a well-brought-up young lady should, by a recoil, and possibly a slap on his face? Yet she was not particularly conventional. Would she, perhaps, have kissed him back...?

He realised that he was day-dreaming, and pulled himself firmly back to reality. He thought it possible that the sudden attack on him had been precipitated by the fear that he might be becoming interested in Eleanor, or in Amy, who was after all a very lovely girl. Once he was married, there would undoubtedly be further heirs, and Hammond's chance would be lost. Somehow, he thought, he must persuade Eleanor that since he was safe in the house, she herself was at greater risk than before. And he must do it without raising either her suspicions or her hopes. He was not ready, yet, to make his feelings known to her. He hardly knew what they were, as yet, and with all this on his mind, romance must take a second place.

Half an hour later Eleanor was calm again, and was just washing her face to remove the traces of tears when Annie came in. Seeing Eleanor, she stopped, and glanced behind her down the corridor before closing the door.

'What is it, Annie. Have you something to tell me?'

The maid nodded, then looked enquiringly towards Amy's door.

'It's all right, she is with Mrs Wyckham. Is it to do with the child?'

Annie nodded again. Eleanor took her hand and drew her to the window-seat, where they might both sit.

'You know that Jane, the housemaid, miss, has been very kindly to me since we arrived?'

'Yes, and I was so glad to see it. I was afraid you would be lonely, moving so far away from everything you know.'

'Oh, no, Miss Nell, not at all! She is the first friend I have ever had, outside the family!' Eleanor smiled her pleasure. 'Well, yesterday was Jane's half-day, and she invited me to go with her to visit her parents in the village. Pleasant souls, they are, and made me welcome. Of course, they have a lot of children, and Jane wanted to hear all the news. They're mostly in service, like Jane, but one of them, Jem, has been taken on by Farmer Hargreaves, not two months since.'

'Farmer Hargreaves? Up on the downs?'

'That's right, Miss Nell. They were pleased, because he's not too clever, like. Not simple, you know, but a bit lacking. A good, steady worker, though, Jane says, once he's understood what he's to do. He's happy enough there, though Hargreaves is a stern master, and sends his money home to his mother every month, proud as proud.'

'Hargreaves is patient with him, then?'

'I wouldn't like to say. Jem wouldn't mind him being silent, you see, for he's not got much to say for himself either. But last time he came home, he had a tale to tell. Seems he'd heard a child, up at the farm, though he'd not seen it, and his master had said nothing. He said he couldn't understand what the voice said, and when he asked his master he got nothing but a beating for his pains, and Hargreaves all the time shouting of sin, and evil, and the devil, so the poor boy was terrified half out of his wits! He thought there was an evil spirit in the house, and was scared to go back.'

'What did his parents say?'

'I think they thought he'd imagined half of it. Hargreaves is known in the village for his views on religion, and since he lost his daughter he's seen the devil's hand everywhere. I kept mum, and came back as quick as I could to tell you about it.'

'A child!' exclaimed Eleanor. 'I, too, heard a child cry out, when I was there.'

'It is not so far away, miss, through the woods. Could that have been the boy that was seen here?'

'Certainly, there are no other boys near enough to come on their own. But why is he there? Where has he come from, and why is he kept hidden? Jem did not say there was anyone else there—the child's mother, perhaps?'

'Oh, no, miss.'

'And the house is not so large that he could keep her existence secret for long. Yet why should he keep a child there? He is not the kind of man who would take in a waif to care for, and you say he speaks of evil...'

'His daughter, miss?' Eleanor reflected that she should have expected Annie to know all about the old scandal, since in a house like this the servants invariably knew all the secrets of their masters. They stared at one another in surmise.

'But that would mean that this child is Sir Ambrose's grandson, by blood if not by name! I must see him, Annie, if he really does exist. But first, I must see the picture of Richard as a child that is in Sir Ambrose's bedroom.'

'Come now, miss. Sir Ambrose is downstairs, and the house is quiet.'

With Annie going ahead to see that no one was about, Eleanor crept into Sir Ambrose's room. The picture was a small water-colour on ivory, placed where Sir Ambrose could see it from his bed. Eleanor gazed at it, trying to memorise it. Then she slipped back to her own room.

'I must go now, Annie, while the picture is still fresh in my mind.' As she spoke she was changing out of her indoor gown, and into a walking-dress.

'Not alone, miss! It's not safe! Let me come with you.'

Eleanor considered, absently biting her lip. She was reluctant to face the angry farmer a second time on her own, and whom else could she take? Not one of the grooms, for they would think it very odd, and besides would tell Charles, which was not to be thought of. Eleanor knew very well what he would be likely to say to such a venture, and she was determined that she would show him that she was not just some helpless female. This was her own discovery, and she must follow it up. Annie was strong, and utterly loyal.

'Very well, then, we will go together. Fetch your things, but be quick.'

CHAPTER ELEVEN

ELEANOR was careful to wear quite different clothes from those in which Hargreaves had seen her before. She put on her riding habit, which was smart but, being old, not too smart, and with it the hat she wore when on horseback. Hats had been out of fashion for some time for everything except riding, and the advantage of this one was that she had a lacy veil that draped from it, which partially obscured her face. She could only hope he would not wonder why she was wearing a habit to go out walking. As they walked briskly through the woods she and Annie agreed to circle round and try to come at the farm from the opposite direction, even though it meant adding a considerable distance to their journey. The days were short, but there were still at least two hours of daylight remaining to them. If they were challenged, they would say that they had come from the village, and had mistaken their way.

In the event their caution was wasted, for they met nobody. From a distance the buildings and the yard looked deserted, and as they approached the house there was not even the barking of a dog to break the stillness. Greatly daring, Eleanor rapped at the door. She thought she heard a scuffling noise inside, but although they peered through such windows as they could reach, they could see very little, and the house appeared to be empty. It had the drab, grimy air of a place where there was no woman to care for it. The walls and roofs were sound, but dingy, and the windows had dirty glass and grimy curtains inside them. What they could see of the rooms was bare and cheerless: not a rug, not a cushion to soften the stone-flagged floors or the old wooden furniture.

Determined not to waste this opportunity, Eleanor began to search through the farm buildings. They contained nothing but what might have been expected: stores of fodder, an old plough, wooden buckets and rakes, and several implements that Eleanor did not recognise. All were old and well-worn, much better cared for than the furniture she had glimpsed through the windows, and stowed away tidily. The innovations that Charles was bringing in to his farming tenants had obviously not arrived here, and from the look of things Eleanor did not believe they ever would, in Hargreaves's lifetime, at least. A few chickens scratched busily round the yard, but luckily for Eleanor there were no geese to give warning of strangers.

She heard Annie call in a low, inarticulate voice, and hurried to her. She was pointing to the ground, and as she looked Eleanor saw, imprinted in the mud and now half-frozen, a footprint. Swiftly she stooped and looked at it. It was smaller than her hand, and had undoubtedly been made by a child, probably no more than five or six years old. It was exactly like the footprint she had seen in the rose-bed at Oaklands Court.

It was at that moment that they heard the sound of voices approaching. Eleanor seized Annie's hand, and together they ran between the buildings and down the path that Eleanor had taken on her first visit. When the bulk of the barn hid them from the yard, Eleanor stopped and, putting her finger to her lips, crept softly back. At first, to her disappointment, all she could hear was the murmur of two men in conversation. One of them sounded surly, and she concluded he must be Hargreaves. The other, from what she could hear, was a gentleman. As she listened, Hargreaves lifted his voice to a shout.

'No, I tell you! I'll not have it! It's the work of the devil, and not to be meddled with. Not by you. Not by me. Not by any man. Vengeance is mine; I will repay, saith the Lord.'

The gentleman's voice appeared to remonstrate, but at once Hargreaves drowned him out with shouted invective, heavily larded with scriptural quotations against sin and evil. Eleanor judged it wiser to be gone.

They were about half-way home, however, when Eleanor heard her name being called. Looking up, she experienced a sudden feeling of *déjà vu* as she saw Mr Jeremy Hammond riding towards her. Her heart gave a thump of apprehension, but she kept her face calm.

'Good day, Miss Hunter. You are far from home! Not in any difficulties, I trust?'

'None, thank you, Mr Hammond,' she replied coolly as he dismounted to speak to her. 'I have not had any air for some days, and have undertaken a longer walk than usual in consequence. You have heard that Ch— the Mr Wyckham met with an accident a few days ago?'

Did his reply come perhaps just a shade too quickly?

'An accident? I had not heard.'

She found this hard to believe. In a country area such as this it was local news that people found most interesting. The important people might have a London paper sent down, but often they were more involved in what their neighbours, or their servants, had to tell them about village affairs. Something as potentially serious as Charles's fall would have been about the neighbourhood in no time, for many of the servants in the different houses were related to one another, and there were always visits being made. When one lady made a morning call on another, her coachman could be relied on to relay any items of interest to the downstairs staff while he was being entertained, and it was next to impossible to keep a secret of any size from one's servants.

'Yes, he had a fall from his horse.'

'That does not sound like Charles Wyckham. He was always such a dashing rider.'

There was a shade of satisfaction in his voice, she was sure, which made her continue, 'Oh, he is. Only this time, you see, there was a patch of ice under the snow, and his horse slipped. It was by the greatest good fortune that he was not killed.'

This time she was positive that she detected a look of chagrin on his face, but he replied merely, 'How dreadful! Of course, these icy patches do occur at this time of year. He is not badly injured, then?'

'Only a broken collarbone and a sprained ankle, and they are mending fast.'

'I am so relieved to hear it. And you have been helping to nurse him? I hope he has not been a troublesome patient?'

'Not at all,' replied Eleanor primly, suppressing the memory of the number of times when only his invalid condition had prevented her from giving Charles the talking-to of his life. 'My sister and I, naturally, have been keeping him company, with his mother, while he is laid up. Of course, it is irksome for him to be confined to the house, but between us we have kept him . . . entertained.'

'He is to be felicitated,' he said with mechanical civility. 'You and your delightful sister have become quite settled then, at Oaklands Court?'

'Oh, yes,' said Eleanor blithely. 'Sir Ambrose is everything that is kind, and we look upon it as our home, now.'

She shivered as she spoke, for the wind was cold. He was all contrition.

'How uncivil of me, to keep you standing in this cold
wind. Should you be so far from...home...in this
weather, and without protection? It seems unwise. I am
surprised that Wyckham permits it.'

'Mr Wyckham has no jurisdiction over me,' she replied haughtily. 'In any case I am, as you see, accompanied by my maid, who is well able to take care of me,
if I should be in need of it,' she added repressively.

'Ah, your maid, yes! An excellent female, no doubt,
but still a female. I would have thought a footman or a
groom would have been more appropriate to your position; after all, you are practically a daughter of the
house, are you not?'

'By no means. I would not lay claim to such an
honour.'

'But you must allow me to accompany you home. I
am sure Wyckham would never forgive me if any harm
were to come to you!'

He spoke lightly, but it seemed to her that he was
watching her reaction closely. He seemed determined to
find out what her relationship with Charles might be,
and she thought back to that unlucky meeting before,
so near to this one. She lifted her chin.

'I am sure your cousin would not expect it. He has
no responsibility towards me, and he knows that I am
well able to take care of myself.' She stifled the recollection that Charles all too obviously thought no such
thing, and would in point of fact be furious if he knew
how she had spent her afternoon.

A quick frown showed her that he had not missed her
knowledge of the family relationship between him and
Charles, but he continued suavely, 'Surely the responsibility any gentleman must feel towards a young and, may
I say, lovely young lady who is living as a member of

his household,' he reproved her. 'You must allow me to insist. It will be a pleasure to further our acquaintance.'

In the face of such bare-faced flattery and determination, she could do nothing but thank him with what civility she could command. He politely offered her a seat on his horse, and, thinking that sitting above him she would be at an advantage, she accepted. Since there was no convenient place to mount, he was forced to bend and offer his hands as an aid, and she had some satisfaction in planting her extremely muddy boot squarely in his expensively gloved fingers. He took it without complaint, and she murmured an insincere apology as he turned to wipe his hand on a tussock of grass. He paused for a moment, staring at the tussock, then turned back to her. Eleanor settled herself with some difficulty on the horse, missing the pommel of her own lady's saddle, and rather wishing she had elected to stay on the ground. He took the horse's rein to lead it, and Annie dropped back behind them, as a servant should.

He began by questioning her closely about the route she had taken, but she was able to plead ignorance of local names, saying only that she had walked along the downs for a while and was now returning by a different route. He mentioned several things she might have seen, and fortunately she remembered enough of the locality to be able to answer that she had indeed passed the old chalk quarry, but that she had not noticed the windmill in the distance. Not much to her surprise, he did not mention the farm, though he did ask her if she had passed any buildings, or met anyone. She summoned up her blankest, most innocent look.

'Oh, no, Mr Hammond. You are the only person whom I have seen up here this afternoon, and as for buildings—it is the beauties of nature that I have come to admire, not the local architecture!' She gave a tinkling laugh that to her own ears sounded false and inane, but he seemed to accept it. Before he could resume his questioning, she countered it by telling him, in great detail, about the buildings in Manchester. She had the satisfaction of seeing that he was extremely bored, but good manners prevented him from interrupting her, and she made sure that she gave him no opening for changing the conversation. He could hardly walk away, either, she thought, when she was sitting, rather precariously to be sure, on his horse!

To her relief he took his leave of her when they reached the drive, saying that he must be on his way, but that he was glad to have seen her safely home. As she walked up the drive she had the uneasy suspicion that he was standing and watching her, and when she turned to look she found that he had not moved. She lifted a hand to wave and he did the same, then turned to mount his horse and ride away.

'If you ask me, miss, he was making sure you really were going back to the house,' said Annie.

'Yes, having first made sure where I had been,' Eleanor replied thoughtfully. 'And he never mentioned the farm.'

'I think he might have come from it, miss.'

'So do I. I certainly heard a gentleman speaking. I wonder what he wanted that upset Hargreaves so.'

'Something to do with the child?'

'I think it must be. Now I come to think of it, he must have been near the farm the other time I was there, when I met him coming back just as I did today. I wish I had dared question him about what he had been doing up there, as he did me. I suppose he would only have said he was out for a ride. I did not think I had better show too great an interest in where he had been, though he certainly questioned me closely enough.'

'I'm afraid he may have known where we had come from, miss. Did you see how he wiped his hands on the bit of grass, after he had helped you up? When you walked on I had a quick look, and there was a piece of straw in the mud.'

Horrified, Eleanor stopped and, lifting the hem of her skirts, examined as best as she could the underneath of her boot. It was all too true. The sound, well-made boots, thoroughly greased and waxed, had kept her feet dry, and she had not hesitated to walk in the muddier patches in them, or bothered to pick her way in the farmyard. For most of their way the paths had been covered with a light layer of snow, which had prevented any dead leaves or grass from adhering, but in the farmyard constant use by man and beast had churned the snow into the chalky mud, and there was a generous layer of this on the sole, to which several pieces of straw had stuck when she had ventured into the barn.

'He had a good look at my foot, too, when he helped me to mount,' she said. 'And I suppose that the fact that I didn't mention the farm at all looks even more suspicious, now. Well, we know how we stand, I suppose. He must be fairly sure that I was there, and I think that he was. But does he know that I know? Or that I know he knows? Oh, dear,' she gave a slightly hysterical giggle, 'it sounds like a conundrum, if only it were not all so unpleasant. Well, it's done now, and can't be undone. Now, not a word of this to anyone, mind, not even Miss Amy. In fact, especially not Miss Amy, for it would frighten her to death. And not to Mr Charles, either.'

As they made their way upstairs, Eleanor was deep in thought. She found herself wishing strongly that she could tell Charles what had happened, but suppressed the thought ruthlessly. She would manage this on her own, and show him! Quite why she was so eager to prove to him that she could care for herself, and find things out by herself, she did not care to give much thought to. On the whole she was pleased with her afternoon's work. She had proved to her own satisfaction that there was, indeed, a child up at Hargreaves' Farm, unlikely though it seemed. She was also certain in her own mind that he was the boy she had seen in the garden, and at the window. That he bore a resemblance to the dead Richard, she was also sure, and it followed that he was most likely Richard's illegitimate son by Lucy Hargreaves. How he had come to be there, and for how long, she had no idea, but it could not have been very long. Even in so isolated a place, the normal sounds a young child made would be bound to excite a certain amount of attention.

She was more bothered by wondering what exactly Jeremy Hammond had been doing at the farm, and, more particularly, what it was he wanted that Hargreaves had refused to do. Nothing good, at least, unless it were good for Mr Hammond. Meanwhile she hated to think of that little boy up there with his half-demented grandfather, at the mercy of a man she believed to be, at least, unscrupulous. Somehow she must remove him from there, and see if Sir Ambrose would not care for him. Though his birth might be doubtful, his breeding was there to be seen in his face, and surely a place could be found for him, if not in this house, then somewhere secure where he could be cared for properly? As she stripped off her muddy habit she gave a wry smile—having set out to make herself a governess, was she to end up caring for her benefactor's dubious grandson? It was not quite what she had intended, but if it should be so, she would be quite content, she thought.

Returning to Mrs Wyckham's sitting-room, she found that her long absence had scarcely been noticed.

'You have missed a treat, Eleanor,' Charles informed her gravely. 'The Miss Jenningses have been here to solace my lonely sick-bed. Well, sick-sofa, I suppose. What a shame you were not here!' His eyes twinkled ruefully, and she understood that he was offering a kind of apology for their earlier disagreement. She smiled back.

'How very good of them! Why, it is only two days since they were last here.'

'Yes, it is certainly an encouragement to be better quickly. The sooner I am on my feet, the sooner I can run away from them!'

'For shame, Charles,' scolded Mrs Wyckham amid the general laughter. 'They are very nice girls, and you should be grateful that they come to see you.'

'Oh, I am, Mama, I am,' he assured her. 'And I am even more grateful when they go away! Surely you would not really like me to become too—too friendly with them? They are charming girls, of course, but complete ninnies!'

She sighed. 'You are far too fussy, Charles. I admit that they do giggle rather a lot, but complete ninnies is going too far. They cannot be called that: they have been taught both music and drawing by the best masters, and they have read all the latest books.'

'Read them, maybe, but as for understanding them...that is another matter. I think there should be more to a girl than an ability to sketch a view, or play through a sonata or two. Don't you think so, Eleanor?'

'I am afraid I can do neither of those things,' she admitted. 'Amy is far better than I at that sort of thing. They are the proper accomplishments of a young lady, though, and you should not mock them.'

'I do not mean to mock the accomplishments as such. Where would we be without ladies to play for us in the evening, and to record the beauties of nature in their sketch-books? But I would rather hear something simple, played with feeling, than their grand duets that just march along with no thought at all.'

Eleanor was pleased, for this seemed to her a compliment to Amy, who loved her music and played with great expression, though lack of time to practise meant that she had never been able to learn anything very advanced. She glanced at Amy, who was scarcely attending to their talk, being engrossed in counting the squares on a design for a church kneeler. Eleanor wished, not for the first time, that Amy would make a little more effort to join in conversations, for it seemed always to be Eleanor who offered opinions, and she wanted her sister to talk with Charles.

'I do not know why you are so hard on those poor Jennings girls,' complained Mrs Wyckham. 'At least they are cheerful, and obliging, and they will have a great fortune, which is not to be sneezed at, after all.'

'Come, Mama, now we are getting to the truth of it. How the possession of money does sweeten the pill, doesn't it?'

'You make me sound calculating and mercenary, but I am sure I am not. It is not as if they are hideous, or twenty years older than you, after all. It just seems such a waste, that is all.'

'I know what you mean,' put in Amy unexpectedly. 'Like taking a piece of bread, when one has eaten enough, merely to finish up the butter one has left on one's plate. I can never see the point of it, when I think of it rationally, and yet I cannot bear to let the butter go to waste!'

Charles laughed. 'I am sure the Miss Jenningses will not be left on the side of the plate for long!'

'Oh dear...I did not mean...not the Miss Jenningses, you know...' Amy floundered.

'We know what you mean.' Eleanor laughed. 'Now what will you give us not to tell them that you are expecting them to be scraped off the plate any day now?'

'And you could say that, like strong butter, a little of them goes a long way. Their visits can never be spread too thinly for my taste!'

Amy had to laugh at this, though she shook her head, for she could see that Mrs Wyckham was quite vexed.

'I am afraid my sister was not really attending to our conversation,' soothed Eleanor. 'You know she would never speak ill of anyone, and she was so busy working out her pattern that it was only the word "waste" that she heard. She has always had strong views on the subject, as you may see.'

'Of course,' Mrs Wyckham was all gracious condescension, 'living as you did, it is very understandable. Not that I am an advocate of wasteful habits—this very morning I told my maid to retrim one of last year's bonnets, instead of buying a new one! And if I find I do not like it, I shall let her keep it, so it will not be wasted, after all!'

'Very economical, Mama,' approved Charles, and Eleanor had to stifle a giggle, thinking as she did so of the five-year-old bonnets that Amy had recently refurbished so cleverly. She did not think that Mrs Wyckham had ever done such a thing in her life.

On the surface, all was well between them, but underneath, the relations between Charles and Eleanor remained strained. Charles knew only too well that he had handled things badly. He himself had for some time entertained suspicions about Jeremy Hammond. As a child Jeremy had been ruthless in pursuit of what he wanted, and although as adults they met but seldom, Charles had no reason to suppose that he had changed. Charles had plenty of time to think while he was convalescing, and a pattern seemed to be emerging that he did not at all like.

He had wondered before now whether Jeremy were the new head of the smuggling group. Such an exploit, where he would make the plans and let other men take the risks, was just like him. It would explain his sudden appearance of affluence. If he had indeed also been responsible for setting the trap for Charles—a trap, moreover, which had very nearly been successful—then he was a dangerous man. It also followed that he might well have been the one who had betrayed Richard to the preventives. Charles clenched his fists at the thought: it was just in Jeremy's style to murder by proxy. A dangerous man indeed. And the last thing that Charles wanted was for Eleanor to put herself into danger.

With a wry smile Charles remembered the moment when Eleanor, in her fear of Hargreaves, had been in his arms. Until that moment he had thought of her simply as a friend, someone who laughed at the same things, felt about things as he did, whom he could tease and joke with. Slightly dazzled by Amy's golden and white beauty, he had never seen Eleanor as an object of desire. Yet in that moment when he had held her in his arms he had felt a surprising urge not only to protect, but to caress. Even bundled in those ridiculous shawls, she had been both feminine and desirable, and he had come perilously close to kissing her.

Then had come his accident. On the night when she had sat up with him he had spoken freely to her, knowing that he could trust her neither to fall into hysterics nor to gossip about what he said. She had been clever enough to see almost at once that Jeremy had a strong motive for wishing him out of the way, and instead of discussing it with her he had done the very thing that he might have known would annoy her. In his anxiety to see her safe he had driven her from him, and now he cursed the weakness that would not let him make sure that she did nothing risky.

About her feelings for him, he was not sure. At the beginning he had derived much secret amusement from watching her attempts to throw Amy at him, while his mother worked equally strenuously to do the opposite. For Amy he felt no more than a sincere liking and friendship. Her beauty he admired, as he did her goodness and sincerity, but he had to admit that after an hour spent in her company he was bored. Eleanor, on the other hand, while she might annoy him, was never dull. She had always been completely natural with him, using no feminine wiles to attract, and treating him, in fact, as the brother he had called himself. Or brother-in-law, he thought wryly. When she was angry with him, as she had been earlier, she tended to treat him with scrupulous politeness, as far as she could, and he found he missed their old stormy relationship more than he would have thought possible.

The days passed slowly for him in his enforced idleness, until at last the swelling was gone from his ankle and he was able to walk and ride again. His first thought was for the estate, and for two days he drove himself hard, riding out all day round the farms. When he returned in the evening he was too tired to do more than eat his dinner and go to bed, so he saw little of the household. He was careful, however, to make sure that there was always a groom with him when he rode out— a sensible enough precaution, since his collarbone was only just knitting. At the same time he ordered Evans, the only man he had taken into his confidence, to keep a watch on the young ladies when they went out. As far as he could tell, all was peaceful. No sudden shots or carefully laid traps occurred, yet he had the feeling that Jeremy, if it was he, was only biding his time.

Lulled, in spite of what had happened, by the apparent quietness, he was quite unprepared for the trap when it came. Arriving home in the early dark of a February afternoon, he found the house in an uproar—Amy weeping uncontrollably and his uncle pacing up and down the hall. Casting aside his coat, gloves and hat, he strode towards them.

'What is the matter, Uncle? The servants are all running around like mad things, and here is Amy in tears. What can have occurred?'

At the sound of his voice, Amy jumped to her feet and ran towards him.

'Find her, please find her, Charles. It is getting so late, and she has been gone for hours!'

'Eleanor? Eleanor is gone? How long ago? Hush, now, Amy, it can serve no purpose to cry. Please tell me what has occurred, sir.' He led Amy back to a chair, where she sobbed in a distraught manner, and turned to his uncle for enlightenment.

'I hardly know, my boy. Eleanor went out for a walk this morning, in the grounds, as I understand. When she did not come in for luncheon we were a little alarmed, and sent some of the men to search the grounds for fear she might have had some mishap. They could find no trace of her, so a search was organised in the woods. So far they have found nothing.'

Charles turned quite pale.

'So she has been missing for five or six hours? You should have sent for me sooner.' He went to kneel by Amy, taking her hand soothingly. 'Think, now, Amy, whether you cannot give us some idea of which way she went.'

'I have thought and thought,' sobbed Amy, 'and I have no idea. She just said she was going for a walk, and I should not come because it was so cold. But she has not come back, and I am so frightened! Oh, Eleanor, Eleanor!' Her voice rose to a hysterical wail and Charles, though sympathetic, wished that she could summon a little more control.

'For God's sake send for her maid, and get her up to her room. I must think.'

'It is her afternoon off, sir,' said Browning quietly. 'I will see if she has returned.' Mrs Martlett was trying to persuade Amy to lie down in her room, but Amy was by now half fainting, sobbing convulsively. With an exclamation of irritation Charles bent and lifted her in his arms, carrying her as he had done on the night of her arrival. Unlike the first time, however, he was totally unmoved by the experience, his only thought to have her out of the way so that he could concentrate on finding Eleanor.

He had just reached the landing when there was the sound of running feet, and Annie appeared, white-faced and still in her outdoor clothes. She went ahead, opening the door of Amy's room for him, and indicating a couch by the fire where he could lay her down. Then she turned to him, her hand coming out to grasp urgently at his arm, trying desperately to tell him something. He took her hand.

'What is it, Annie? Is it Miss Eleanor?' She nodded. 'Do you have some idea where she might have gone?' She nodded again, more violently, and he tried to understand her nasal speech. Abruptly she turned from him and ran to the table, snatching at paper and pencil, scribbling in her haste. He leaned over her, watching the words forming.

'At Hargreaves? The child? What child? Are you sure she went that way? No, I see, but it is certainly worth trying. Blast the girl, what was she thinking of?' Annie was already pushing him from the room, wordlessly urging him to hurry, but Charles needed no urging. Downstairs the hall was momentarily deserted, as Browning had taken his master to sit down in the study. Charles snatched up his coat and gloves, then ran to the stables for a horse and a lantern. It was a clear evening, with some light still coming from the sky, and he set off on the most direct path, through the woods. He could not understand why Eleanor should suddenly take it into her head to go up to Hargreaves' farm, where she had been so frightened once before, and he had no idea what Annie meant by 'the child'. He wondered, too, why Evans had not been guarding her, and remembered that he himself had left no word where he was going. He could only hope that Annie would be able to tell them, for there was no time to turn back now. He did not know how unstable Hargreaves really was, but the thought of Eleanor up there, alone and perhaps afraid, was more than he could bear. He urged on the horse, regardless of the danger of a fall in the uncertain light. As he neared the farm he slowed his horse, then stopped in a group of trees and bushes and tied it up in their shelter. It might be better, he thought, to try to approach unobserved, and find out what he could about Eleanor's presence, and Hargreaves' state of mind. He made his way through the glimmering dark as quickly and as quietly as he could.

CHAPTER TWELVE

SCARCELY had the sound of Charles's departing hoof-beats died away before there came a knocking at the door. Such was the uproar and distress in the house that it was several minutes before Browning answered it, but for once the caller was not impatient, nor did he appear to be surprised at the delay.

'Ah, Browning. How is your master?' Suavely Jeremy Hammond nodded to the butler, holding out his hat and gloves, and waiting to be relieved of his outdoor coat.

'You'll have to forgive me for keeping you waiting like that, Mr Jeremy. I am afraid we're all at sixes and sevens just now. I don't know whether my master...' He paused, knowing that the visitor was not particularly a favourite with anyone in the household.

The visitor was all concern.

'Nothing serious, I trust? Sir Ambrose is not ill? Or my aunt? Mr Charles has not been riding carelessly again, and had another mishap?'

Browning frowned at the slur, but let it pass.

'No, no, Mr Jeremy. Nothing like that. It's Miss Eleanor—she cannot be found!'

'Good heavens! Of course, the young lady has been staying here for so short a time, we have hardly had time to get to know her. Perhaps she was not all that we had thought. She may have run off with some man, you know—such things can happen.'

Browning drew himself up.

'You must pardon my plain speaking, as one who has known you since you were a boy, when . ll you that

188

you have no business thinking such a thing, let alone saying it. If there had been anything like that, do you think we would not have known of it? Miss Eleanor is a very nice young lady, a very nice young lady indeed, and it's more than I can bear to hear such a suggestion.'

Jeremy Hammond saw that he had gone too far.

'Forgive me, Browning! Of course I had no business saying such a thing. You must believe that I spoke out of concern for my uncle. I should hate to think of him being taken in like that. Of course, if you vouch for her, I am sure that the young lady is everything that is proper. But where can she be? Has she been missing long?'

Browning, reluctantly, relented.

'She has not been seen since this afternoon. We are very much afraid that she may have met with some mishap when she went out for a walk. She was only intending a stroll in the grounds, but she may have been tempted to go further, and if she should have had a fall, with no one by to see her...' He paused eloquently.

'No one by? Surely so proper a young lady would not go far on her own?'

'It was too cold for Miss Amy, and it is the maid's afternoon off, she had gone out. That is why Miss Eleanor only intended to walk in the gardens. But they have been searched, and there is no sign of her!'

'Good heavens! This is serious, then. If she has been missing for several hours, and in this icy weather...tell Mr Charles that I will accompany him on his search.'

'Mr Charles is not here, sir.'

'Not here? But I am sure I saw him returning home, not more than twenty minutes ago! That is why I am here—I wished to ask him something.'

'Yes, he did come home, Mr Jeremy, but he seems to have gone straight out again. I don't know what happened, for I was directing the menservants to go and search further afield, but he is not in the house now. He must have gone to join in the search himself.'

A look of chagrin, unnoticed by Browning, crossed Jeremy's face.

'But he did not go with the men, or you would have seen him. Why should he rush off like that, without a word? Did he speak to no one?'

'I wouldn't like to say, sir. Miss Amy was in a terrible way, crying and carrying on about her sister, and he carried her up to her room. Mrs Martlett was there, but I believe she is with Mrs Wyckham now. She doesn't know where Mr Charles has gone, though, for Mrs Wyckham was asking about him, and worrying that he had gone without a word.'

'If Mrs Martlett is with my aunt, who is with Miss Hunter? She is not left on her own, surely?'

'Her maid will be with her, Mr Jeremy. She'd be back from the village by now.' The butler's bewildered tone showed that he thought this concern over Miss Amy pointless.

'Don't you see, man, that someone must have said something to Mr Charles to make him go off in such a hurry, without leaving word with anyone. It isn't likely to be Miss Hunter, but the maid, if she had just come back from the village, might have given him some idea. Have her sent for!'

'But Mr Charles is not likely to have got lost, sir. It is Miss Eleanor we are looking for.'

Jeremy Hammond fought down his rising irritation. He could not allow himself to appear too eager to find his cousin. He strove for, and achieved, a tone of calm reasonableness.

'Mr Charles may have some clue to Miss Eleanor's whereabouts. But he has only recently recovered from his accident. He should not be out searching on his own.

If I can find him, I can help him. After all, if Miss Eleanor has by any misfortune sustained some injury, she may need to be carried, and his shoulder is only just healed.

'Yes, of course, sir, I should have thought. I'll have Annie fetched straight away.'

Browning hurried off, and Jeremy strode impatiently to the fireplace, kicking abstractedly at the burning logs so that the flames leaped up, casting an orange glow on his frowning face, and setting sparks dancing in his eyes. He had not expected to find Charles absent. Biding his time, he had listened for his cousin's return, and had hoped to arrive, as if by chance, just at the right moment to accompany his search without occasioning any surprise. Now he must be off after him, as soon as might be. He could not lose him now, when everything was falling into place so well. He cursed under his breath, and turned as a rustle of skirts told him he was not alone.

He remembered Annie at once—the woman who had been with Eleanor up on the downs, the day he had been sure she had been to the farm. He eyed her with disfavour. Annie stood composedly before him, her hands clasped at her waist, her eyes correctly and demurely lowered. He could read nothing in her face.

'Now, then. Annie, isn't it?' She nodded, and he forced a friendly note into his voice. 'You must be very worried about your mistress, I suppose? I am going to help find her, but I want to know where Mr Charles went. Can you tell me?'

She did not look at him, but spoke in a low voice. The sound was odd, and he could not understand what she said.

'What is that? Speak up, girl.'

She spoke again, incomprehensibly. He found that his hands were clenching into fists, and relaxed them. The butler spoke, his voice expressionless.

'I am afraid Annie cannot talk very well, sir.'

'So I apprehend. Can you understand her?'

'I'm afraid not, Mr Jeremy. Only the young ladies understand her properly.'

'Then why the devil did you fetch her down?'

'You did insist on seeing her, Mr Jeremy.' The butler's voice was smooth, bland. Did he imagine there was a note of satisfaction in it as well? He bit his lip.

'She must have some other way of communicating. If nobody understands her, in the servants' hall . . . can she not write?'

'I would not like to say, sir. Mrs Martlett is in charge of the maids, of course. Can you write, Annie?'

No doubt about it, the man was taking an insolent satisfaction in being obstructive. When I become master here, just look out, old man, he thought, and the idea helped him to stay impassive. This was no time to show too much impatience.

'Yes, can you write, Annie?' She nodded unwillingly, still not looking at him. At his nod, Browning fetched paper and a pencil. She took them in both her hands and, turning her face away from Hammond, she lifted up her eyes and shot a sharp glance at the butler, a look that held both fear and a command. He did not react, but stood quietly by as she held the pencil in her right hand and slowly, laboriously, traced shaky letters on the paper. As soon as she had finished Jeremy snatched at the paper.

'Dont no. Mite hav gon to villig, i think.' In a spasm of irritation, he crumpled the paper and tossed it into the fire.

'The woman's not much more than an idiot. I can see I'm wasting my time. I'll just have to go after him, and see what I can do.' He thrust his arms into the coat that Browning held out for him, snatching hat and gloves and striding to the door, waiting with a tapping foot while Browning pulled the heavy oak slowly open, then he was gone at a run.

Browning turned to look at Annie, who had not moved. She looked at him and their eyes met in complicity. She smiled.

'Well, I hope you have good reason for that. Don't tell me you can't write properly, for I have seen it many a time, and I know very well that you're left-handed.' Her smile widened, and she took another piece of paper, holding the pencil this time in her left hand and writing with ease.

'Thank you. I do not trust him, and nor does Miss Eleanor.'

'Nor do I,' he answered her, 'or I would never have kept quiet while you played that charade. But why should he be so keen to find Mr Charles, I wonder? Surely it's Miss Eleanor he should be looking for? She's the one that's lost.'

His words brought an end to Annie's smile, and her eyes darkened with worry.

'There, now,' he patted her awkwardly on the shoulder, 'you get back to Miss Amy. There's nothing you can do down here, and worrying won't mend anything. Miss Amy's the one who needs you now. I'd say Miss Eleanor can look after herself.' He watched Annie turn and walk away, adding under his breath, 'I hope.'

Eleanor woke slowly, not sure at first whether she was not still trapped in some horrible dream. Her eyes were open, she was sure, and yet she saw nothing and, as in nightmares, she was unable to move. It was pitch dark and very cold, and she appeared to be lying on something hard and lumpy, that was certainly not any bed she had ever known. The hope that she might be dreaming died as consciousness returned more thoroughly; surely no dream had ever been as complete as this? She moved her head a fraction, wincing as a stab of pain shot through it. Confused, she tried to think back.

At first her memory was as blank as the darkness in front of her eyes. The day should have started, surely, as any other day: rising, dressing, breakfast? It seemed likely that she had done those things, she even remembered doing them, but one day was so like another; was it the same day she was remembering, or a composite of all the others that had begun in a like manner? And afterwards, what? A ride? That was quite possible. Perhaps she had fallen from her horse, and hurt herself. She could have tumbled into some hole in the ground— that would account for the darkness, for surely no night was ever as dark as this? She tried to pull up the memory of riding from the maelstrom of her muddled thoughts. The feel of the horse moving beneath her, the smell of leather tack and horse... She breathed, testing the air.

No scent of horse here. Nor was it such air as she might have expected in a hole or cave. There was no dampness, no breath of cold earth or sour stone, but a dry dustiness, even a whiff of summer. She could not have been unconscious for so long. It must be hay, the faint fragrance of last summer's harvest, and she was in some kind of building. A spark of triumphant pleasure lit up the blackness for a moment. Her head, though it might ache, was still working, then.

If she had not been riding, then she must have gone out walking, for nothing but the most severe weather

would keep her indoors for the whole day. Yes, that
seemed to fit. She had a hazy recollection of dressing to
walk—but surely only in the garden? She was sure that
she had been going out on her own, and that she had
intended to go no further than the shrubbery. Painstak-
ingly she thought back, going with her shadowy-
remembered self along familiar paths, down the walks
and alleyways she would have been bound to take. A
face swam out of the mists—the face of the dead
Richard. She could not have seen him, and yet...surely
she recalled following a figure that retreated before her?
If not Richard, then...the child? Yes, that was it.
Glimpsed in the distance, and followed...and then?
Nothing. It was like walking headlong into a wall.
Whatever had happened to her had happened then, it
seemed.

The pain in her head was subsiding, and she ventured
to move again. She tried to put out a hand to feel what
was around her, and found that she could not. There
was a moment of panic when she thought she was para-
lysed, that her limbs would not respond to her com-
mands, then common sense returned and she realised
that her muscles were working, and that something was
constricting her. Her cloak, she thought, was wrapped
tightly round her, and when she flexed her limbs to free
them she learned that she was in fact tied, a rope wound
round and round her so that she could free neither arms
nor legs. There had been no fall, no accident, then.
Someone had tied her very securely.

She gave a little sob of terror, and at once there was
a rustling sound, not far off. She held her breath, her
skin crawling and tingling with horror. Rats? The rustling sounded like the straw or hay she had guessed at,
and nothing could be more likely than that such stores
would be alive with vermin. Desperately she struggled,

pushing with her feet and straining to sit up, to get her head and face at least away from the floor. The rustling came again, and she froze. Out of the musty darkness came a whisper, a thin thread of a voice that sent icy shivers down her spine, the voice of a child so far gone in terror that all feeling was lost.

'*Qui est là? Il y a quelqu'un?*'

Not rats, at least! Eleanor summoned her schoolgirl French to answer.

'*N'aie pas peur. Je m'appelle Eleanor. Qui es tu?*'

'*Richard. Je m'appelle Richard.*' He pronounced the name in the French fashion, but for a moment her flesh crept again at the sound of that whispering voice. Then the child continued. '*Vous... vous n'êtes pas le Diable?*' he enquired tremulously. Eleanor felt a bubble of hysterical laughter rising in her throat. Perfect she might not be, but no one had ever mistaken her for the devil before.

'*Non, Richard,*' she whispered back. '*Je ne suis pas le Diable. Pourquoi dis-tu ça?*'

'*C'est mon grand-père,*' the small voice insisted. '*Il m'a dit que je suis le fils du Mal, le fils du Diable, et que le Diable viendra me chercher. Il m'a montré des dessins, dans un livre.*'

Eleanor felt her heart contract with pity and terror. 'He' could only be Hargreaves. She had already heard him ranting of the devil, knew of his obsession with guilt and sin, but what sort of man could terrify a child like that? To tell any child that he was evil, the son of the devil, was wicked, for she knew well that young children would believe what adults told them. To show him pictures in a book! She herself, as a child, had once seen a copy of *Foxe's Book of Martyrs*, and had had nightmares for a week as a result, and she could well imagine the kind of book that Hargreaves might have had in his possession. If this was, as seemed possible, his own daughter's child, how could he treat him like this?

'*Ce n'est pas vrai, mon enfant,*' she said gently. '*Ne le crois pas, ce n'est pas vrai. Tu es le fils du Bon Dieu, comme nous le sommes tous.*' She thought of her own father, who had built his life on that belief: that all people were God's children, however miserable and debased. How much more this poor innocent, be his birth what it might?

'*Vous êtes sûre?*'

'*Parfaitement.*' She put all her conviction into that whispered assurance, and it seemed it was enough. He gave a little sigh, the sound of one laying down a burden too heavy for his years. Suddenly she was angry, furiously angry, that anyone could treat a child so. It was a glorious feeling, that sent the blood pulsing through her cold, stiff body, and banished all fear. She struggled against her bonds, but to no avail. She called the child to come to her.

'*Richard, viens ici,*' she whispered urgently.

'*Je n'ose pas. J'ai peur.*'

She thought at first that he was simply frightened of the devils in his imagination, and, struggling with her small vocabulary, she explained that she could not move, was tied up, and that he must come and loosen the rope so that they might escape. He replied with a torrent of French and she had to make him go slower, and when she finally understood her heart sank.

It appeared that they were, as she had thought, in a farm building, the big barn at Hargreaves' farm. But they were up high, in the hayloft, which was old and had holes in the floor, and was not much used. The trapdoor was open, but the ladder had been removed. In the darkness there was a risk of falling through the trapdoor, or through a rotten piece of planking, and it was a very long way to the ground below. It was a place where Richard sometimes hid, when he was able to get out of the house, for Hargreaves usually locked him indoors. That very morning he had been locked in, but someone had undone the door—not Hargreaves, but another man—and had said he could go to look at the big house. He liked doing that, had done it whenever he could, so he had been quick to take advantage of the offer.

Eleanor's own memories came back more clearly. Had he seen her, that morning, she asked? He had, and had been frightened, and started to run away. He did not know what had happened to Eleanor, for he had come back and hidden up here, in the hayloft. Not long after, to his horror, the man had come back, and carried a big bundle up here on his shoulder. He had not seen Richard, but had rolled the bundle on to the floor and left. Richard had heard the ladder being removed, but had not dared to call out.

Trying to hide her own fear and desperation, Eleanor told Richard to crawl slowly towards her, feeling his way carefully with his hands, and testing the floor as carefully as he could. She herself lay perfectly still, for her own weight must be considerably greater than his, and she could not risk rolling on to a piece of rotten timber. It was difficult for him, for he had no very clear idea of where she was, and she dared not speak out loud, but at last his shuffling grew nearer, and then he was beside her. She felt his hand on the ropes, and for a moment it touched her face. It was icy cold. Then he found the knots in the rope, and began tugging at them.

'C'est dur,' he muttered. 'Je ne sais pas si je pourrai.' She talked to encourage him, keeping her whispering voice steady and calm. He could speak a little English, she found, doubtless learned from Hargreaves, for it was

larded with scriptural words. She felt that it bothered
him, however, and reverted to French, which it was a
relief to him to speak, as he had not been able to make
himself properly understood for some time. He did not
know how long he had been at the farm—it seemed to
him a long time, but since he said it had been autumn
when he arrived it could not have been more than a few
months. Nor could he remember his mother, though he
spoke of her with tender respect. The couple who had
cared for him, whom he called aunt and uncle though
he was careful to point out that they were not related to
him, had spoken of her often, and he felt as if he knew
her.

In reply to a further, tentative question, he said that
yes, he had been told that Hargreaves was his grandfather, the father of his mother. He, himself, did not
believe this, for he could not allow that this harsh, vi-
olent man could have anything to do with the sweetness
and gentleness of the young girl of whom he had been
told, and besides, the old man seemed to hate him, and
should a grandfather hate his own grandson? No,
mademoiselle, it was surely a mistake. Would she perhaps
be able to put it right for him?

All the while he kept on picking at the knot, while she
mastered her impatience and lay still. She was so cold
that her feet were quite dead, and her head was
throbbing, but she clung to the remnants of her anger,
and added to it her determination to help this poor child
who pulled at her rope, now with his fingers, now with
his teeth, in an attempt to loosen it. Suddenly he gave
an exclamation of pleasure, and a moment later she felt
the rope slacken. Her muscles protested as she moved,
but she fought herself clear of the entangling cloak and
reached out her numb hands towards the child. He was
trembling with cold and fear, and clumsily she gathered

him into her arms, cuddling him close and pulling the cloak round them both as well as she could.

For a moment his skinny little body was stiff and un-yielding, then he let her pull him on to her lap, and he buried his face against her, his arms clinging desperately round her as he wept out some of his fear and loneli-ness. She murmured soothing words in both French and English, and let her own tears roll unheeded down her cheeks, holding him to her and rocking him until his sobs died away.

The blood was returning to hands and feet, burning like needles of ice, and she welcomed the pain, flexing and rubbing at her fingers, and wriggling her toes inside her boots. The child was relaxed now, almost sleeping after his storm of emotion, and together they created a little cocoon of warmth inside the good, woollen cloak. Her mind was racing. Who had brought her here, and why? She was sure she had been in the garden when she was knocked out, and it was certainly not Hargreaves who had fetched her, but some other man who had used the boy to attract her deeper into the shrubbery, out of sight and earshot from the house. She must get out of the barn, and Richard with her. She was sure now that he must be Lucy Hargreaves's son, the illegitimate child of Richard Hammond, and named for his father. She felt a surge of protective tenderness as she pressed her cheek against the hard roundness of his head. Reluc-tantly she roused him, for they could not afford to rest now.

'*Il faut que nous nous sauvions,*' she whispered. They must go—and soon, before Hargreaves came looking for them. Richard shook his head, still pressed into the hollow of her neck, and she felt him tremble.

'*C'est trop haut sans l'échelle.*' His voice was de-spairing, and she had to accept the fact that he knew the building well. If he said it was too high without the ladder, then he must be right. They could not jump but, she thought with an uprush of hope, they might climb. They had the rope that had tied her up. Feverishly she pushed aside the folds of her cloak and felt for it, tugging it between her hands to test its strength. It was not very thick, but seemed quite strong. It would surely hold the weight of a child, and if she could lower him down perhaps he could replace the ladder, or at the very least go for help.

At that moment, just as the prospect of escape seemed imminent, there was a tiny flicker of light. They froze, not daring to move or speak. They were sitting near the wall of the barn, and the light was coming through a gap in the cladding. Slowly, trying not to make a noise, Eleanor turned so that she could peer through the hole she could now see was there. Her heart leaped, for down in the yard was Charles, surely Charles, with a lantern. She drew breath to call out to him, but at that moment there came a great bellow of rage, and Hargreaves appeared. In the flickering lantern-light he was a huge, shambling figure, his face dominated by two wide, staring eyes and a black cavern that was his mouth, shouting, 'Devil! Black fiend from hell! Thine hour is upon thee!'

Charles laid down the lantern in one hand, and started to lift the pistol that he held in the other, but the demented farmer was too quick. He swung his thick stick and caught the other a sharp blow on the side of the head. Eleanor winced as she heard the crack of wood against the skull. Charles dropped where he stood. Hargreaves remained still for a moment, looking down at the motionless body at his feet, then he lifted his head to the sky. Eleanor drew instinctively back as his face turned towards her, then reason conquered her fear and she put her eye to the gap again. Richard's hands clutched at her, and she shuddered as the wild laughter rang out. She watched in horrified fascination as Hargreaves picked up Charles's lantern, and with the other hand took hold of Charles by the back of his coat and dragged him towards the barn. He muttered as he walked.

'Death! Death! No more than he deserved. His blood be upon my head.' He disappeared from her view, and almost immediately the square of the trapdoor was illuminated. Eleanor could still hear his muttering, interspersed now with shrill giggles, but she could no longer hear what he was saying. She had no need to, however. Charles had fallen without a word, and his body had been limp as he was dragged through the yard. Charles was dead, and she could not spare the time even to weep for him—that must come later, if she and the boy were to escape at all. She heard a rustling, as if he were moving some fodder, then there came the sound of footsteps outside.

'It is done already, then? Good. I did not know whether he had come up here. And the child?'

The muttering broke off. Eleanor's first instant of relief at hearing Jeremy Hammond's voice was swamped by the realisation that he had expected to find what he had. Richard, who had replaced her at the gap in the wall, was pulling at her hand, and she bent so that he could breathe into her ear.

'C'est lui! C'est l'homme qui vous a portée ici. Je le reconnais.'

It was no surprise to her that it had been Jeremy Hammond who had lain in wait for her and brought her to this place. She saw only too well that, having failed in his first attempt on Charles, he had resolved to be rid of both possible heirs in one last try. Somehow he knew

about Richard, and he had used her as bait to get Charles
to come to the farm, inciting Hargreaves to a frenzy of
rage to do his evil work for him. Now Charles was dead,
and nothing stood between Jeremy and his inheritance
except a child, of whose existence the world knew
nothing, and cared less. She, of course, must die also,
for she had seen and heard too much. Already the top
of the ladder was scraping against the frame of the
trapdoor. Hargreaves had resumed his muttering and his
laughter down below, so the footsteps climbing up must
be Jeremy's.

Once again she felt that heartening lift of anger.
Charles might be dead, but the child lived, and she realised suddenly that Jeremy did not know that he was
with her, nor that she was not still tied up. With Richard
following her, she crept to the trapdoor, making as little
noise as possible, and hoping that the sound would be
covered by Hargreaves down below. Jeremy was clearly
silhouetted against the lantern-light, while she, if she were
careful, could remain hidden in the darkness of the loft.
He was about half-way up. Urgently she gestured to
Richard, and he nodded. When Jeremy was within a few
rungs of the top, she took hold of the ladder and pushed
as hard as she could, the child helping with all his
strength. At first nothing happened, but the ladder had
been set at a steep angle, and its feet were on a scattering
of slippery straw. Suddenly it moved, almost dragging
her into the hole, and crashed against the far side of the
trapdoor. For a moment she looked down into Jeremy's
face as he clung to what was now the underside of the
ladder. Then the bottom of the ladder skidded away,
and she turned her face away, hands pressed to her ears
to block out the cry he gave as he fell, and the heavy
thud as his body hit the ground.

Hargreaves gave another cackle of laughter.

'Fallen angel! Fallen angel! The imp of Satan was too much for you,' he shrieked. Eleanor realised that he could have no idea that she was up there, and that he thought Richard alone was responsible for Jeremy's fall. To her surprise he made no attempt to put the ladder back and come up after Richard. Instead he seemed to be heaping a mound of hay and straw in the middle of the barn, surrounding the big wooden timbers that supported the upper level and, ultimately, the roof. His giggling and muttering were louder now, and a few words reached her with horrifying clarity.

'Hell! Hell! Everlasting damnation! Eternal fires! Burn in Hell for evermore!'

Before she realised what he was doing, the demented man took up Charles's lantern and swung it round, smashing it against one of the wooden uprights. There was not much oil left in it, but it was enough. The burning drops ignited, and at once tongues of flame licked through the heaped-up fodder. The madman cried out wordlessly in delight, drowning Eleanor's own scream, then turned and lurched out. Eleanor heard the scrape of the barn door as he pulled it shut behind him, and heard his voice receding across the yard.

'Burn in Hell! Burn in Hell, the Devil and all his works!'

CHAPTER THIRTEEN

THE dry fodder burned quickly, and it would not be long before the wooden building became an inferno. Already they were both coughing in the smoky air that came up through the trapdoor, and flames were licking at the wooden supports, fringing them with a sparkle of gold where the rough edges caught the fire. The timber was old oak, as hard as stone, and might be slower to catch than softer wood, but soon it would burn and bring the barn crashing to the ground.

The crackling flames at least made more light. Careless now of the rotten floorboards, Eleanor hurried back to the wall for the rope. She had to bend low, pulling a fold of cloak over her face, for the open trapdoor was acting like a chimney and the space under the roof was already thick with smoke. Unable to see out of her streaming eyes, she groped for it, dragging it back to the light of the trapdoor. Now that she could see it she was afraid it would not be strong enough, for it was not new, nor was it very long. It would have to do, though. Squinting her eyes against the burning air, she struggled to tie a loop in one end of it, as small as she could make it to keep as much length as possible.

When it was made she slipped it over one of Richard's wrists, pressing his hands round the knot. He was crouching at the opening, his face buried low in his knees to protect it as far as possible from the smoke. He did not need telling what to do: sitting at the side of the trapdoor, he gripped the knot firmly, then nodded to her, and she braced herself to take his weight as he let himself slip down. The thin rope cut into her hands as she paid it out as fast as she could. When she reached the end, Richard was still some feet from the ground, and she let her crouching body come forward as far as she could, then lay with her arms through the hole, bracing her body to let him as far down as possible. He glanced up at her, then gave a quick look down and let go.

He fell as he landed, but was up again at once. The fire was spreading fast; its roaring filled her ears. Each breath burned in her lungs and she fought not to cough, lifting the edge of her cloak over nose and mouth once again. The little boy ran to the ladder, but as he tried to lift it she knew that it was hopeless. He was so small, so thin. He would never be able to lift it enough, for the length alone made it unwieldy even for a man, and it was of solid wooden construction. She looked at the rope in her hands, useless when she had nothing to tie it to. The flickering light of the flames showed nothing but loose hay around her.

The child stood helplessly, tears cutting clean runnels through the dirt on his face as he looked up at her. At the back of her mind she was filled with pride for him: child though he was, he would not save himself and leave her to die. Then she caught sight of a pitchfork stuck carelessly in a pile of hay. She gestured towards it. He looked puzzled, but fetched it obediently, while she hastily stripped off one of her petticoats and with hands and teeth tore off a long strip, which she tied to the end of the rope to lengthen it. Hastily she held up the knotted end of the rope and pointed to the pitchfork, then to the loop, putting her hand through the circle of rope. He nodded and pushed the handle of the fork through the loop until the metal end caught and held. She pulled it up.

When he saw her wedging the wooden handle across the opening of the trapdoor his face lit up, and at once he set about collecting a pile of unburned hay underneath the rope that now dangled down. Eleanor dropped her cloak down first, and, wishing she were not so hampered by petticoats, sat on the edge of the hole and leaned down to take a grip of the rope. It felt so insubstantial in her hands, but she did not give herself time to think about the consequences if it should break. Wrapping her legs as best she might round her lifeline, she began to climb down.

The handle of the pitchfork creaked and bent, but it held. Her hands could hardly grip the thin rope, and she could feel them beginning to slip. Try as she might, she could not halt the slide, but she hardly noticed the pain as her hands were burned by the friction. Suddenly her legs were gripping nothing, and then she hit the ground with a thump that knocked all the breath from her body.

She lay gasping and coughing on the pile of hay, but already Richard was tugging at her. She staggered to her feet. Around them the flames were licking at the walls. Near her lay Charles, and further away Jeremy, his head at an unnatural angle and his eyes staring sightlessly upwards. She gave a sob and, giving Richard a push towards the doorway, went to Charles. She could not leave his body there to burn. A trickle of blood ran down his cheek from the side of his head, and she grabbed the back of his coat, twisting her sore hands into the fabric and pulling him. He was so heavy. Her head was swimming, every breath an agony, but slowly the body slid across the floor.

Behind her she could hear Richard struggling with the heavy door. Perhaps Hargreaves had locked it. There was no knowing what he might have done in his state of madness—to lock the door on a burning building might seem a perfectly logical move to him. That he might be waiting for them outside the door was an idea she would not allow her mind to dwell on. She sent up a wordless prayer. Surely they could not get this far only to find themselves locked in the barn?

She was nearly at the door, and saw Richard straining at the heavy latch that held the door in place. As she was about to go to his aid the latch lifted, and with a creak from the old hinges the doors swung wide, so that Richard almost fell out into the yard. There was a blast of cold air that was the most delicious thing she had ever experienced. Her head cleared, and her energy was renewed. Behind her the fire roared up, flames driving through the trapdoor to the roof, fed and impelled by the same rush of air. For a moment her thin lifeline of rope showed as a long line of fire, then it shrivelled and was gone. The heat of the flames was intense now. The walls were well alight, and the black hole that was the open doorway was surrounded by fire. Suddenly Richard was beside her, grabbing Charles's arm and adding his childish strength to hers. Together they dived through that doorway into the blessed cold and calm of the deserted farmyard. Charles's body bumped over the stones and frozen ruts as they dragged him away, foot by foot, inch by inch, to the far side, for there was still danger from the falling timbers when the building should collapse.

After what seemed a lifetime, they reached the flint wall that made the far boundary of the yard, and collapsed into its lee. Eleanor laid Charles's head gently down into her lap as she sat, her head thrown back to breathe in the pure, icy air that was lit now with a lurid orange glow, extinguishing the pale gleam of the stars. Richard came round to huddle at her other side, and together they sat, beyond all thought or action. All at once the yard was full of people, running and shouting. A face looked down at her and she gasped in terror, thinking it was Hargreaves, but as the man moved she saw in the glare from the burning building that he was a stranger. He was shouting at her, incomprehensibly, and she only shook her head dumbly. The man left her and ran to join the others who stood, staring helplessly at the conflagration, knowing that the barn was too well alight to be saved. In a dream she sat on the hard cobbles, shivering now, though not with cold, for the heat was fierce on her face.

'Miss Eleanor! Miss Eleanor!' Slowly, almost reluctantly, she looked round. The idea of time passing had no meaning for her then; her existence was bounded by the hard wall behind her and the burning barn before her. Nothing else had any reality. Evans was bending over her, taking her hands, exclaiming over the weals on her palms that she looked at without interest. He turned from her to Charles, running his hands over him, and her heart smote her. She had almost forgotten him.

'I'm sorry, Evans.' Her voice was no more than a croak—he had to bend over her to hear above the shouts of the men, the roar of the fire, and the bellows of terrified animals that had already been led to safety. 'I'm so sorry. He killed him. He's dead. I couldn't do anything.'

'Who, Mr Charles, miss? He's not dead, just knocked out.'

'No, no, I saw it. Hargreaves hit him, and he hasn't moved since. He's dead.'

'Look at him, Miss Eleanor. There's blood running from that cut. Dead men don't bleed. I've felt his head; his skull's not harmed, though he'll have a mighty headache later! But his heartbeat's as steady as my own, and a sight steadier than yours by now, I'd say.'

'Are you sure?'

'Quite sure, miss. You'll see.'

Her eyes filled with tears.

'I nearly couldn't move him, Evans. He was so heavy. I nearly left him. He would have burned, burned to death, Evans. I might have left him!'

'But you didn't, miss.' His calm voice called her back from the edge of hysteria. At that moment there was a great crack and a shooting fountain of sparks as the roof of the barn fell in. A groan went up from the watching men. Eleanor felt Richard flinch. She held him more closely to her.

Charles's eyes opened, and he moaned. At once Evans was beside him.

'My head,' said Charles, lifting his hand to the bump and hurriedly removing it, 'hurts like hell. Must find Eleanor. Up at Hargreaves'. Must find her.'

'It's all right, Charles. I'm here. Don't move.' She did not know that tears were pouring down her face until he put out one shaky hand and touched her cheek.

'Mustn't cry, Eleanor,' he murmured. 'Mustn't cry, darling. You're safe now. I'll look after you.'

'More likely the other way round,' said Evans gruffly, hiding his pleasure and forcibly preventing Charles from rising.

'Damn it all, Evans, let me sit up, at least! I'm all right, I tell you.'

Between tears and laughter, Eleanor wiped her face, neither knowing nor caring that she added mud to the soot already griming it.

'I'm not crying, not really. Only I thought you were dead, when Hargreaves hit you like that.'

'So that's what happened. You saw me, then?'

'Yes. Jeremy Hammond put me up in the loft, tied up. Oh, Charles... He is in there—Mr Hammond, I mean.'

'Too late to save him now, miss,' put in Evans, glancing at the flames.

'It would be too late anyway,' she responded soberly. 'He is dead already. He came up the ladder, and I pushed him down. I think his neck was broken.'

'I can't say I'm very sorry. I suppose he and Hargreaves were working together. I don't remember much beyond coming out to look for you. Disappointed you, have I? I feel a little odd, but I can assure you I aim to live for many years yet.'

She had never thought she would be so happy to have him tease her. Satisfied that Charles was indeed almost unhurt, Evans allowed him to move, and helped him to a sitting position. As Charles moved, Richard lifted his head from Eleanor's side and looked at him with alarm that vanished as he realised there was no threat. Charles's eyes, which had been fixed on Eleanor's face, travelled to the boy's and rested on it. He frowned, and at once the child withdrew into Eleanor's shadow.

'It's all right,' whispered Eleanor, 'it's only Charles.'

'That bang on my head must have addled my brain. I thought for a moment...' Charles's voice tailed away, and he leaned forward to look again. Gently Eleanor moved the boy forward into the light, and encouraged him to lift his face.

'You thought what?' she prompted. She wanted to hear him say it himself, before she had given any explanations.

'I thought for a moment I was seeing—Richard. Richard when he was a child. That boy is the image of my cousin at that age. At least, that's what I thought just now. I must have been mistaken. It's so long ago...'

He reached out and put his finger under the boy's chin, lifting his face and turning it to the light of the fire. 'It is. I cannot be mistaken. Do you see it, Evans?'

'Of course I do, Mr Charles. Spit and image of Mr Richard, God rest him. Reckon I know who he is, then.'

'I believe he is Richard's child. He was here, hidden by Hargreaves. He hasn't been here very long—since the autumn, he says. He can't speak much English, only French. I didn't have much time to ask him about himself, but he has been told that Hargreaves is his grandfather, and also that his father came from the big house,' explained Eleanor.

Charles held out his hand, and, after some hesitation, Richard moved closer and took it. They looked at one another.

'He was very brave.' Suddenly Eleanor wanted more than anything that Charles should accept the child as his relative. 'We were trapped up in the loft, above the fire. I let him down on the rope, and he didn't run away, but stayed to help me down, though the flames were so bad. And he helped me to save you, too. I don't think I could have moved you on my own.' She fell silent, realising that Charles was scarcely listening. He spoke in swift, colloquial French, and Richard's eyes sparkled as he answered in a rush that Eleanor could not understand. Charles was obviously questioning, and it seemed that the answers did not displease him, for he nodded encouragingly and Richard relaxed, moving confidingly closer to this man to whom, at last, he could make himself properly understood. At last Charles leaned forward and put his hands on the boy's shoulders, studying the thin, dirty face that looked so trustingly up at him. Then he pulled Richard to him and kissed him, holding him closely in his arms.

'As you thought,' he said huskily, 'this is poor Richard's son. And to think that I searched for his mother and did not find her. Poor child, I believe when Richard did not return she thought he had forsaken her. She did not dare to return home, knowing that her father would never allow her into the house, so she moved inland and took lodgings with an old couple in a village near Chartres. Richard had given her money, and she had enough to live on for quite some time. She died soon after the child was born, leaving the money to the couple who promised to care for her son. They must have been good people, for they cared for him as if he had been their own, but the old man died a few months back, and the old woman was ill. She managed to contact the smugglers, and arranged for Richard to be brought back to England. She hoped that he would be taken to us, to his father's house, but instead he was brought here, for some reason. If only we had known! What a place for a young child to come to!'

He fell silent, and Richard spoke again.

Je ne veux pas rester ici. J'ai peur de l'homme, mon grand-père. S'il vous plaît, je voudrais rester avec vous et la demoiselle.

'He must come back with us, Charles!'

'Of course he must. No one who sees him can doubt that he is Richard's son, and even if he is not—legitimate—we must care for him. I cannot understand why he was not brought to us in the first place. My uncle might not have been pleased that Richard fell in love with Lucy, but no one who knows him could doubt that he would care for Richard's child.' He hugged the boy again. *'Tu vas venir chez moi, dans la maison de ton père,'* he told him. Richard smiled and chattered back. Charles laughed. 'He says he has already seen the house. Apparently his mother talked a lot to the old couple, and they have told him all about his father's fine home. He says he sometimes escaped from Hargreaves and found his way down there, but did not dare let anyone see him because his mother had said that Richard's father had been angry, and did not approve of their marriage.'

Charles and Eleanor stared at one another, the full import of the words striking them only after he had finished speaking.

'Their marriage?' repeated Eleanor. 'But surely...?'

Charles questioned the boy, who replied confidently.

'He seems convinced that they were married. He says he has her wedding ring, but that he hid it so that Hargreaves would not find it.'

'Perhaps,' suggested Eleanor delicately, 'she told the old couple that she was married, for fear that they would not let her stay otherwise. Poor girl, they had meant to marry, and would have done if Richard had lived. Or do you think they were actually man and wife?'

'I cannot think so. I made enquiries everywhere, and no one knew of any ceremony. It would not have been easy to arrange a runaway marriage in France and keep it hidden, and they could not have been married in England without news getting out, surely? No, it is as you think. She must have lied to protect herself, and her unborn child. Who can blame her for that? I only wish it were true, for it will be a sadness for him, later on. We must teach him still to honour the memory of his mother, in spite of it.'

There was a shout, and a rumble of wheels. Evans had ridden swiftly back to Oaklands, to take word that Eleanor and Charles were safe, and bring some means of conveying them home, for neither were in a fit state to ride or to walk. None of the more comfortable carriages could use the steep, winding lanes, most of them hardly more than tracks, which led to the farm, so he had brought a small cart, its inside hastily made more comfortable with a layer of clean straw and some blankets. Soon the three of them were wrapped warmly, and huddled together in the cart.

Eleanor looked back at the farm as they left. The flames had died down now, the barn was no more than a large heap of glowing timbers that lit the sky with a lurid orange glare. The animals had been moved out of nearby buildings, but fortunately the barn had stood on its own, separate from the farmhouse and the byres. These were all safe, for luckily the night was still enough not to spread the blaze, and the roofs were not of thatch, but of Horsham stone which was impervious to the flying sparks.

Charles left instructions that the house and stock were to be guarded against looters, for the light of the fire had shone like a beacon and a large crowd, some known, some unknown, had collected. No one knew whether Hargreaves had any other living relatives—certainly he had never spoken of any, and as far as anyone knew the child was his only heir, if it could be proved that he was indeed Lucy's son. At least, thought Eleanor, he would be assured of some kind of living for the future. She was glad when the twisting lane carried them out of sight of the farm. She thought she would be happy never to see the place again.

Despite the jolting and the throbbing of her head, Eleanor slipped in and out of sleep on her way back, happy to know herself safe at last. She was aware, when she woke, of Charles and Richard speaking. With the resilience of childhood, Richard seemed to have cast off his fear. Eleanor thought that he must have had a happy childhood, and been kindly treated, for in spite of his experiences with Hargreaves he was immediately ready to trust himself to Charles and herself. He had no thought or anxiety for the future; it was enough that he was with someone who was kind to him.

Never had Oaklands Court looked more welcoming than it did as they drew up outside the front door. All the windows blazed with light, and the moment their wheels were heard on the drive the door was flung open.

'My uncle must be warned,' said Charles in a low voice. 'The sight of this boy, looking as he does so like my cousin, might be enough of a shock to endanger his reason, if not his life. Will you stay out here with Richard for a few minutes, while I try to prepare him, and tell him what has happened as well as I can?' Eleanor nodded, and Charles ran up the steps to the hall.

The boy looked up into her face. He looked apprehensive. She supposed that Charles had told him he was to meet his grandfather, and it was not surprising that he should be worried; certainly his experience of grandfathers to date had not been such as to inspire confidence in the breed. She smiled reassuringly, and Richard clung to her hand, determined to hang on to such safety as he had.

When at last Charles returned, he helped Eleanor and then Richard down from the cart. As Eleanor looked a question he gave a brief nod, then bent to look into Richard's eyes.

'*Tu vas voir ton grand-père. Il est vieux, et il a été malade. Tu comprends?*'

The boy nodded, but clung more tightly to Eleanor in mute anxiety. She knelt to bring her face on a level with his, and struggled in her schoolgirl French to make herself understood. She explained that his grandfather had been ill and sad since his son, Richard's father, had died. The boy's face cleared. Here was something familiar, something he understood.

'*Comme Maman, alors,*' he said.

'Yes, like your mama,' she repeated softly. 'But he is old, and ill. You must be quiet, and gentle.'

'Bien sûr. Monsieur Victor, lui, il était souvent malade. Je serai sage.' Brought up by elderly people, he knew how to behave, she thought. He slipped his hand free of hers and drew himself up to his full height, squaring his shoulders. She watched with pride as he walked up the steps with Charles, disdaining any support.

Together they walked into the hall. Everyone was there but Amy, who had been given a sedative and was asleep in her bed, but Eleanor had eyes only for Sir Ambrose. White-faced, he sat on a chair near the great fireplace. As they walked, he fixed his eyes with painful intensity on Richard's face. He started to rise, then almost fell back into the chair. Richard did not hesitate, but walked straight up to him. Halting by the chair, he made a small, formal bow.

'Good evening, *Grand-père*,' he said carefully. 'Stay sit, you must be *tranquille*.' He laid his hands confidingly on the old man's knee, looking anxiously up into his face. 'You be ill, *Grand-père*? You be sad, like *Maman*?'

His hands trembling, Sir Ambrose reached out and gathered the child into his arms.

'No, I am not ill now, my child. My little Richard, my dear son, you have come back to me. You did not leave me alone, after all. You left me your boy.'

There was a sudden choking gasp. Eleanor looked round. Mrs Wyckham was collapsed in a chair, her lips blue.

'Her drops! Fetch her drops quickly, the shock is too much for her!' Eleanor hurried to her side, and Mrs Wyckham clutched at her hand.

'I did not know,' she said urgently. 'I did not know there was a child! I did not know!'

'Of course you did not, ma'am,' said Eleanor soothingly. 'How should you have done, when nobody knew?
You must not excite yourself. Just let me give you your
drops, and you will feel better.'

'He did not tell me.' Mrs Wyckham ignored Eleanor,
the words coming painfully on each harsh breath. 'I
would not have kept quiet if I had known. He should
have told me!'

'Who should have told you what, Mama?' Charles
had moved to Eleanor's side, and stood looking down
at his mother, his face intent. She shrank from him. Mrs
Martlett came at a run with the medicine, and Eleanor
took it, saying at the same time a few quiet words which
set the housekeeper clearing the room of an interested
audience of maids and menservants, who had gathered
in the hall when they first returned. Soon the family were
alone but for the butler and Mrs Martlett. Sir Ambrose
ignored them, in a world of his own, gazing at the play
of firelight on the dirty little face of the boy who now
sat enthroned in his grandfather's lap.

'Who is "he", and what should he have told you?'
Charles reiterated roughly.

'Richard. Told me about . . . the girl.' Charles leaned
forward and gripped his mother's shoulders.

'What are you saying? What have you done?'

'Charles, she must have her drops!' Eleanor protested. 'This is no time to be questioning her, she is very
unwell!'

He would have ignored her, but she pushed his hands
away and bent to hold the glass to Mrs Wyckham's lips.
She drank, then leaned back and closed her eyes. After
a moment Eleanor was relieved to see the blue colour
recede from her lips, and her breath coming more easily.
She took the older woman's hands and held them firmly.

'What did Richard tell you, ma'am?' she asked gently, silencing Charles with a fierce look.

'That they were married.' She spoke in a whisper, but it rang like a shout in the silent, listening room. 'I did not say, for he was half out of his mind, and I was not even sure it was true. After all, there was no proof! He just talked of Lucy, and said she was hidden in the castle, or something, and it made no sense, so I just—forgot it. Do not look at me like that, Charles. I meant no harm. It was for you, only for you!' She dissolved into tears.

'You knew that they were married, and you did not tell us?' His voice was harsh, and she looked up at him with fear.

'I did not see that it could matter! After all, Ambrose never approved of her, at least not as a wife for Richard, and it would have made everything so uncomfortable.'

'Uncomfortable! She was perhaps not the wife his friends would have wished for him, but if he married her then she was his wife! A good, sweet girl, and hardly more than a child herself. When I think how she must have lived, and died, not knowing what had become of him, not daring to come home to that madman of a father, believing herself cast off by us, his family...and you—you talk of uncomfortable!' His voice was low, icy cold; there was hatred in his eyes.

'I am sorry, so sorry,' she wept. 'I did not think—I did not know about the child. They could not have had more than a few days together. And you looked for her, you know you did. You were gone for weeks!'

'Child or no child, they were married. I searched for her, yes, but do you think I would have given up so soon if I had known? I have been at fault in this, too, and this poor boy has suffered because of it.'

'Enough.' Sir Ambrose's voice was tired and weak, but it stilled both Charles's angry voice and his mother's sobs. 'We have all been at fault, but the time for anger and recriminations is over. Let the dead rest in peace—our business is with the living. I am as much at fault as you, Charles, for I discouraged you from looking for the girl. I hated her, blamed her for Richard's death. Even if I had known they were married, I do not think I could have forgiven her, then.' Again he hugged his grandson to him. 'Against all hope I have a young Richard again. That joy is enough to cast out all the shadows of past misdeeds. Let this house become a happy home to him, and to us all.'

'Amen to that,' Eleanor agreed. 'Let us all renounce past disagreements and quarrels.' She glanced shyly at Charles as she spoke, and he smiled at her.

'I am glad,' he said simply. 'Come, Mama, no more tears. Richard is found, and thanks to Eleanor we are all safe, with no more than bumps and bruises to show for our adventure.'

'And I am very hungry,' said Eleanor in some surprise, 'and no wonder, for I have not eaten since breakfast. I am sure young Richard needs to eat, as well. He looks half-starved.'

'I will inform Cook at once,' said Browning imperturbably. Eleanor hurried upstairs, and saw her own appearance with horror. Annie had thoughtfully prepared a bath, and with much relief she stripped off the filthy, torn dress, extravagantly consigning almost every stitch she had on to be burned, since nearly everything bore evidence of the ordeal she had passed, in terms of spark-burns and holes. Dressed in a fresh gown, her still damp hair neatly arranged, and with light bandages over the palms of her hands where the rope had rubbed them raw, she hurried down. An informal supper had been spread in the little dining parlour. Richard, looking much cleaner and very angelic in one of his father's old night-gowns, was already eating.

'We suggested bread and milk, but the little fellow seems ready to tackle a full-sized meal,' said Charles with a mixture of pride and amusement.

'This is probably the first good meal he has had for some time,' said Eleanor. 'He should not eat too much, though, or he will suffer for it later. I, on the other hand, will not, and I intend to eat a great deal!'

'How is Amy?'

'Very relieved to see me back. She has a bad headache, however, and prefers to stay in bed. She asks me to apologise to you for being a little overwrought.'

'Overwrought! I should think she was! Screeching like a barn owl,' he said callously, helping himself to a large portion of chicken. Eleanor was about to remonstrate over this description when she was silenced by an enormous yawn. Now that her hunger was beginning to be assuaged, she was finding it hard to keep her eyes from closing.

'Tired? I'm not surprised. I should go to bed now, and tell me off in the morning when you have more energy. You will be able to make a better job of it then.'

'I wouldn't,' she started to protest, and yawned again.

'Wouldn't you just? But in gratitude for saving my life, I shall allow you the luxury of abusing me to your heart's content for saying unkind things of your precious sister. And when you have done, Miss Eleanor Hunter, I have a few things in mind that I wish to say to you!'

CHAPTER FOURTEEN

IT WAS late when Eleanor woke the following morning, and she was surprised to see Amy sitting beside her bed. For a moment she remembered nothing, and wondered why her sister was so pale, and looked at her so anxiously; then she moved and felt her muscles protest. Her hands felt clumsy and she lifted them, seeing the bandages that had been renewed before she went to bed.

'How do you feel, dearest?' Amy leaned forward in concern.

'A little stiff and sore, but otherwise I feel very well,' replied Eleanor. 'I must have slept for hours. Is it very late?'

'Nearly midday. You were exhausted, and no wonder. You should have gone straight to bed as soon as you came home.'

'I don't think I could have done. I had to see everything settled at last. I would not have been able to sleep straight away—besides, I was very hungry!'

Amy shuddered.

'Hungry, after what you must have been through? I don't know how you could!'

'Well, you know I am lacking in sensibility,' said Eleanor prosaically.

'No, I am afraid you are just more sensible than I. Oh, Eleanor, when you disappeared yesterday I was frantic with worry! I am afraid I was very silly, and no help at all to anyone. I am ashamed.'

'Nonsense, there is nothing to be ashamed of. I should probably have been just as bad if it had been you who had disappeared—worse, even. It is terrible to be left waiting for news, not knowing where someone is or what they are doing. Nobody blames you for being so upset.'

'Can you bear to talk of it all? I am so longing to hear what happened, but I know it has all been very terrible, and maybe you would prefer just to forget it?'

'I don't think I ever could forget, however long I live. But I don't mind telling you about it. It was terrible, yes, but somehow, now I am safely back here, it is already becoming a bit unreal, as if it had happened to someone else and not to me. Will you ring for some tea, though, first? My throat is so dry this morning.'

'Of course—I sent a message as soon as I saw you were stirring, for I knew you would be thirsty. Annie will be bringing it any minute. May she hear what happened too? I think it is thanks to her that Charles came to find you, for she was the one who told him where you might be. Whatever possessed you to go up there on your own?'

Annie arrived at that moment with the tea, and Eleanor was glad to swallow two cupfuls before telling her tale. Her throat felt rough and dry, and she could feel the effects of the smoke with every breath she took. Nevertheless, she motioned Annie to stay and listen while she recounted what had happened to her the previous day. Amy's already pale face turned whiter still when she heard what danger her sister had been in, and her eyes filled with tears.

'You could have been burned to death! I do not know how you could have slept so soundly all night.'

'Quite easily, for I was worn out. Besides, the greatest danger is gone, now that Jeremy Hammond is dead.' Her face clouded. 'Oh, Amy, I killed him. Am I a murderer? I did not mean to kill him, only I had to keep him away. There was nothing else I could do.'

'It was his own wickedness that killed him,' said Amy with unwonted firmness. 'Besides, you saved not only your own life, but little Richard's, and Charles's too, and he must have meant great harm to you, or why should he take you there, and try to get Charles there also? No one could possibly blame you for what you did, only praise you for your bravery.'

'How is little Richard today? Have you seen him?'

'Yes, he came down to breakfast. Is it not wonderful? His grandfather is so happy, I have never seen him so well—it is as if he had shed twenty years in a night! And he is the boy you saw before?'

'Yes, the very first day we were here, and then again at Christmas. Oh, Amy, if you call me brave, there are no words to describe his courage! Such a small child, and with no education as we know it, and yet the instincts of a gentleman. It is really he who saved us all, for without him I would never have been able to get down from the loft, and Charles would have died as well. He will be a great man, I am sure of it. And he is up already, and breakfasted?'

'Yes, with Uncle Ambrose. Mrs Wyckham keeps to her room today. No one says very much about her, but I hear there was some kind of upset yesterday evening?'

'Yes, I did not really understand it, but she suffered a severe spasm when she saw the boy. It was terrible, she was very ill and I really thought she might die of the shock, and Charles was so angry with her! It seems that when Richard, the boy's father, that is, came to their house the night he was wounded and died, he told her that he had married Lucy, and after he was dead she did not tell anyone.'

'Would it have made much difference if she had?'

'I do not know. Certainly Charles was very angry, but he already knew that his cousin had run away with the girl, and I am sure he searched for her as diligently as he knew how. I do not think she wished to be found, for she must have been very frightened of her own father, and probably doubted her own welcome here, even though they were married. Of course, if he could have found her, the boy would have been brought up here, and none of this would have happened. However, it is too late to think of that now.'

'But she could not have known there was a child. She would not have kept quiet then.'

'No, that is what she kept saying, that he should have told her. But he himself cannot have known—the poor young things had only so short a time together, Lucy cannot have been aware of her condition herself until after Richard had disappeared.'

'She might have been afraid that her baby would not be accepted as Richard's child. After all, he cannot have been born until nearly nine months after his father's death, and many children bear no very strong resemblance to one or other of their parents. If the baby should have taken after her in looks, she could have feared that slanderous tongues might suggest that she was attempting to pass off some other child as Richard's.'

'Yes, and even if it was not said, it might still have been thought. Then, of course, with her dying so soon after the boy was born, nothing could be done. I suppose if she had lived, and seen how like his father the boy was, she might have brought him back here. As it was, I believe, from what he said, that he had a happy childhood with the elderly couple who gave her a refuge. They certainly treated him very kindly, and I do not believe he is any the worse for it. Who knows, if he had been brought up here, doted on by his grandfather, he might have turned out quite differently, and not even as well.'

'As you say, there is no knowing what might have been.'

'I hope Charles is no longer angry with his mother.'

'I think he still is, a little, though he did not say much at breakfast. It was for him, of course, that she did it. The temptation of seeing him inherit all this was very great, and, in her eyes, whether Richard was married or not made little difference.'

'No, I really believe that the possibility that he might have left a child behind him never occurred to her. She was certainly very much shocked last night. I only hope that it has not made her ill.'

Eleanor put down her cup, and pushed back the bedclothes.

'I absolutely must get up now, I so long to see the boy again.' She was surprised to find how stiff and weak she was, and Annie and Amy came to help her. Amy laughed at her sister's expression.

'If our positions were reversed, how you would scold me for trying to get up! I feel sure you should stay in bed for today, at least, but I also feel sure that I am quite unable to make you do so.'

'Stay here all day? I could not do so. But I own I should like another bath. I can still smell the smoke about my person, and I feel I will never be clean of it again.'

Annie, eager to care for Eleanor, whom she had feared never to see again, hurried to fetch mats and towels and the big bath. Soon a procession of cans of hot and cold water arrived from below, and for once Eleanor did not feel guilty at making the servants carry so much upstairs. When all was prepared Annie set screens round the fireplace, to keep off wandering draughts, and soon Eleanor was luxuriating in the warm, scented water. To have so large a bath was still a novelty and a treat—at home they had only used a small one, and then very often in later years they had crept down to the kitchen to bathe, for it was so much warmer and less work for Annie, though they knew that most people would be shocked at their behaving thus—only poor people took baths in the kitchen.

Now Eleanor languidly washed her limbs, pink from the hot water, with the fine soap that was such a treat after the coarse, cheap stuff they had used for the sake of economy at the vicarage. She felt her aching muscles relax in the welcome heat, and the water, stinging at first, soon soothed the raw skin on her hands.

Annie washed her hair for her, more thoroughly than there had been time for the night before, and the last of the smoky smell vanished in the fruity scent of the camomile she put in the rinsing water. It was bliss to sit, wrapped in fluffy towels, before the glowing fire, while Annie brushed out her drying hair as if she were a small child again.

Dry again, she found herself not tired, but languid and disinclined for much action. In spite of her earlier protestations, she did not now feel she wanted to dress and go downstairs, and was content to put on a loose gown of fine wool over her clean shift and petticoats. Her chest still felt tight when she breathed deeply; she did not think she could bear the constriction of her stays just yet.

A light meal of soup and chicken awaited her in their upstairs sitting-room, and Amy fussed over her, enjoying the reversal of their usual roles.

'You must not spend all your time up here with me,' protested Eleanor. 'The rest of the family will think you are neglecting them. I will be all right up here; you should go down and take luncheon with them.'

'Certainly not,' responded Amy indignantly. 'Besides, Mrs Wyckham is staying in her room, as I told you, and Charles has gone out.'

'Gone out? Is that wise? After all, he was hit over the head only yesterday, and he is scarcely recovered from his earlier fall.'

'I know, but there was no stopping him. You know what he is! He is sure that that terrible Jeremy Hammond was the organiser of the smugglers, and he wants to get to them quickly, before the news of their leader's death is too widely known. He has taken Evans with him, of course.'

Eleanor felt rather shy of talking of Charles. Last night had been so strange, so outside all normal experience, that she hardly knew how to meet him. Certainly nothing between them could ever be quite the same as it had been before. She had to admit that, for all her frequent irritation with him, she had always found him attractive, though she had never before allowed herself to admit it. He would not be likely, after all, to look at her when Amy was there, and she had had no wish to make a fool of herself languishing after an indifferent man. Better to encourage Amy to like him. But seeing him struck by Hargreaves, seeing him lie so still and believing him dead, had made her at last confront her own feelings. The pang of despair that had shot through her at that moment, the knowledge that her life could never again be complete without him, held up to her the reflection of her own heart, and she could no longer dissemble. Then, afterwards, in the darkness and confusion, had he or had he not called her his darling? She had not imagined it, surely? He must have been confused by the blow on his head. She would put the memory out of her mind, she decided, together with her new self-knowledge.

The sound of the door opening made her look up in confusion, but it was Sir Ambrose and young Richard. The boy, cleaner than she had ever seen him, and smartly dressed in some hastily assembled clothes of his father's childhood that had been laid by, ran to her.

'The boy has been wild to come and see you,' said Sir Ambrose fondly, following his grandson more slowly. 'I told him he must wait until you had rested and got up, but I thought you would allow us the licence of visiting you here, in your sitting-room.'

'My dear sir, how can you ask?' exclaimed Eleanor, unable to rise and greet him since Richard had flung himself bodily into her lap, and was clinging round her neck and babbling a torrent of words into her ear. 'We are so happy to see you both. Will you not sit here comfortably by me?'

He came to her, taking the hand she held out to him, and bending to kiss her cheek fondly.

'Are you well today, my dear Eleanor? You have slept, and eaten?' He turned for confirmation to Amy, who was arranging a chair for him near to her sister.

'I am very well—only a little lazy today, as you may see!' Eleanor indicated her robe with a laugh. 'Besides, Amy is so strict with me, it was as much as I could do to get permission to leave my bed!'

'Eleanor is a better nurse than she is a patient,' Amy averred with her gentle smile. 'I do believe that, though she may not be as well as she claims to be, she has taken no real harm from her adventure. She is so very brave, Uncle! She has been telling me the full tale of yesterday, and I wonder whether I shall ever sleep soundly again.'

'I have heard Charles's story, and I know that you acted with the greatest fortitude, my dear. I should be glad to hear your own tale, if it will not distress you too much to repeat it again, for of course he did not know the whole, and last night it was impossible to take in all that happened.'

Rather unwillingly, Eleanor once again embarked on her saga, keeping as far as possible to a bare recital of the facts, but putting full emphasis on Richard's courage. He was still in her lap, one arm round her neck, the other hunched childishly under his chin. Eleanor was glad that he would not be able to understand most of what she said, for though he was clean, fed and rested there were still shadows beneath his eyes, which held from time to time a haunted look in their depths. She dropped a kiss on his head, and saw with some amusement that his thumb had crept into his mouth as his eyelids drooped.

Amy and Sir Ambrose listened in silence as Eleanor talked. When she recounted the end of Jeremy Hammond, Sir Ambrose sighed, and shaded his eyes for a moment with his hand.

'I am very sorry, sir,' faltered Eleanor. 'I am afraid it pains you to hear of his death.'

'It pains me more to think that any kinsman of mine should be so evil. It is as well he died when he did. How much worse if we had been forced to have him apprehended by the police, to stand his trial for kidnap and attempted murder! As it is, no one outside the family need ever know what happened. The main thing is that you and the boy are safe.'

'What about the man Hargreaves?' put in Amy. 'He played a part in this also, and it sounds as though he really meant to kill Charles, if not the others. He cannot be allowed to go free, but he will surely reveal Mr Hammond's place in all this. The poor man is obviously quite out of his mind, he is a danger to himself and everyone else. Where is he now?'

'I forgot that you had not heard. A message was brought to me early this morning.' Sir Ambrose glanced at the boy, seeing with some satisfaction that he was now fast asleep. 'Hargreaves is no danger to anyone now—he is dead. The men were out at first light searching for him, and found his body in the old flint workings. He must have run off in the dark and fallen, for his neck was broken. It may be, of course, that he threw himself down on purpose, but we shall never know.'

'I do not think he knew what he was doing, by that time,' put in Eleanor soberly. 'I think he was quite mad by then, you know. I suppose he had been for some time, and the attack on Charles was just the climax of his demented state. I have never heard such laughter.' She shivered.

'Poor man.' Amy showed her customary compassion. 'He had lost his only daughter, and living up there, all alone, he had nothing else to distract him, and give a more cheerful turn to his thoughts.'

'It is only too easy to allow one's whole life to become bound up in an only child,' agreed Sir Ambrose sadly. 'I believe we were both guilty of being too protective, too possessive of our children. I do sincerely pity him, but, for young Richard's sake, I am glad the man is dead. He must otherwise have been put into some kind of custody, and that is a terrible burden for a child to bear. As it is, we can only hope the boy will forget all about him.'

'Forgive me, sir,' put in Eleanor, 'but I do not think it is possible that he can ever forget the events of the last few months. Would it not be better to talk to him of it, not just at first, perhaps, but when he grows older? He can be made to understand that his grandfather did not hate him, but only the sin he believed he represented. I think it quite possible that Jeremy Hammond, to further his own designs, stirred up and encouraged the anger and hatred Hargreaves already had. It would not have been difficult to do. Hargreaves must have loved Lucy very much, and I think Richard is able to understand that, and realise that such love can easily turn to hate.'

'You may be right. I wanted only to protect the boy.'

'I believe Eleanor is right,' Amy inserted. 'He cannot be protected from something that he has already experienced. It might be better to confront it, and to learn to understand it. I do believe children can understand such things better than we think.'

Eleanor, alone of them all, had heard a firm, hurried tread in the corridor, and when the sitting-room door opened she did not need to turn to see who had entered.

'Charles! My dear boy, you are back!'

Eleanor was suddenly acutely conscious of her state of relative undress, and that her hair had merely been bundled into a net instead of its usual neat arrangement. She felt the warm rush of blood to her cheeks, and bent her head to hide her face by looking at Richard, still fast asleep in her arms. The sound of his voice made her suddenly tingle; she could not bring herself to meet his eyes.

'Forgive me, ladies, for coming to your sitting-room like this. I hope I do not intrude?'

Amy murmured dissent, and Eleanor remained silent. Charles strode to his uncle.

'I felt I must come to you at once, Uncle, to show you this!' He thrust a slim package into Sir Ambrose's hands. Eleanor was relieved to find that he was scarcely aware of her, but at the same time she could not help feeling piqued that he had not even looked at her, let alone asked after her health. Sir Ambrose's words, however, drove all such thoughts from her head.

'What is this, Charles? That is Richard's signature, surely? A certificate of marriage? Where did you get this?'

The older man's hands were shaking again. Eleanor looked up to see Charles take them in his own.

'Do you remember what my mother said, last night? That Richard said that Lucy was hidden in the castle? She did not know what he meant, and took it for the ramblings of a mortally wounded man. It was not so, of course, though she could not have known it. Richard knew the risk he ran in returning, and he had taken care to put this in a safe place—a place that Jeremy Hammond did not know of, but I did. I think he had guessed, by then, that his cousin was somehow involved in his betrayal, and was determined to safeguard Lucy's position.'

'Where did you find it?' Eleanor could not contain her impatience. He glanced up at her, his eyes glinting, and she thought she saw a warmth in them that she had not seen in the past.

'Richard and I had our own secret place, as I think I once told you. It was a hollow tree in the woods, and we used to tease Hammond, I am afraid, by hiding there. We called it our castle. I hadn't thought about it for years, until I was telling you about it the other day, and it is so deep in the woods that I wasn't even sure if it was still there, for I never go that way at all. When my mother said that Richard claimed Lucy was hidden in the castle, I wondered. Of course, he was not talking clearly, and I imagine that what he actually said was something like "Lucy...the castle", meaning that there was something there which concerned Lucy and her well-being. How he did it I do not know, in the dark, and wounded as he was, but somehow he must have climbed up and found our old hiding-place. I had other enquiries to make this morning, or I would have been back sooner, but as soon as I had done what I could I went to look for our tree.'

'And this was there?' Sir Ambrose stroked the precious piece of paper.

'It was. It took me some time to find it, for the trees have grown up since those days, and the old oak has crumbled away some more. We used to think it so huge, but it seemed quite small to me now. I was not even sure it was the right tree, until I climbed up it and found the remains of our old rope still tied at the top. There was a deep crack some two feet below the opening, where we used to store things, and that was where I found it. Luckily it had been well wrapped in oiled silk, and placed in a small box, or it would never have survived. There can be no doubt. They were married by the old vicar before they went to France. Richard must have persuaded him into doing it—the old man always adored him.'

'But how was it that he never told anyone? Surely, after Richard died, he should have spoken, and in any case the marriage should be in the parish records?' It was Amy who spoke this time.

'Poor old fellow, it can only have been a few months before his own death, and at that time he hardly knew the time of day. He never remembered what he had done or where he had been, and if Richard roused him in the night to perform the ceremony, as seems likely, he might well have thought the whole thing was a dream.'

'Is it a legal marriage?'' Sir Ambrose's voice was hungry, hardly daring to hope.

'I think so. They must have been planning a runaway marriage in any case, for Richard had procured a special licence. Of course, Lucy was under age, but I do not think that makes any difference. They even had witnesses: two French fishermen, contacts of the smuggling ring, who had come ashore to fetch Richard. It may be possible to find them, though I hardly think it would be necessary. Richard must have sworn them to silence, for none of the other smugglers knew of the marriage.'

'You have spoken to them, then?'

'To some of them, yes. There is no doubt that their true leader was Jeremy Hammond. He was organising the whole group, and making a tidy profit out of it, too, with virtually no risk, since he never went on a run, only provided the finance for the original purchases and planned the movements. When Richard became involved with them it was a heaven-sent opportunity to be rid of him, without any suspicion attaching to himself. What could be easier than to drop word in an Excise Officer's ear, telling him as a good citizen should that he had heard rumour that a drop was to be made at a certain time, in a certain place. He need not even have appeared in the matter—an anonymous tip-off would have been enough. It was his bad luck that Richard was not killed outright.'

'He knew about Lucy?' Sir Ambrose seemed incapable of speech, and Eleanor preferred to hide in silence, but Amy was innocently eager to hear all the details.

'He must have done, though not that they were married. He certainly did not know about the child, until very recently. I do not think young Richard would have lasted long, legitimate or not, if Hammond had known of his existence. Unprotected as he was, with only the old couple to care for him, Hammond would have found it easy to trick him away from them and arrange a quiet accident somewhere. I think that getting the child to England was done without his knowledge, too. He would never have allowed the boy to come so near to this house, looking as he does so like his father. It must have been an unpleasant shock to him when he found what had happened. However, it does not seem to have taken him long to turn things to his advantage. By all accounts, the child's arrival was the thing that turned Hargreaves' obsession into the beginnings of madness, and Hammond obviously saw his chance to use the man as a pawn, as his executioner.'

Amy shivered.

'That is horrible.'

'As you say.' He turned to Sir Ambrose. 'I should tell you, Uncle, that also included in the package was a letter, sealed, with your name on the outside.'

'A letter? To me?' He seemed hardly able to take it in. He had scarcely listened to their conversation, contenting himself with reading and re-reading the precious document in his hand.

'To you, in Richard's hand. He must have known the danger he ran, and left word for you. Do you want to see it now? I have put it on your table in the study.'

Sir Ambrose stood up.

'I will go down at once.' Charles hurried to steady him with a hand under his elbow, for his uncle suddenly looked very frail. He was obviously in no fit state to go downstairs on his own, and Charles cast only one glance back towards Eleanor, where she sat with the sleeping heir in her lap. She, however, did not see it, for her head was lowered and her face hidden. He had to content himself with a speaking glance to Amy, before he left the room.

Amy went to her sister.

'Are you all right, dear? You are very pale again.'

'It is all so strange, so sudden, I can scarcely comprehend it. So this child really is Sir Ambrose's legal grandson? There is no need to worry for his future, then.

See how peacefully he sleeps, with no idea what is in store for him.'

'Is he too heavy for you? Shall I take him?'

'No, it would be a shame to disturb him, let him lie. He weighs so little, poor fellow. I hope he will be all right. What a strange, dramatic beginning his life has had! I hope the rest will be more peaceful for him.'

As she spoke the boy stirred and opened his eyes. After a wondering moment he smiled up at her, and she felt her throat tighten at the trust in that open look.

'J'ai faim,' he announced prosaically, and she gave a shaky laugh. Trust a child to bring one back to earth! And why should he not be hungry? He must have missed many meals in the last few months, he had plenty of catching up to do. Amy held out her hand, and he seemed quite happy to go to her.

'I will take him down to the kitchens,' she said. 'They are all so thrilled—Cook will stuff him like a goose if we are not careful! You do not mind if I leave you for a while?'

'No, but I think I will go back to bed,' said Eleanor hastily.

'So soon? Perhaps it is best, but I am sure Charles will wish to speak to you. He had to go with Sir Ambrose, but I know he would like a chance to see you. I am sure there can be no impropriety if he should find you alone— after yesterday he must surely be counted as family.'

The possibility of Charles's return was what had driven Eleanor into retreat. To be alone with him, now, was more than she could do. She felt so weak, so stirred in all her emotions, that she was sure she could not be with him without betraying herself. That she should do so, and learn that her feelings were not returned, was something that she did not think she could bear.

'I feel a little unwell,' she said mendaciously. 'I am sure Charles will not mind waiting until tomorrow.'

Amy left the room with the blithely chattering child. Eleanor sought her bed, and lay for some time feigning sleep, her mind revolving endlessly and uselessly until she fell into a disturbed slumber.

CHAPTER FIFTEEN

MUCH to her own surprise, Eleanor slept right through the evening and the night. Accustomed to strength and health, she had underestimated the effect of shock and exhaustion on mind and body, both of which needed to withdraw into sleep to recover. At length she drifted into wakefulness, sleepily aware of past and present, but reluctant to rise and face them. She wished she could stay like this forever, lapped in warmth and safety, with no demands from the outside world.

When Annie came in to see if she were awake, Eleanor was only too pleased to agree with the suggestion of breakfast in bed. She still found the thought of meeting Charles almost insupportable. Part of her longed to know how it was to be, whether there was any change in their relationship, but mostly she wanted to hide away, too terrified of a possible rejection to risk her fragile equilibrium on the possibility of happiness.

She was up and dressed, but still sitting by the fire in her room, when Amy came to see her. If her sister seemed a little distracted and reluctant to speak, she did not remark on it, for she herself was in a pensive mood. There was a radiance, a quiet happiness, about her, of which Eleanor was dimly aware, but unable to account for.

After the expected enquiries into her health, Amy fell silent. Unusually for her, her hands lay in her lap, without their usual knitting or sewing. It was rare for Amy to be unoccupied, and even more rare for her to be restless, rising after a few minutes and pacing to the window. Eleanor waited, aware that her sister had something on her mind. When at last Amy said nothing, Eleanor asked after the child.

'Richard? He is well. He is asking after you again, but I said he must wait until later before coming to see you. Already he is using more English in his speech—he seems such a clever boy, he will soon be speaking perfect English.'

'We must see that he does not forget his French, though,' said Eleanor. 'It is such an advantage to have learned it so young, but he could easily lose it all, which would be a pity.' She stopped, struck by a sudden thought. 'Do you realise, Amy, that our old ambitions may at last be fulfilled? Here is a child much in need of a governess! He shall have two, for we can both teach him—though your needlework might not be needed!' She laughed, but to her surprise Amy blushed and turned away her head.

'For a while, perhaps,' she said shyly, 'but I expect to have . . . other duties, quite soon.'

Eleanor stared at her in silent surprise. Her skirt rustling, Amy came back to her sister's chair, and sank on to a low stool by her side. She took her hand, and smiled tremulously.

'You cannot have failed to notice that my feelings have lately been growing into something warmer than friendship,' she said shyly, her eyes lowered. 'Knowing me as well as you do, I knew I did not need to tell you in so many words.'

Eleanor felt her body grow cold. Her fingers moved to press Amy's, and it was as much effort as if they had indeed been made of the marble she felt they resembled. She could not say that she had noticed nothing of the sort. Recently she had been so absorbed in her own feelings, her own changing emotions, that she had hardly given her sister's a thought. At first, of course, she had watched all the time, hoping to see a growth of sympathy and love between her sister and their eligible host, but Amy had several times denied any possibility of such a thing.

'Has he spoken?' Her voice, which she would have thought would come out as a croak, sounded in her own ears peculiarly calm.

'He has said nothing, but I hope...I am sure...he very soon will.' Amy blushed more deeply, and buried her face in her sister's lap, not noticing how white Eleanor's face had turned.

'I am sure he will,' she said, her lips and mouth dry. 'How could he fail to love you?' She leaned forward to embrace her sister, and tried to calm her trembling voice. 'I hope...I am sure...you will be very happy. And you know I am happy for you.' This, she told herself, this was what you wanted, what you hoped and schemed for.

'How could I not be, with such a husband?'

How indeed, thought Eleanor numbly.

'He is all goodness, all nobility! I am humbled to think that, with his powers of intellect, he should choose me. I only hope that I can be worthy of him.'

Eleanor felt a little surprise at her sister's words, but dismissed it at once. Naturally Amy, in love, saw in her beloved every good characteristic, and certainly Charles was an intelligent man, though not scholarly in his habits. Obviously Amy saw a different side to Charles's character.

Amy raised a glowing face to her sister's embrace. 'I am so glad you are pleased, dearest. I was not sure that you appreciated him, as I have long learned to do.'

Eleanor chose her words carefully.

'If I have sometimes appeared—less than friendly— it must have been that I have had other things on my

mind. Certainly I have always valued him as a friend.
Henceforth, I shall love him as my brother.' Her lips
trembled as she spoke, and Amy was quickly contrite.

'Do not believe that I will love you any the less,' she
said, kissing Eleanor. 'You will always be my dearest
sister, and I will always want and need you. I hope you
will always be with me, or at least very nearby. I cannot
imagine life without you there to help and support me.
Particularly in my new responsibilities.'

Eleanor had scarcely thought of the implications of
her sister's marriage. They might stay here, of course,
but with Richard's return Charles was no longer the heir,
nor did he need to care for his uncle as he had previously
done. Presumably he would continue to run the estate
for the time being, but after his wedding, surely he would
choose to take his bride to his own house? She did not
know which would be worse. To live in the same house,
to watch her sister happy with the man they both loved,
would be torture, but to have them living elsewhere might
be even worse.

Wordlessly, Eleanor hugged her sister. Her mind and
body still felt stiff, frozen. Thus, once her dearest hope,
had come about, and it was as if a knife had stabbed
her. She had just learned that she loved Charles, that
she had loved him almost from the moment she first saw
him. She relived the anguish she had felt when she saw
him fall to the ground beneath Hargreaves' blow. And
afterwards, he had called her darling. But it had meant
nothing, no more than the relief of finding her safe and
alive, a relief that probably stemmed as much from his
care for Amy as for herself. She had learned to love him,
and now she must put him out of her heart. And worse,
she must learn to see him happily married to another.
For a hideous fraction of a moment she hated Amy,
hated her for her beauty, her gentleness, her very

goodness. Then she put her hate, and with it her love, sternly from her.

'I am so very happy for you, darling,' she said. 'It is such a marriage as I have always wished for you.'

'I knew that you would say that, for you have always known what would make me happy,' responded Amy warmly. 'I feared, sometimes, that you were ambitious for me to make a great match, but you know I have no inclinations in that direction. This is the kind of life that fits me, where I belong.' She paused, and gave a little laugh. 'You must think me rather forward and presumptuous, when he has not even asked me yet! But I am so sure of my own feelings, and I do not think I can be mistaken in his. I am going to see him now. He asked me to meet him this morning, and I think he has been speaking to Uncle Ambrose already. I think, when you see me again, it will be as his promised wife!' The sisters clung together again, wordlessly, then with one final kiss Amy flitted from the room.

Left alone, Eleanor paced the length of her chamber, biting her lip and clenching her fists to keep the tears at bay. She would not give in to them. Her pride alone would not allow anyone to see how she had been hurt. After all, no one but herself was to blame. She had fallen into a trap of her own devising. Presently the door opened stealthily—the housemaid had come to clean her room, and she was in the way. Wanting to be alone, she went swiftly to the blue sitting-room at the end of the wing. She could not be still, but fidgeted round the room, taking up and laying down her needlework, her book, her sketching block, all the time wondering how she was to live her life.

One thing was certain: she could not stay here. That would be too hard. Surely she could find some useful work, in London perhaps, that would keep her, and give her an excuse to stay away. The problem would be explaining her absence to Amy, and the rest of the family. Perhaps she could stay for a while with Lady Haywood? There could be no problem without Amy there, and she would have time to think, to look around her. Feverishly she tried to plan, but all she could think of was Amy, perhaps at that very moment in Charles's arms, kissing and being kissed.

Her ears, finely attuned to his tones, heard Charles's voice in the hall downstairs, and Browning's soft reply. Then the unmistakable sound of his feet hurrying up the stairs and towards the door. Not now! Not yet! It seemed to her that she had screamed the words, so strongly did they ring in her own mind, but the steps, almost running, came ever nearer. She drew back, scarcely knowing what she did, but aware that she could not now escape, for there was only one door to the room, which he had nearly reached. She looked round, childishly, for somewhere to hide, and had a hideous vision of him discovering her crouching beneath a table, or the piano. She was at the window-seat, and hurriedly collapsed into it, snatching up some needlework so that she would not have to look at him, and in an effort to appear happy and relaxed, though the bandages on her hands made it impossible for her to sew.

He burst in, his face alight with pleasure, and she clenched her hands on the cambric, hardly feeling the pain of the needle as it pricked her finger. His first words, however, surprised her, for he made no mention of Amy.

'There you are at last! I have been trying to see you alone ever since yesterday.' She made no reply, keeping her head lowered over the mangled sewing. 'Are you feeling better now? It was a terrible experience for you, and you were so brave.'

'So were you.' Her voice was low, but controlled.

'It is due to you that I am still alive. You must let me thank you for that, at least.'

She shook her head, wordlessly.

'Ah, you do not like to be thanked. I know just how you feel, but you have to let me, all the same. Only consider my feelings in the matter! But for you, I would have been burned to death, and probably little Richard, too.'

Eleanor found her voice, seizing on a safer subject of conversation.

'Of course, I would have helped him whoever he had happened to be, but now that we know he is really Sir Ambrose's grandson, it is wonderful. He is a dear little boy.'

'He is, and if you will not allow me to thank you for myself, let me do so on my uncle's behalf. He really is a changed man. It is as if he had shed ten years overnight, and though he was very moved to read his son's letter, I think it helped him, too.'

'The letter—I had forgotten about that! Richard wrote to his father, then?'

'Yes, he must have done it before leaving France, knowing that he was putting himself into danger. He wanted to be sure that his father would take care of Lucy, and also to warn him about Hammond. As I thought, he had made the connection for himself, and guessed that his cousin was behind the original ambush when he killed the Exciseman. More than that, however, he wanted to beg his father's forgiveness. He knew he had not behaved as he should and, though his father made him angry, he never ceased to love him. My uncle always blamed himself for Richard's death. I think it was the guilt, rather than the sorrow, that made him so strange at times. Now he knows that Richard understood, and forgave, he is suddenly free of the past, ready to care for Richard's son, and bring him up as his heir.'

'And you? How do you feel?' She had to ask, though she still could not bring herself to look at him.

'I can never quite forgive myself for not finding Lucy,' he said soberly. 'I know I searched, and advertised, and that she must have made efforts to hide from me, but even so...so much misery could have been saved if I had brought her home to us then.'

'You must not blame yourself. I am sure you did your best.'

'I think that I did. I must always regret it, but now we must put the past behind us, and enjoy the present and the future. Of course I am no longer my uncle's heir, but you know that I never wanted that. I shall continue as his steward until Richard is of an age to take up his duties. I still have my own estate, small though it is in comparison with this, and I, for one, have no regrets in giving up the responsibilities of this one. You know I have never wanted more than my patrimony. But shall you mind? The house is comfortable, even spacious, but of course it cannot compare with this one.'

Eleanor looked up at him at last. He had pulled a chair round to her, and sat in it. His eyes were warm, concerned, and she stared at him, confused.

'I? Why should I mind? I shall not make my home there.'

It was Charles's turn to look surprised.

'You wish to remain here? For a while, perhaps, but surely not for long? Now that my uncle has less need of me, I hope to go back to my own house. I need hardly say that my mother will be staying here, if that was worrying you. She is better with her brother, nearer to her friends, and I admit I am unable to keep her in the level of luxury she enjoys at Oaklands. In any case, I do not think it advisable for a man to have his wife and his mother living in the same house. It never answers.'

Eleanor fixed her eyes on the crumpled needlework in her lap, and said with as much composure as she could muster, 'When you are—married—I intend to seek some useful employment, perhaps in London, I am sure I can find something.'

'I am not quite a pauper, you know! I said that my house and estates could not compare with this one, but I think I can manage to support you with all the comforts, and most of the elegances, of life.'

'I prefer not to be supported by you,' she said stiffly. 'As I said, I can work for my living in London, or perhaps back in Manchester. I do not expect you to keep me.'

His eyes glinted with amusement.

'That would raise some eyebrows—I should never be able to show my face again. It is usual, you know, for husband and wife to spend at least some of their time under the same roof!'

She looked at him without comprehension.

'Darling crosspatch, are you angry with me because you have not received a proposal in form? I had thought after the other night we understood one another better than that, but I see that I have been remiss, and must rectify it immediately.' Rising from his chair, he came towards her, and she found herself like a mesmerised rabbit, unable to move as he knelt before her, taking gentle hold of her bandaged hand. 'Miss Eleanor Hunter, will you do me the inexpressible honour of accepting my hand in marriage?'

To his horror she burst into tears, burying her face in the needlework. He instantly removed it, and substituted a large handkerchief, rising quickly from his knee.

'Not that, dearest, you might put your eye out with the needle. Are these tears of joy, or of horror at the thought of spending your life with me?' He thought to tease her out of her tears, thinking them no more than an excess of emotion, but realised that she was really upset and could only sob. When he tried to take her into his arms, she pushed him violently away, saying, 'No! No! Think of Amy!'

'What has Amy to do with it? Surely she likes me well enough to accept me as a brother-in-law?'

'She doesn't like you! At least, I mean, she more than likes you. She loves you—she is expecting you to propose to her today, this morning!'

She did not see the beginnings of a smile on his face.

'You surprise me profoundly. How do you know?'

'She told me so herself. She said that lately her sentiments had grown from friendship into love, and that you are all that is good and noble. She said she was quite sure that you share her feelings, though you had said nothing, and hoped that she could be worthy of you!' Eleanor broke into fresh sobs.

He threw back his head and laughed out loud.

'How can you laugh? She reveres you, and admires your intellect. She is so good and sweet, you must not hurt her!'

He sat down beside her, pulling her firmly into his arms. Eleanor tried to resist him, but her strength was no match for his, and against her will she found herself pressed to his side. Almost without being aware of it, she let her head droop on to his shoulder, so invitingly near and so reassuringly solid, and gave herself up to grief.

'Eleanor!' He gave her a little shake. 'Eleanor, you must stop crying and listen to me. Darling girl, do you mean to tell me she said that, and you still thought she was talking of me? Oh, Eleanor, can it be that you love me more than I thought?'

'Of course I do,' she wailed into his coat-front, abandoning all maidenly modesty. 'I love you quite terribly, but I don't think you are particularly noble or good. And I don't care that you aren't, or anything about your intellect.'

'Quite rightly,' he agreed equably. 'I am none of the things that Amy said, and she was most certainly not speaking of me. Tell me, did she once mention my name?'

Startled, Eleanor thought about it. 'No,' she said slowly. 'She just said "he", and I suppose I thought it must be you, because to start with I wanted you to marry her.'

'I know you did, and very amusing it was too, watching that speculative look in your eye. But Amy is nothing to me, nor I to Amy. Poor little goose, most of the village has been prophesying for weeks that there would shortly be a new mistress at the vicarage.'

'At the vicarage? You mean—Edgar Lutcome?' In her surprise she raised her head to look up at him, and found that she could not look away.

'I do indeed. In fact he was here this morning, speaking to my uncle. He is a very good man, and will give her precisely the kind of life she wants. I know you had ambitions for her, but you must admit that she never shared them. She is very beautiful, I know, but she is not cut out for life in the great world. A country vicarage is just where she longs to be.'

'But—Edgar Lutcome! He is a very good man, of course, and all the things she said of him were true, though they are not of you, Charles. But he is so very... very plain!'

He laughed again, but tenderly.

'What matter? She has beauty enough for both of them. And now I think we have spoken enough of Amy. It is not her life we need to arrange, but ours. If there is to be an "ours", for you have not given me your answer yet.'

His look burned into her, but though she was uncomfortably aware of her reddened eyes, she did not allow her own glance to fall, but let him read her joyful acceptance in her face.

He gave her no opportunity to speak, for before she could do so his lips descended on hers. His kisses burned her, coursing through her body as the flames had devoured the burning barn, his arms around her like steel bars. She struggled to free herself, and at once he let her go.

'I am sorry. Was I too fierce? I did not mean to frighten you.'

'You have never frightened me,' she said softly, freeing her arms so that she could put them round his neck, and pulling his face down to hers again. Gently nurtured though she had been, his passion held no fear for her, and her response was immediate and uninhibited. As his kisses moved from her lips to her neck, and then to the soft swell of her breasts as he pushed aside the modest draping of lace that masked them, she neither shrank from him nor repulsed him. Her body melted towards him, and she held him as fiercely as he had her, murmuring his name.

Presently he raised his head, looking down at her as she lay within the circle of his arms, his eyes caressing her. He smiled. 'You still have not given me your answer,' he pointed out with mock severity. Eleanor smiled boldly back at him.

'I think I shall keep you in suspense,' she teased. 'Who knows, I might change my mind!'

He silenced her with more kisses, until she was breathless and begging for mercy.

'Very well, my answer is yes!'

'I think we should be married as soon as possible,' he said meditatively.

'If you wish, but why?'

His eyes laughed at her.

'Partly because if you are going to kiss me like that, I cannot promise to behave as a gentleman. And partly because you will have to promise to obey me. At last I shall be able to make you do as you are told!'

She laughed back at him.

'You are the most annoying man! But I should not count too much on my ability to keep such a promise, try though I might. I am by no means as biddable as Amy.'

'Which,' he replied, kissing her again, 'is precisely why I wish to marry you, darling crosspatch!'

THE COMPELLING AND UNFORGETTABLE SAGA OF THE CALVERT FAMILY

| April | August | November |
| £2.95 | £3.50 | £3.50 |

From the American Civil War to the outbreak of World War I, this sweeping historical romance trilogy depicts three generations of the formidable and captivating Calvert women – Sarah, Elizabeth and Catherine.

The ravages of war, the continued divide of North and South, success and failure, drive them all to discover an inner strength which proves they are true Calverts.

Top author Maura Seger weaves passion, pride, ambition and love into each story, to create a set of magnificent and unforgettable novels.

WORLDWIDE

Widely available on dates shown from Boots, Martins, John Menzies, W.H. Smith, Woolworths and other paperback stockists.

Without a Doubt – *Risa Kirk* £2.99

In this latest novel by the best selling author of *Beyond Compare*, successful businesswoman Valerie Stafford faces a double dilemma... The worrying arrival of a smooth, dynamic management consultant at work, and her teenage niece's drastic transformation into a punk rocker!

Elizabeth – *Maura Seger* £3.50

This sequel to "Sarah" is the second novel in this captivating trilogy about the formidable Calvert family women. In the aftermath of the Civil War, Elizabeth moves to the elegant social whirl of Boston, to find that shadows from the past threaten her marriage and future happiness.

By Special Request – *Barbara Kaye* £2.75

Five years after scandal rocked Audrey Hamilton's socially prominent family, renewed publicity threats leave her only one option – to accept Boyd Benedict's offer of refuge. But can she maintain her anonymity in the face of his curiosity?

These three new titles will be out in bookshops from August 1989.

W❤RLDWIDE

Available from Boots, Martins, John Menzies, W.H. Smith, Woolworths and other paperback stockists.

VOWS   *LaVyrle Spencer*   £2.99

When high-spirited Emily meets her father's new business rival,
Tom, sparks fly, and create a blend of pride and passion in this
compelling and memorable novel.

LOTUS MOON   *Janice Kaiser*   £2.99

This novel vividly captures the futility of the Vietnam War and the
legacy it left. Haunting memories of the beautiful Lotus Moon fuel
Buck Michael's dangerous obsession, which only Amanda Parr can
help overcome.

SECOND TIME LUCKY   *Eleanor Woods*   £2.75

Danielle has been married twice. Now, as a young, beautiful widow,
can she back-track to the first husband whose life she left in ruins
with her eternal quest for entertainment and the high life?

**These three new titles will be out in bookshops from
September 1989.**

W🌐RLDWIDE

*Available from Boots, Martins, John Menzies, W.H. Smith, Woolworths
and other paperback stockists.*

FRUIT SALAD WORDSEARCH
COMPETITION!

How would you like a years supply of Mills & Boon Romances ABSOLUTELY FREE? Well, you can win them! All you have to do is complete the word puzzle below and send it in to us by Dec. 31st. 1989. The first 5 correct entries picked out of the bag after that date will win **a years supply of Mills & Boon Romances** (*ten books every month - worth £162*) What could be easier?

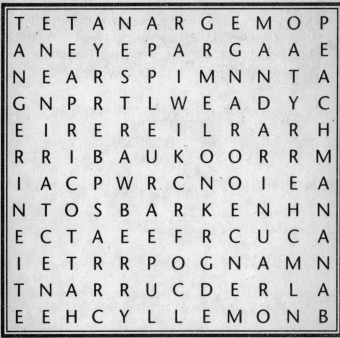

```
T  E  T  A  N  A  R  G  E  M  O  P
A  N  E  Y  E  P  A  R  G  A  A  E
N  E  A  R  S  P  I  M  N  N  T  A
G  N  P  R  T  L  W  E  A  D  Y  C
E  I  R  E  R  E  I  L  R  A  R  H
R  R  I  B  A  U  K  O  O  R  R  M
I  A  C  P  W  R  C  N  O  I  E  A
N  T  O  S  B  A  R  K  E  N  H  N
E  C  T  A  E  E  F  R  C  U  C  A
I  E  T  R  R  P  O  G  N  A  M  N
T  N  A  R  R  U  C  D  E  R  L  A
E  E  H  C  Y  L  L  E  M  O  N  B
```

RASPBERRY	ORANGE	LYCHEE
REDCURRANT	MANGO	CHERRY
BANANA	LEMON	KIWI
TANGERINE	APRICOT	GRAPE
STRAWBERRY	PEACH	PEAR
POMEGRANATE	MANDARIN	APPLE
BLACKCURRANT	NECTARINE	MELON

PLEASE TURN OVER FOR DETAILS ON HOW TO ENTER ▶

HOW TO ENTER

All the words listed overleaf, below the word puzzle, are hidden in the grid. You can find them by reading the letters forward, backwards, up or down, or diagonally. When you find a word, circle it or put a line through it, the remaining letters (which you can read from left to right, from the top of the puzzle through to the bottom) will spell a secret message.

After you have filled in all the words, don't forget to fill in your name and address in the space provided and pop this page in an envelope (you don't need a stamp) and post it today. Hurry - competition ends December 31st. 1989.

Mills & Boon Competition,
FREEPOST,
P.O. Box 236,
Croydon,
Surrey. CR9 9EL

Only one entry per household

Secret Message _____

_____

Name _____

Address _____

_____

_____ Postcode _____

You may be mailed as a result of entering this competition
Please tick the box if you are a Reader Service subscriber ☐

MAILING
PREFERENCE
SERVICE

COMP7